Red Bush and Lemon

Alysia D Evans

Published by Alysia D Evans

Chapter 1

Horns blared as Wes pushed his way onto the motorway, forcing the Volvo in between two lorries. His hands slammed the steering wheel, and he cursed as he brought the car to a sudden halt, joining a line of stationary traffic.

Lucy looked at him. "Can we stop for a cup of tea?" she asked, feeling trapped by the confines of the car.

"No time, sorry. I've got to drop you at the airport, then get to this bloke's house before one o'clock to pick up some stuff I've bought off eBay."

Lucy sighed, hating the control Wes had on her life. "What have you been buying?" she asked.

"Can't say it's a secret."

"You're full of secrets." Wes's irrational behaviour concerned Lucy. "You won't go back on the alcohol while I'm on holiday, will you?"

"Don't be stupid," he muttered, shaking his head.

"Good and remember AA is on Tuesday."

Wes sneered at her. "Yeah, I won't forget."

Lucy yawned, closed her eyes, and fell into a light doze.

The traffic started moving and Wes trailed close behind a car in the fast lane. He flashed his headlights, swerved across lanes, and used sign language to vent his frustration on the other driver. Then he hit the next traffic jam.

"Fucking roadworks," he yelled.

Lucy jumped out of her dreams and looked around. "Look, I need a drink and the loo."

"Oh okay." Wes pulled into the next service station.

The road delays meant it was noon when they arrived at the airport. Wes pulled Lucy's silver Gucci suitcase and matching cabin case out of the Volvo trunk and carried them into the airport.

"Well, have a pleasant holiday." Wes gave her a quick kiss on the cheek.

Lucy sat on a bench next to her suitcases. "Are you going straight away?"

"Yeah, if I'm quick I can collect my stuff." Wes gave her a quick wave from the door and disappeared.

Lucy carted her luggage to a coffee shop and bought a flat white and a pastry. As she drank, she observed people wander into the airport, and glared at a rude female traveller lying across the seats.

The woman woke, stretched, and grinned at Lucy. Embarrassed, Lucy looked away and checked her wristwatch. It was time for her to check in her luggage and go through customs.

In a quiet cafe on the main concourse, Lucy sat and ate her sandwich. She noted that the young woman who'd been sleeping on the seats was now sitting in the cafe writing in a book. Ignoring her, she continued being irritated by Wes's thoughtless goodbye kiss, and his slight wave as he rushed out of the airport doors. She knew he'd looked forward to her leaving, and that he didn't love her anymore. Tears gathered in her eyes, and she searched in her handbag for a handkerchief, unable to find one she wiped her eyes with her hand.

"Are you okay?" said the woman with the notebook.

"Are you talking to me?" asked Lucy, looking around for other people who may need help.

The tall, young woman nodded her head, her curled auburn hair bouncing with each nod.

"Oh, I'm fine," said Lucy. "I think!"

The woman put her pen and notebook into a tan leather satchel. She picked up her sandwich and cup and moved over to Lucy's table. "This might help." She held out a paper napkin in place of a handkerchief. "Jaz, the name's Jaz."

"Thanks." Lucy took the napkin and cleared her nose. "I'm Lucy." She pushed her fingers through her short black hair, the soft fringe framing her deep brown eyes.

Jaz couldn't help gazing into them, her own eyes lighting up as a mesmerised Lucy stared back at her.

"Did something dreadful happen?" asked Jaz.

"I'm not sure." Lucy blinked and looked at her cup. "My husband drove me here at stupid miles an hour, it's a wonder I survived the journey. He dropped me off with my luggage and then left. Married for twenty-seven years, and he didn't even say he loved me. Can you believe that? He's changed, I don't think he cares for me anymore."

"Sorry to hear that." Jaz tried to change the topic. "I've been here most of the day, since six o'clock this morning, bloody coaches. I had to have a nap on the seats by the draughty airport entrance. It was heaven getting into here. But I'm starving now." Jaz tucked into her sandwich and drank her coffee. "What are you eating?"

"Oh, melted cheese and ham toasty. I shouldn't have married the soft git." Lucy's anger resurfaced.

"Wow, he's upset you. You should chat with him later and sort out what's going on." Jaz drained her cup. "What time's your flight?"

"Four o'clock, not long now."

"That's good. Well, I hope you get things sorted." Standing, Jaz smiled and collected her things.

The relaxed, generous smile Jaz gave her absorbed Lucy's mind. "What are you going to do now?" she asked.

"I'll sit and draw people; us artists do peculiar things. Creativity takes your mind away from the chaos of life," said Jaz dreamily.

"Can I buy you a drink when you're finished? You can show me what you've drawn."

The suggestion threw Jaz. People weren't usually interested in her artwork. "Err okay, three o'clock in the Sunshine Bar?" Jaz pointed across to the other side of the lounge, then walked off. She sat on a bench, pulled out her pencil and sketchbook, and drew. Lost in her own world.

Lucy finished her tea and for the next hour wandered from shop to shop trying to entertain herself. She smelt a choice of perfumes, deciding she still preferred her Chanel No.5. Then she browsed the paperbacks in the bookstore sale aisle; with vague thoughts of Wes, she bought a murder mystery. Standing in front of the expensive luxury chocolate, Lucy wondered if Jaz preferred milk or plain chocolate.

Trying to be creative, Lucy decided to compile a photographic scrapbook of her journey. Foraging in her handbag Lucy realised she'd forgotten her camera, visualising it sitting on the dining table at home.

An electronics store sign stood out from the row of shops. Inside, Lucy perused the mid-priced cameras. She plumped for a Nikon that came with a free camera pouch. A bargain, she thought.

Out of the store, Lucy looked around to see where her artist friend was working. Not seeing her anywhere, she entered the bar and bought herself a small white wine. She sat and sipped it, not expecting to see Jaz again.

"Sorry to be late, I got carried away," said Jaz, arriving ten minutes later. "Only a quick drink, we can go through to the plane in half an hour." She winked at the barmaid. "Just a half pint of bitter, please." She delved in her pockets for change.

"I'll get that, it was my idea." Lucy tried to reclaim Jaz's attention.

"Okay, thanks." Jaz never ignored a free drink.

As she turned the pages of her sketchbook, Jaz showed Lucy her drawings. Lucy enjoyed looking at them and attempted to make sensible artistic comments.

"I rarely show people my sketches," said Jaz.

"Is it because you're feeling sorry for me?" said Lucy, touching her heart with her hand.

Lost for words, since what Lucy had said had been true, Jaz took a drink. "I think we're on the same flight. Where are you going?"

"South Africa."

"There you go, I was right," said Jaz, pleased with herself, her mouth curving upward into a serene smile.

Jaz's smile enchanted Lucy. She quickly brought herself back to reality. "I've just bought a camera; do you think it's any good?" She removed the camera from its packaging.

"A Nikon, that's nice. Can I..." Jaz held out her hand and waited for Lucy to pass her the camera. "Do you mind?"

"No, sorry, here you go."

Jaz switched on the Nikon and pointed it at Lucy, pressing a button. "Look, takes a great photo." She handed the camera back, showing Lucy the smiling picture of herself on the screen. "You'll need a big SD card, though, to capture your holiday photos."

Lucy smiled a more relaxed smile and put the camera into its free pouch.

Jaz drank a mouthful of malty ale. "So, what's your job back home?" she asked.

"Oh, I work in a library in Manchester."

Jaz giggled. "Do you go around shushing people?"

"Well sometimes, but there's lots to do in a library; sorting books, submitting orders, helping people," said Lucy in defence of her role.

Hilary strode along the concourse.

Emma scurried behind. "There's Lucy," she said pointing to the bar.

Hilary looked over. "Come on Lucy, planes on the tarmac," she shouted.

Jaz looked at the two older women. "Are they your friends?"

"Yes," sighed Lucy. "I'd best join them. It was lovely to have met you today, and thanks for showing me your artwork."

Jaz was infatuated by Lucy's calmness and enjoyed talking to her. "Nice to meet you too, maybe I'll see you later."

Lucy nodded. "I bought you some chocolate." Lucy handed a package to Jaz, then stood and wandered over to her friends.

"Thank you," mumbled Jaz.

Emma put her arm around Lucy's shoulders. "Have you made a friend?"

"Yeah, she cheered up my awful day," said Lucy, telling Emma about her dreadful journey with Wes.

Dazed, Jaz stared at the box of chocolates, and finished her beer. Savouring the last taste of draught bitter she'd have for a few weeks. She took a deep breath, smelling the perfumes Lucy had been wearing. Then, at a distance, she followed Lucy to the departure gate.

Chapter 2

On her way to her allocated seat at the rear of the plane, Jaz waited patiently while Lucy seated herself, apologising for getting in Jaz's way.

"No problem, shall I put your bag in the locker for you?" said Jaz.

"That'd be nice, if you don't mind." Lucy handed over her cabin case, and Jaz deposited it in the overhead locker.

"Catch you later." Jaz wandered along the plane aisle. She settled herself into her seat, secured the seatbelt and clung on to the armrest as the plane took off.

During the flight Jaz saw Lucy standing in the aisle surveying the plane. Their eyes met and Lucy smiled. Jaz smiled back and looked back at the in-flight magazine she was reading.

They changed planes in Qatar to travel onward to Johannesburg, and Lucy tried to sit closer to Jaz. But Hilary directed her to a row of three seats and sat her next to the window. Disappointed, Lucy placed the airline's spongy earplugs into her ears, muffling the constant hum of the engines, and fell into a light sleep.

When she woke Lucy walked past Jaz as she headed to the tiny bathroom. "Morning," she said.

"Oh, hi," said Jaz, her mouth full of chocolate.

The plane landed in Johannesburg, and there was a brief wait before the flight to Gaborone. Lucy went to buy a coffee at the machine in the waiting lounge and got herself into a panic. She had pressed the buttons and then realised she didn't have the correct currency.

Jaz wandered up by her side. "My round this time." Jaz put the correct coins in the slot. "Are you staying in Joburg?" Jaz asked, smiling at a cute woman sitting nearby.

"No, just changing to another plane, we're getting off in Gaborone."

"Oh, me too." Jaz paid Lucy more attention. "We're on the same journey."

"Can I sit next to you on the plane?" asked Lucy.

"That'll be nice, I can tell you what places you should visit."

Once on the plane Hilary took control again, forcing Jaz to sit on her own. Lucy looked over the heads of her friends and caught Jaz's eye. She waved and shrugged her shoulders. Jaz looked at her and winked, sending a shiver through Lucy's body.

Safely on the ground at Gaborone's major airport, Lucy departed the aeroplane. She walked out onto the tarmac. The coolness of the air conditioning on the plane wore off immediately, and Lucy realised that the overwhelming heat was making her sweat excessively. She looked up at the bright blue sky and then at the dazzling Indian red ground. Suddenly her head was spinning.

"Are you okay?" Jaz caught Lucy's arm as her legs crumpled beneath her. "Here best have a drink of water." She handed Lucy an opened bottle.

"Thanks, felt odd then."

"Best get you inside out of the heat," said Jaz leading Lucy into the airport closely followed by Hilary and Emma.

Lucy sat herself on a bench and convinced everyone that she was alright.

"Well, if you're okay, I'll leave you to it, hope you enjoy your holiday," said Jaz. "Oh, I got you a present." Jaz produced an SD card from her pocket and handed it to Lucy.

"Thank you, you shouldn't have," said Lucy queasily.

"There's my lift, might see you around." Jaz shot off, hugging a woman with curly blonde hair and getting into her car.

Having taken the hotel minibus from the airport, Lucy, Hilary, and Emma walked into the airy, fake marble interior of the Grand Sereto Hotel.

Lucy was edgy as she expected Wes to appear behind her and totally ruin her holiday.

"Are you okay?" asked Emma, putting her arm around Lucy's shoulders.

Lucy sighed. "Yes, I think I'll go for a nap," she said, checking in and receiving her door key.

"Don't forget we're going out this evening with my pen-friend, Bernard," said Hilary.

"Oh okay, I'll meet you at six o'clock," said Lucy.

"We'll see you later," said Emma.

Lucy woke hot and sweaty. She showered and dressed herself in a thin cream skirt and t-shirt printed with African elephants. After spraying herself with perfume she felt more refreshed.

She grabbed her jacket and handbag and left the room to join Hilary and Emma downstairs. Not finding them in the lounge or by the poolside, she waited in the foyer, browsing the tourist pamphlets.

"Hello, are you staying here?" said a vaguely familiar voice.

Lucy turned to see Jaz walking toward her. "Oh, hi, yes," replied Lucy, fanning herself with a leaflet.

"How are you feeling?" Jaz breathed in a waft of Lucy's perfume.

"Good, yes, better now."

"It's good to get away from home, you'll have time to consider your life," said Jaz, looking around the foyer.

"I suppose so," sighed Lucy, placing the leaflet back in the rack. "What are you doing here?"

"I'm collecting a group of people to take them to my uncle's flat."

"What's your uncle's name?"

"Bernard," said Jaz.

"Well, that'll be me, Hilary and Emma. Bernard is Hilary's pen-pal."

"What? My uncle writes letters to Hilary," said Jaz, a perplexed look on her face.

Lucy giggled as Hilary marched into the foyer, with Emma wandering behind.

"Hello again," said Jaz, shaking Hilary's hand. "I'm Bernard's unofficial tour guide, picker-upper and taker outer."

"We didn't realise we'd get a tour guide, I'm Hilary O'Brien."

"How do you do, Jasmine Page, but people call me Jaz."

"Jaz is Bernard's niece," Lucy told Hilary and Emma.

"It's so nice to meet Bernard's family," purred Hilary.

"I'm Emma Manu." Emma shook Jaz's hand.

"Lucy, we've already met."

"Pleased to meet you," said Jaz, formally shaking Lucy's hand and giving the sexy smile that had captured Lucy's thoughts yesterday.

Jaz directed them outside to the red twin-cab pickup she'd borrowed from Bernard. She helped Lucy climb into the front seat of the cab, admiring Lucy's elegant legs as they emerged from her short skirt. "That's a cool t-shirt you're wearing," Jaz stuttered. "Hopefully, I'll find you a herd of real elephants."

"Excellent," said Lucy.

Jaz set off, pointing out interesting aspects of the city as they headed to Phakalane, an affluent suburb on the other side of Gaborone.

When they reached a block of flats, Lucy stepped out of the pickup, and dirt from the running board smeared onto her leg.

"Oh no, sorry," said Jaz. "I'll get a cloth."

"It's okay, I'm fine," said Lucy, wiping the dirt away with a tissue.

"Okay, if you're sure," said Jaz, leading the group up the stairway to Bernard's flat.

Bernard greeted them at the front door and led them inside. The rooms in the flat were spacious, and paintings hung on the pure white walls, their bright colours allowing them to stand out against each other.

"Are any of the paintings yours?" Lucy asked Jaz.

"A couple, that one there, oh and that one." Jaz pointed out two pieces which showed the activities of village life.

"They're lovely, very vivid," said Lucy.

"Thank you, the colours over here in Botswana are incredible, bright blues, dazzling ochres, a rainbow of hues."

In Bernard's sitting room, they nibbled biscuits and drank South African wine. Hilary explained to Jaz that the three of them were members of a book club. They had been reading stories written by the author Alexander McCall Smith, concerning a lady detective who lived and worked in Botswana.

"That's why we came to Gaborone," said Lucy, joining in the conversation.

"Oh, that makes sense," said Jaz, more relaxed now that Lucy had appeared.

"Have you read any of his books?" Hilary asked.

"Well no, but I'll get Bernard to fill me in on the stories, people and places, then I can plan relevant trips."

Hilary saw Emma and Bernard sitting on the sofa, deep in conversation. "I must talk to Bernard, excuse me." She arrived at Bernard's side and listened to him and Emma discuss the perils of living in a foreign country.

Jaz and Lucy stood by the open balcony doors enjoying the cool breeze and watching Hilary nodding and agreeing with everything Bernard said.

Jaz topped up Lucy's glass.

"Cheers," said Lucy.

"I think Hilary's on a losing streak, Bernard's entranced by Emma," whispered Jaz.

Lucy laughed, choking on the red liquid. Jaz tapped her lightly on the back.

"Thanks," Lucy spluttered. "Should I tell her?"

"Well, I suppose you could, but it's amusing to watch, and Bernard's enjoying himself. I hope you're not feeling left out of your little group, though."

"No, I'm always on the outside looking in, I don't really fit into the gang."

"Yeah, you're a welcomed observer but not a comfortable participant," said Jaz finishing her drink. She put the wine bottle on the table and headed over to the sofa, doing a winding-up gesture to Bernard.

"Well ladies, time you returned to your hotel," said Bernard in response to Jaz's cue. "We can meet up again on Tuesday after Jaz has taken you around Mochudi, the heroine's traditional home."

"Oh, that will be wonderful," said Emma. "Thank you for a lovely evening."

Hilary took Bernard's hand and thanked him profusely, saying she looked forward to Tuesday and seeing him again.

Feeding Hilary's obsession, Bernard kissed the back of her hand and said he couldn't wait. Then he winked at Jaz.

In the pickup, Emma leaned forward. "Lucy, it's nice to see you looking more relaxed. You need to forget Wes and think of yourself."

"Yes, you're right," agreed Lucy.

"Remember he isn't here; he's not watching you." Emma rubbed Lucy's shoulder and sat back.

Lucy nodded in agreement and took a deep breath. "I don't suppose you fancy meeting for a coffee tomorrow?" she asked Jaz. "I can help you plan our visits."

"Oh, yes, excellent suggestion, eleven o'clock on the terrace bar at the Provincial Hotel? It's in the middle of Queen Street, you can't miss it; any taxi will take you there." Jaz tried to sound as if she hadn't been debating the possibility of inviting Lucy out for a drink.

"Great, I'll see you there," said Lucy as they pulled up at the front of the hotel. "I'll get these two to their rooms, if I can get them passed the bar!"

"Hang on, I'll help you." Jaz ran around to Lucy's side of the pickup and opened the door. "Watch the muck this time." She held out her hand to assist Lucy.

Lucy's stomach fluttered.

Chapter 3

In the indoor coffee lounge, wearing a denim cotton dress and misted with perfume, Lucy sat drinking a latte. On her tablet computer, she used the details that Masego, the receptionist, had given her to log onto the Internet. She read Wes's dull email and dropped a reply. "*Arrived safely, have a pleasant room in the Grand Sereto Hotel. I'll try to message you regularly. Love Lucy x.*"

There were other emails in her inbox, including a bank statement. Lucy didn't know how secure the Internet was in Botswana so decided not to open it. In the search engine she typed *Jasmine Page* then pressed enter. There was a reference to Jaz's exhibition at an art gallery two years ago. A picture showed Jaz standing in front of a large painting of a village in Botswana. Lucy did a screenshot of the image and saved it in her tablet's gallery.

Outside, a taxi collected Lucy and took her to Queen Street, where she wandered along the rows of shops. She ventured into the bookshop where she bought a map of Botswana which had a zoomed-in plan of Gaborone.

Reaching the Provincial Hotel early, Lucy spotted a pair of seats by the fenced edge of the terrace bar. She ordered a pot of tea and waited, convinced that Jaz wouldn't arrive.

The bar overlooked the shopping square, Lucy watched the people below and took a series of photographs for her scrapbook. Including a picture of a woman selling home-made trinkets. Through her lens she saw Jaz standing by a girl who was drawing a group of stall holders. There was an unusual tightness in her stomach and Lucy closed her eyes for a few moments to calm her nerves.

Jaz hovered in the doorway looking at Lucy, wondering what made her so alluring. It could be her openness and the accepting warmness of her brown eyes. Jaz reminded herself to keep her distance and not let her feelings get carried away.

Lucy tried to appear laid back as she politely waved over to Jaz.

"Sorry to be late," said Jaz, who had sat in the pickup for half an hour deciding that maybe it wasn't a brilliant idea to meet up with Lucy, she was far too enticing.

"It's okay, I haven't been here long," said Lucy. "What do you want to drink?"

"A cola, please."

The waiter took the order, and the two women sat quietly until the drink arrived.

"Thanks." Jaz downed the cola and smacked her lips. "That's better, this heat makes me thirsty." She looked up at Lucy as she put the empty glass on the table. "So, what places have written on your 'I must visit' list?"

"Well, I bought a map," said Lucy, laying it on the table, moving her cup to make room.

"Oh great, I've got a pen here. Is it okay to write on it?"

"Yeah, I suppose," said Lucy, unnerved at the thought of Jaz scribbling on her new map. She pulled out her tablet and studied her notepad. "Let's see, Mma Ramotswe's office is in a garage on Tlokweng Road."

"Office and garage, interesting," said Jaz, finding it on the Gaborone map and circling it.

Lucy cringed. "Then there's Zebra Drive where she lives."

"That's over here." Jaz added another circle.

"And Mochudi where she was born," sighed Lucy.

"Oh yeah, we're off there tomorrow." Jaz moved to the map of the country and marked off Mochudi. "Then we could go to Thamaga, Lobatse, and Mokolodi." Jaz drew more pen circles.

"Mma Ramotswa goes to Lobatse and Mokolodi to examine criminal cases. I'm not sure about Thamaga though," said Lucy, thinking out loud.

"Well, it's an enjoyable trip, and there's a pottery," said Jaz tapping the table with the end of her pen. "Any other places come to mind?"

"Not that I can think of. I'll ask Emma and Hilary where else they want to go."

"We've made an excellent start. Tomorrow we can search for the garage, drive up Zebra Drive to look at houses, and then carry-on to Mochudi."

"That sounds wonderful," said Lucy.

"Great," said Jaz, beaming. "Would you like an iced tea?"

"That sounds pleasant," answered Lucy.

Jaz ordered the drinks as Lucy attempted to fold her map. She ended up with a bulky rectangle of paper, which she stuffed into her handbag.

"I was nervous about meeting you," said Jaz. "But it's been enjoyable."

"I didn't mean to make you uneasy. To be honest, I didn't think you'd show up."

"I'd never leave a girl standing," said Jaz smiling, a glint in her eyes.

The iced teas arrived, and Jaz told Lucy which of the shops in the street were worth popping into and informed her that the museum down the road was interesting to visit.

Lucy took a drink. "Oh, that's refreshing." She swirled the liquid in her cup and smelt its subtle, earthy aroma.

"On Saturday me and my friends are jumping out of an aeroplane to raise funds for the local orphanage," said Jaz. "I could ask Bernard to bring you over to watch my dramatic fall to earth if you're interested!"

"That sounds dangerous!"

"It was a mad idea I came up with one day, and Bernard organised it." Jaz was terrified about the jump but tried to sound cool.

"Well, that'll be an exciting day out, I'll definitely be there," said Lucy, humoured by Jaz's death-defying exploit.

Jaz looked nervously at the amusement in Lucy's eyes.

"The most dangerous thing I've ever done is place a book on the wrong shelf," said

Lucy.

"It's a wonder they didn't frog-march you from the library and take your ticket away," Jaz replied.

Lucy giggled, then stifled a yawn.

"Am I boring you?" said Jaz, gazing at Lucy's lips and her tired eyes.

"No, I'm sorry, I didn't sleep too well last night."

"It was the prospect of meeting up with me." A cheeky grin appeared on Jaz's face.

"No, I don't think so," said Lucy, smirking.

"Well, I'll meet you at your hotel tomorrow morning, is half-past nine okay?" asked Jaz, trying to decide how to say goodbye. Handshakes were formal and the British just didn't do kisses. She wished she could be more continental.

"Yes, that's fine," said Lucy, exhausted but enjoying spending time with Jaz. "I don't suppose you're going home via the Grand Sereto?" she asked.

"Yeah, I guess I can go that way." The hotel wasn't on Jaz's route, but not wanting to be offensive, she agreed to give Lucy a lift. "This way," said Jaz as she led Lucy around to the rear of the hotel where she'd squeezed the pickup into a parking space. "Watch the muck?"

"Yeah, I'll be more careful this time."

"I must wash you, Big Red."

"Who's Big Red?"

"That's my pickup's nickname," said Jaz. "Because she's big and red."

"Imaginative," said Lucy, laughing at Jaz's peculiar ways and looking around Big Red's interior. "She's roomy inside, that's a handy space." Her hands wandered into the compartment above the windscreen, finding maps and dirty cloths.

"Sorry, she needs a tidy," said Jaz setting off. She switched on the radio and hummed to the tunes. "Your dress is lovely, it suits you," she said, attempting to be sociable.

"Thank you." Lucy smoothed the fabric and picked at a loose thread. "So, do you live here on your own?"

"Yeah, but I've got a few friends in town. Aileen, who picked me up from the airport, and Naledi, who puts my paintings in her gallery. Sometimes, if I'm lucky, I pick up strangers along the way." Jaz grinned at Lucy.

"I bet lots of lost and aimless people fall into your hands."

"Well, yeah, I have to be choosy who I take on," said Jaz, enjoying their unusual conversation.

Arriving at the hotel, Jaz took Lucy's hand helping her climb out, cautious of her dirtying her tidy dress.

"Thanks for the lift, it was lovely meeting up with you," said Lucy holding Jaz's hand.

"We should do it again," said Jaz. "If you're interested and enjoy dancing and music, I could take you to an excellent club," she said, trying not to be too forward.

"Well, I'll consider your offer," said Lucy.

"Great." Jaz gently pulled her hand free. "Have a nice evening."

Chapter 4

Lucy was excited about today's trip, but the heat was sweltering, and she couldn't decide what to wear. She tried on several outfits, finally choosing a jade-coloured t-shirt, blue paisley wrap-around skirt, and white pumps. Downstairs in the lounge she joined Emma on the comfortable soft seats.

Jaz arrived on time, dressed in beige cotton trousers and a short-sleeved white shirt. As she entered, she removed her sunglasses and smiled at Lucy. "Oh, it's nice to be in the air conditioning," she said as she admired Lucy's outfit. "It's getting hot outside." Jaz pulled her collar away from her neck.

"We're waiting for Hilary. She was here earlier, but had forgotten her hat," said Emma.

"Well, there's no rush," said Jaz. "Lucy, are you alright?"

Lucy stopped gazing at Jaz. "Sorry, oh yes, fine."

Hilary appeared wearing a straw hat, its wide brim covering her short white hair. "Good morning, Jasmine," she said.

"Morning Hilary, ready to go?" asked Jaz.

Hilary nodded and walked toward the hotel door.

"After you." Jaz shepherded Lucy and Emma outside and toward the pickup.

Lucy jumped into the front seat, leaving Hilary and Emma to sit at the back.

"You still looking forward to your day trip?" asked Jaz putting the vehicle into gear and driving out of the car park.

"Oh yes," said Lucy as she tucked her skirt around her legs.

"First, I thought we'd drive along Tlokweng Road, see if we can recognise Mr JLB Makatoni's garage. Then we can head to Zebra Drive to find Mma Ramotswa's house, and after that we can head out to Mochudi to explore her origins." Jaz winked at Lucy for helping her plan day one.

"That sounds marvellous, Jasmine," said Hilary.

Jaz winced and pulled her face at hearing her full name. Only her granny called her Jasmine.

Lucy covered her mouth as she tried not to giggle at Jaz's perturbed face.

Glancing at her, Jaz grinned and turned the pickup onto a wide main road. "So, we're now on Tlokweng Road with its range of garages."

"Oh, that one is Speedy Motors," said Emma.

"No, no, it's definitely that one," announced Hilary.

"Do you have a preferred garage, Lucy?" asked Jaz, trying not to sound sarcastic.

"Well, I agree with Emma," said Lucy in a serious tone, taking a photograph of the garage.

"Over there is Riverwalk Mall, it's got a few useful shops." Jaz pointed over to an arcade.

"We need to go there, it's where Mma Ramotswe does her shopping!" shouted Hilary. Emma and Lucy nodded enthusiastically.

"Okay, we'll put it on the trip list, now off to Zebra Drive," said Jaz

They arrived in the street and the three book lovers studied the buildings through the pickup windows.

"Oh, it's got to be that house there, the one setback in the garden with the small tree," gushed Emma.

"You're right, I can visualise Mma Ramotswe sitting under that tree drinking tea," agreed Hilary.

Lucy took more photographs.

Jaz drove along Zebra Drive and then joined the road that headed toward Mochudi. The tourists surveyed the scenery as they travelled along the tarmac covered roads. Passing metal shacks on the street side, which sold fast food and offered haircuts. The road surface grew grimmer as they drove across the wide sandy landscape, dotted with odd-shaped trees.

As she drove Jaz told them the story of the local currency. "It's called the Pula, that means rain in Setswana, and it's the most precious thing in Botswana, other than diamonds."

"What's Setswana?" asked Lucy.

Hilary looked at Lucy as if she was stupid and tutted.

Jaz didn't appreciate Hilary's impudence. "That's a good question. Setswana is the native language of Botswana. There's also Khoisan, the language of the Bushmen, a fascinating vocabulary of clicking sounds. And everyone learns English, as the country was a British protectorate until 1966."

"Very interesting," said Emma, glaring at Hilary.

Jaz turned off the main road onto a bumpy, pot-holed road. The tourists bounced around as Jaz drove as carefully as she could.

"No wonder Mma Ramotswa's white van struggles," moaned Hilary.

As they entered the village of Mochudi, they saw traditional rondavels and a few shops.

"They build the rondavels with clay bricks and cover it with a mud-based outer plastering. The men put up the walls and the women group together to thatch the roof," said Jaz.

"They're charming," said Lucy, clicking the shutter of her camera.

"A few rondavels have decorative designs painted on their walls," said Jaz, pleased at Lucy's interest in the architecture. "The shops here are hardware stores and bottle shops."

"Bottle shops?" asked Hilary.

"Yes err, I suppose they're a cross between an off-license and a bar," answered Jaz.

"That's why men are sitting around outside," said Emma.

"This is the Kgotla," said Jaz, pointing to a sheltered compound. "That's where the chief of the village and his advisers meet to discuss local issues."

"The same as a council?" suggested Emma.

Jaz nodded in agreement. "We'll travel up the hill to the museum now."

Big Red steadily climbed up the steep road, encouraged by Jaz's choice words of support. When they arrived, the passengers got out and went inside the ramshackle building to investigate the local artefacts.

Jaz sat herself on a rock and looked down at the view of Mochudi. Although she liked the historical stories in the museums, Jaz preferred to sit and use her artistic skills to capture the environment and create her own impression of the landscape. She took her sketchbook from her satchel and drew the rondavels, adding trees, goats and people doing their daily tasks.

Lucy came out of the museum and sat in the shade, watching Jaz paint purposeful watercolour strokes onto the paper.

Jaz noticed that Lucy had joined her. "Could you take a photograph of the view for me, please?" she asked. "For future reference, in case I do a bigger painting."

Lucy focussed her camera and took the shot. "It's such a talent being able to paint the scenery and have it in your sketchbook forever."

Jaz blushed and thanked Lucy for her comment, and they sat enjoying the peaceful scenery. Emma and Hilary joining them shattered the moment.

"An interesting museum. Thank you, Jasmine." Hilary closed her notebook. "Now I'm ready for my lunch."

"Well, it's back to Gaborone, we're meeting Bernard at the garden centre cafe. I hope you're not too starved, it might take an hour to get there," said Jaz.

"It's okay, I brought biscuits for us to share," said Emma, delving into her oversize handbag and removing several packets.

As they drove Jaz gave the group a lesson in Setswana. "Well, *dumella* means good day. So, when you meet someone you say *dumella*."

"Dumella," they repeated in unison.

"Now if you are speaking to a lady you say *mma*, hum the *m* and add an *a*."

"Mma. Dumella mma," said Lucy.

"Now if it's a man, you're speaking to you say *rra*."

"Ra."

"Roll the *r*, *rra*."

"Rra, dumella rra."

"When you're leaving you say *go siame*, it's spelt with a *g* but you say *h*," Jaz explained.

"Go siame," repeated Lucy with an 'h', enjoying learning something new.

"Now you can say *ke ithuta Setswana*."

"What does that mean?" asked Lucy as they pulled up at the garden centre.

"It means I'm learning Setswana." Jaz winked at Lucy.

Bernard was waiting in the car park and helped Emma out of the pickup, while Jaz assisted Lucy. Hilary glared at them as she clambered out unaided.

The garden centre was a hive of coloured flowers and grasses which they admired on their walk toward the restaurant. Once there they sat and chatted under the large shady umbrellas, eating the delicious food served to them.

When she'd finished her food, Jaz drained her teacup and stood. "Well, I'll see you on Thursday for our trip to Thamaga."

"Oh," said Lucy. "Can I come with you to the pickup? I left my jacket on the seat."

"Oh, okay," said Jaz, trying to remember if Lucy had brought a jacket with her.

They walked to Big Red, admiring the blossoms on the plants. Lucy stopped to sniff the jasmine flowers.

"I wonder if my mum likes the smell of jasmine," said Jaz.

"She must have loved it to name you after something so captivating." Lucy paused after saying something so forward, her cheeks reddened, and she apologised.

"No, it's okay, I'll take any compliment I can get."

Arriving at Big Red, Jaz opened the door and looked inside. "No jacket here. Are you sure you brought one?"

"Well, I thought I did. Sorry, my mistake."

"No problem. Well, I'll catch you on Thursday."

Lucy stared at Jaz with a melancholy look in her eyes.

"Hey, is your husband still upsetting you? Do you need a hug?" Jaz held her arms open and comforted Lucy with her embrace.

"He hangs around inside my head, depressing me," sighed Lucy into Jaz's ear.

"Life's a bitch, especially with relationships," said Jaz, trying not to enjoy their hug too much. "Look, I can't leave until you smile."

Lucy looked up at her, the edges of her mouth turning upward.

Jaz stroked Lucy's cheek with the back of her hand. "Good, that's better. I'm sorry, but I've got to go."

"That's okay, you're busy."

"Bye then."

"Yes, go siame."

Jaz smiled, impressed by Lucy's grasp of the new language.

Lucy felt lost as Jaz drove away. She waved, and an arm came out of the window, waving back.

Re-joining the others, Bernard gave Lucy a hug. He detected Lucy's depressed aura and poured her another cup of tea. "It's good that you're getting on with Jaz," he said.

"Yeah, it's been nice making a friend," said Lucy.

"Someone cheerful like Jaz is just the person you need to hang out with," said Emma. "Since Carly died you've lost your lively spirit." She patted Lucy's hand.

That evening, the three ladies of the book club visited the casino. Lucy set herself a limit of one hundred Pula, which she quickly gambled away. She spent the rest of the evening watching Hilary waste her money on the one-armed bandits and Emma regularly winning at the solitaire table.

Emma paid for a round of drinks and they sat and watched other punters make and lose from their gambling.

"I'm off to bed," said Lucy. "See you for breakfast." Exhausted, Lucy left Hilary and Emma talking and drinking with a man they'd just met.

"I can lend you more money if you want to carry on playing," said the man.

"No thanks, I'm fine. Goodnight."

Chapter 5

When she opened the curtains, Lucy viewed a dull overcast morning and decided to visit the gym.

While she cycled on the exercise bike she reflected on her relationship with Wes and the inconsiderate way he'd abandoned her at the airport. A tear joined the sweat on her face. She sniffed and wiped it away.

Lucy's mind wandered to her friendship with Jaz. A hot flush crept through her body when she recalled the peculiar feelings that had zoomed around her body when she was in Jaz's arm. She needed a cold shower.

In the cool morning air, a lonesome Lucy walked along a dusty road to the small square of shops next to the hotel. She popped into the mini supermarket, checking out their range of chocolate bars, purchasing two bars of fruit and nut; it was excessive, but she was on holiday.

Back outside Lucy found a telephone box and phoned Wes, just to say hello and have a chat. She missed talking to him; it was the most amiable thing they did together. Lucy put coins into the machine and rang the flat. There was no answer.

Across town, Jaz was at the garden centre with Aileen and Naledi. They met every Wednesday, admired the flowers, and sat amongst them with cakes and coffee.

"I need some more of your paintings to hang in the shop," said Naledi, proprietor of an arts and crafts shop in Broadhurst, a tourist area of Gaborone. "They're selling well."

"That's good to hear, I'd best some work done," said Jaz.

"It's a wonder she's got time, our Jaz has been busy flirting with a lady," said Aileen, a hint of sarcasm in her voice.

"I couldn't help it, she fainted into my arms," Jaz replied, re-enacting the event.

"Tell me more," spluttered Naledi, as she choked on the crumbs of her carrot cake.

Jaz blushed. "There's nothing to tell; anyhow, she's married, not happily, though."

"Oh no, I sense a disaster," sighed Aileen, winking at Naledi.

"Shut your face, it's purely professional."

"Whatever." Aileen sneered at Jaz.

"Is Jeremy looking forward to the parachute jump?" asked Jaz.

"No, he's terrified, I shouldn't have let you talk him into it," moaned Aileen.

"Don't be awful," said Naledi. "I wish I could have done it, but baby says no," she said stroking her baby bump. "At least hubby's looking forward to the challenge."

"Good old Frank, at least we've got one hero," laughed Jaz.

"Hey Jaz, invite your visitors to come camping with us on Friday. They can meet everyone and enjoy a night in the wild, and you can spend more time with Lucy!" said Naledi, grinning.

"No, I don't think they'll enjoy camping," said Jaz.

"Oh, go on invite them. I'm dying to meet your friend." Aileen patted Jaz's arm. "Naledi, will Frank be able to get hold of spare tents and bedding?"

"Yes, that's not a problem, he can borrow it from the Scout store."

Jaz scowled.

The three members of the book group had lunch and drinks by the pool.

Lucy told them about the outings Jaz had planned. "Thamaga tomorrow, then a visit to the airport on Saturday to watch a sponsored parachute jump that's raising money for the orphans."

"Oh, how exciting," said Emma.

"Is Jasmine one of these parachutists?" asked Hilary.

"Yeah," answered Lucy.

"Then I suppose we should go, give her our support," said Hilary.

Lucy stood and dived into the freezing cold swimming pool.

"We're off to the casino now," shouted Emma to Lucy. "Hilary wants to win her money back."

"Okay, have fun," gurgled Lucy as she floated to the side and clambered out of the pool. She adjusted the umbrella, lay on the sunbed, and began reading the mystery book she'd bought at the airport. Lucy identified who the killer was, then tried to focus on the words to prove her ideas correct, but her eyes slowly closed.

Lucy's sleepy mind dreamed that Jaz and Wes were walking together along the corridors of a grim grey building. Lucy was sitting on a train, heading for the building, but she never reached her destination.

When she opened her eyes, Lucy thought she was still dreaming. Jaz was sitting on the sunbed by her side, studying her and drawing in a sketchbook.

Jaz shut her sketchbook when she realised Lucy had woken. "I've ordered us an iced tea," she stuttered. "Hope that's okay, they do a good version here with lemon and honey."

"Yes, that's fine." Lucy established reality by pinching her arm as she pulled on her t-shirt and covered her breasts. "Why are you drawing me?" she asked. "I'm almost naked for goodness sake."

"I just saw you there and thought..." Jaz didn't have a plausible excuse for wanting to draw Lucy's body.

"You should ask if it's okay?" The tone in Lucy's voice was terse, and it stunned Jaz into artistic silence. "Well?"

"Sorry, I'll ask next time," said Jaz, fidgeting with the shoulder strap of her satchel.

"Good," said Lucy.

The drinks arrived, and they sat in a tense silence.

"What are you doing here?" Lucy asked, trying to calm her tone.

"Well, I was chatting with Aileen and Naledi, and they wanted to invite you to camp at the kloof near Molepolole on Friday night. But I can sense you won't want to go, so it doesn't matter."

"A kloof?" said Lucy, questioning Jaz's weird word.

"Oh sorry, the kloof is a ravine, the same as a valley."

"Well it sounds interesting," said Lucy being calmed by Jaz's mesmerising eyes. "I'll mention it to the others later, but count me in, I've never been camping." Lucy didn't know if she'd enjoy sleeping in a tent. She remembered that Wes had suggested trying it in the past, but she had refused. "The others are in the casino, so I won't find out until this evening."

"That's okay, I can let Naledi know in the morning, and her husband can get the camping gear ready," said Jaz. "Have you been in the casino yet?"

"We visited it last night, I lost a hundred Pula in ten minutes, unbelievable," said a disgusted Lucy. "I kept a chip as a memento though."

"That's casinos for you, they're fixed. I only ever gamble on the Grand National, a pound each way, and that's my lot."

Lucy laughed. "Hilary's losing loads of money, Emma's doing well though."

"I'll have a word with Bernard, he can ask Emma to stop gambling before her luck runs out."

"Does he fancy her?" Lucy asked.

"There might be love in the air."

"Oh, that's nice."

They finished their drinks, and Jaz sensed Lucy's temper had eased. "What are you up to now?" she asked, hoping they could go for a walk and continue their conversation.

Lucy was bored sitting around the pool, but she didn't want Hilary and Emma to think she was avoiding them. "Nothing, just reading."

"Fancy a trip to the lake?"

"I'm not sure, I said I'd wait for the others and we'd have a meal in the restaurant."

Jaz's shoulders drooped, and she stared at the pool. "Oh okay. Well, I'll catch you tomorrow to go to Thamaga," she said in a quiet voice.

"Yeah, that'll be nice," said Lucy.

"Bye then." Jaz picked up her satchel and left. She had a quick chat with Masego at the reception desk and amused her by dinging the reception bell every time Masego tried to speak. The next time she tried to ding it, Masego snatched the bell from underneath Jaz's hand and they both laughed.

From the poolside Lucy watched their joviality and felt a pang of jealousy. She saw Jaz waving to her as she left the hotel, but ignored her, pretending to be busy reading.

In her room Lucy realised how rude she had been and promised to apologise to Jaz when she saw her again. Showered and changed, she arrived in the restaurant and saw Hilary and Emma chatting to the man they'd met in the casino last night.

"Oh Lucy," Hilary shouted. "We're over here."

"Hi everyone," said Lucy as she took a seat.

"This is Ian," said Emma, introducing the chap with them. "You remember him from the casino."

"Hello," said Ian, holding out his hand.

"Oh hello," said Lucy, shaking his thin, scrawny fingers.

"Ian won lots of money on the roulette wheel," said Emma. "It was so exciting to watch."

"Oh well done," said Lucy, observing his lank black hair and wide rimmed glasses.

"Ian's staying in the hotel, he's working on an engineering project with the water company," said Hilary giggling. "Lucy, do you mind if he joins us for supper?"

"No, that'll be nice. Before I forget, the parachutist's we're watching on Saturday have invited us to go camping with them on Friday evening."

"That sounds fun. What do you think Emma, you up for it?" said Hilary.

"As long as you're both there."

"Good, the three-go camping!" announced Hilary, as if they were in a children's book.

"Okay, I'll let Jaz know tomorrow," said Lucy.

Ian sat next to Lucy as they ate supper, telling amusing stories of engineering disasters he'd encountered. Finishing his meal, Ian's tall thin body stood, and he headed for the bar where he bought the ladies a bottle of wine. He poured a glass for Lucy and handed it to her, then he gave the bottle and two glasses to Hilary and Emma. "Goodnight everyone," he said. "Enjoy the wine."

"Goodnight," Hilary and Emma said together.

Lucy put her glass on the table. "I'll give it a miss and get myself rested before tomorrow's outing."

"Can I have yours?" asked Hilary.

Lucy nodded and wandered into the lounge where she saw Ian lingering at the bar looking as if he were waiting for someone.

"Hi," said Ian as Lucy walked past him. "Did you enjoy your wine?"

"Oh, Hilary's drinking mine, I'm too tired."

He manoeuvred himself in front of her. "Do you fancy a walk in the garden?"

"No," said Lucy, frowning at his strange request. She swerved around him.

"Do you want a coffee?"

"No thank you, goodnight," she said, shaking her head as she hurried away.

"Yeah, goodnight." He walked back to the bar and slouched onto the bar stool.

Chapter 6

There was a loud rapping on Lucy's door. She rolled over in bed, stretched, and yawned, then had a sudden thought it might be Jaz. "Hang on, just coming," she shouted, putting on a dressing gown and checking her hair.

When she opened the door, she found Emma in a panic.

"Lucy, I can't get hold of Hilary, she's not answering her door."

"Oh dear, come in, try ringing her from here while I get dressed."

Emma dialled and waited. "Still no answer."

"Let's visit her room again," said Lucy.

As they travelled in the lift to the next floor, Emma told Lucy what had happened last night.

"We were tipsy from drinking the wine. Ian helped me get Hilary up to her room, and I made sure she had a glass of water and got her into bed. She fell straight to sleep."

Reaching Hilary's room, Lucy hammered loudly on the door and listened. There was silence. "We'd best ask reception to let us in," said Lucy.

Emma hurried away and returned with a concerned Masego. Lucy stared at her, still envious of Masego fooling around with Jaz yesterday. Masego unlocked and pushed open the door, unsure of the scene she might find.

"She's dead," cried Emma, seeing Hilary lying still on the bed.

"No, she's breathing." Lucy prodded Hilary as she spoke. "Look."

Hilary's chest rose and lowered.

"Oh good," Emma sighed. "What should we do now?"

"Thank you Masego, we'll take care of Miss O'Brian," said Lucy, filling and turning on the kettle to make a restorative cup of tea. "Emma, can you find Hilary's mobile phone? You'd best call Bernard and tell him that Hilary's not feeling well."

Emma rooted through Hilary's handbag, found her phone, and dialled. "Hello, Bernard, its Emma here...Yes, it's nice to talk to you too...I'm just phoning to say Hilary's sick...We can't wake her, she's fast asleep...Lovely, see you in a while." She hung up the phone. "Bernard's on his way."

When he arrived, Bernard stared at Hilary and shook her shoulders. There was no response. "I'd better phone Jaz and ask her to re-arrange our trip to Thamaga."

Emma made Bernard a coffee and Lucy listened to Bernard's phone call.

"Yeah, she's pissed...No she's fine...Can you re-arrange the trip...okay...Bye." He looked at Lucy and smiled. "There, she'll do that, then come over."

They sat for a while, talking, and waiting for something to happen. Bernard's phone rang with its 'God Save the Queen' ringtone. Hilary sat bolt upright, saluting the national anthem, then she fell back to sleep.

"Blimey," said Bernard as he answered the phone and told Jaz the number of Hilary's room.

A few moments later there was a light tap at the door, and Jaz wandered in. "Hi, what's going on?"

"Hilary partook in too much alcohol last night," said Bernard, stifling a laugh.

"You two must be to blame!" Jaz looked at Lucy and Emma, as she tried to keep a straight face.

"Not to blame your honour, I was in bed," announced Lucy.

"Oh, what have I done!" cried Emma. "I've turned Hilary into a zombie!"

Bernard put his arm around her shoulders. "Now then, don't you worry, Hilary will sleep it off. Let's go and have breakfast."

"She'll never talk to me again," wailed Emma as Bernard escorted her from the room.

"See you later," said Jaz, winking as he left. "That's Bernard's day sorted. Would you like a drink by the pool?"

"Sure, why not?" said Lucy.

Lucy sat at the outside bar, drinking an iced latte, and eating a piece of toast.

Jaz sipped her lemon tea. "You know, you've got to be careful with alcohol over here. The heat does strange things to your metabolism, it can really mess you up," she said. "I've re-arranged the trip to Thamaga for next Tuesday, so you have a free day. If there's anywhere you'd like to go you have me and Big Red at your service."

"Well, I want to apologise for being grouchy yesterday. I was in an odd mood, I'm sorry," said Lucy.

"That's okay. I think you'd have enjoyed the lake, though. It was stunning." Jaz went quiet as she recalled her visit last night. She'd sat on a rock overlooking the rippling water, feeling a slight breeze waft over her face. When she got up to leave, she told the lake she'd be back soon, and hoped to bring Lucy with her. In response, the wind had ruffled her hair.

Lucy's lips pursed, and she glared at Jaz through narrowed eyes.

"Are you alright?" asked Jaz. "You seem tense."

"I'm not tense, I'm fine." Lucy frowned and folded her arms, resting them on her crossed legs.

"Look, I'll be going to the lake again, maybe you'll come with me next time."

"That'll be nice, thank you," said Lucy tersely.

"You should try to relax more," said Jaz.

"I am relaxed." Lucy waved her arms in the air and threw a serviette at Jaz.

"Good," giggled Jaz, catching the paper napkin and throwing it back into Lucy's face.

"Stop it," huffed Lucy, swatting the napkin onto the floor. "So," she said, changing the subject. "I asked the others, and they agreed to go camping."

"Oh, excellent." Jaz phoned Naledi and spent a while talking of art sales before telling her about the additional campers. "There that's arranged," said Jaz, an enormous smile on her face.

"Shall we go to the museum today?" suggested Lucy.

"Sure, brilliant idea, are you ready now?"

"I just need to get my handbag from my room." Lucy stood, walked into the hotel, and travelled up in the lift with Jaz in tow.

Jaz followed Lucy into her room and looked around. "Ooh, it's lovely, you've got a telly, and a better view than Hilary."

"Yes, it's alright," said Lucy. "I just need to send Wes an email," said Lucy, switching on her tablet and clicking the email app.

Wes had replied to her last message saying he was well and hoping Lucy was enjoying herself. She typed back. *Hi Wes, I'm having an interesting time. I'll be going camping tomorrow! Hope you're okay. Love Lucy x.*

"Oh, Coronation Street," said Jaz.

Lucy took the remote control from Jaz and switched off the TV.

They parked at the top end of Queen Street and walked along the row of shops, passing the bookshop.

"Can I go in?" asked Lucy.

"You can do anything you want." Jaz held the door open.

They browsed the books and Jaz pointed out a bird and animal book in which Lucy could record her safari sightings. After purchasing it, they continued along the shopping street.

"Do you eat pies?" asked Jaz, disappearing into the Pula Pie shop without waiting for a reply. She re-appeared with a paper bag containing two pies. "I got you steak, is that okay?"

"Yeah, that's fine." Lucy considered whether there were any positive points to Jaz's dining options.

When they reached the museum, they toured the exhibits.

Lucy learned about the landscape, the cattle industry, tribal histories, traditional arts and crafts, and the story of diamonds.

"Can we eat our picnic now?" Jaz asked as her stomach rumbled.

"I told you to have breakfast with me."

"I know, but I wasn't hungry then."

They found a shaded spot under a large-leafed tree and sat on the dry yellow grass. Jaz produced Lucy's steak pie and a can of cola from her satchel.

"Thanks." Lucy took a bite from the pie, it was tasty, and she smiled while savouring the flavours before taking another bite.

"I thought you'd enjoy it."

They relaxed and observed the world go by as they finished eating and drinking.

"Where shall we go now, tour guide?" asked Lucy.

"Well, there's a small safari park we can visit. It'll give you an idea of what you might see if you were out in the bush, and you can tick off the animals in your book!"

"Great." Lucy stood, walked to the pavement, and stepped into the road.

A motorbike drove straight toward her.

"Lucy," shouted Jaz.

Lucy turned and saw her reflection in the rider's visor.

Jaz's arm wrapped itself around Lucy's waist and pulled her backward. "Bloody hooligan!" Jaz ranted after the biker. "Are you okay?"

Lucy rested her head back against Jaz's shoulder, gasping for breath. "Yes," she sobbed. "He could have killed me!"

A few locals gathered asking if Lucy was alright and cursing the motorcyclist. Lucy told them she was fine, and Jaz released her, guiding her to a bench where Lucy sat. A bottle of water emerged from Jaz's satchel, which appeared to carry everything.

"Here." Jaz handed her the bottle. "We'll do the safari park another day, I'll get you back to the hotel?"

"No, I don't want to go back yet, I'm alright honestly. I could do with a proper drink, though, steady my nerves."

Jaz admired Lucy's response to her near-death experience. "I know the perfect place." Jaz took Lucy's hand. "Can you make it to the car park?"

"Yes, you grabbing my waist hurt more than he did." Lucy linked Jaz's arm and walked closely next to her.

Jaz carefully helped Lucy climb inside Big Red, before driving her to an unfamiliar part of the city.

"You'll love this place, it's full of cool dudes," said Jaz, grinning like a naughty teenager. "Cocktail?" she asked as she parked.

"Lovely, just what I need," said Lucy, observing the outdoor dance floor and bar.

They sat at a small table with a *Sunset Over the Cape* wine cocktail for Lucy and a cola for Jaz.

"Cheers." Jaz held her glass in the air.

"Cheers, to the worst motorcyclist in Botswana," said Lucy chinking her glass to Jaz's.

"Hey up, don't drink it that fast." Jaz watched Lucy drain the whole glass. "I'd better get another."

After three cocktails Lucy was dancing with Jaz to the traditional music beating out of the huge speakers. Jaz was creating strange angular dance moves and swinging her head manically.

Lucy couldn't help but laugh. "I'll get more drinks, grab a table. You'd best have a rest after your gyrations."

Jaz sat in a nearby seat and studied Lucy at the bar. She was lively, unpredictable, a total flirt, and utterly gorgeous. Jaz was desperately trying to stay professional and not fall for Lucy.

Lucy returned with her cocktail and a cola. "I asked them to put a cherry in your drink." She pulled the cocktail stick out of the cola and moved the cherry toward Jaz's mouth. "There you go."

As Jaz's tender lips took hold of the cherry, the phone in her satchel started ringing, distracting her from her amorous thoughts. "Must be my agent," she laughed. "Hello. Hi Bernard. Yeah. okay. Bye." Jaz put her phone in her trouser pocket. "Bernard's invited us to join him for supper at the Bull and Bush Diner."

"Sounds great, I'm hungry now."

"Time for one more dance," said Jaz, pulling Lucy up from her seat.

Lucy staggered into the restaurant and joined the others at the table. As they ate their steaks and ribs, Lucy told everyone how she was almost killed by a motorbike and kept thanking Jaz for her life-saving reaction.

Jaz told her she was exaggerating because if she hadn't been there, someone else would have saved her.

"And this afternoon, to cheer me up, Jaz took me dancing," said Lucy, her hand holding Jaz's.

Jaz's heart fluttered. "So, Hilary, how are you feeling?" she asked.

"Oh, my head was fuzzy earlier, and I can't remember last night. I'm sure I didn't drink more than I usually do," said Hilary.

"You're just worn out," said Bernard. "While you were sleeping, me and Emma had a delightful walk around the hotel gardens and viewed the birds."

Emma smiled at him. "It was lovely; we saw a crested barbet and a fairy flycatcher."

"How nice," said Hilary, unable to look happy for them.

The two pairs of friends sat looking at each other whilst Hilary continued to scowl. When Lucy stood and headed for the toilets Hilary followed her.

"You know she's gay," said Hilary scathingly as she walked past Lucy, who was holding the bathroom door open for her.

"Who's gay?" Lucy asked.

"Your friend, Jasmine, she's a lesbian," Hilary spluttered, strangely sounding out the letters. "Bernard told me."

"Well, you shouldn't base a person on social labels. Remember our book club rule, we must accept diversity."

"Yes, sorry, but watch yourself she might be after you! Lucky you've got Wes waiting at home for you!"

Lucy flushed the toilet and left the toilet block.

"You alright?" said Jaz, noticing the pained expression on Lucy's face.

"I'm fine, bit tired, today's drama has caught up with me, and far too many cocktails." Lucy looked dejectedly at Jaz and drank a mouthful of wine.

"Yeah, it's been a wild day, hasn't it?" muttered Jaz.

Hilary returned and sat watching Lucy and Jaz. Bernard sensed the uneasy atmosphere, and distracted Hilary by asking her if she wanted a pudding.

Jaz sighed. "I'd best go. I need to prepare for tomorrow's tour of Molepolole." She kissed Bernard's cheek and squeezed Lucy's shoulder. "Goodnight everyone, see you tomorrow."

"Goodnight," said Emma.

"Bye," said Lucy. "Thanks for today."

"No probs."

Lucy sat and stared at the others. In her head she was dancing wildly with Jaz, but now Hilary was watching her every move.

Chapter 7

The next morning Jaz collected the members of the book club. Lucy handed over her cabin case and Jaz secured it into the rear of Big Red beside her rucksack and tent. Emma and Hilary got into the pickup with just their handbags.

They headed away from Gaborone towards Molepolole. There wasn't much to see on the forty-minute journey except sand, trees, and a few rondavels. They sat silently as they travelled.

Lucy's mind flashed back to last night's conversation with Hilary and the possibility that Jaz might fancy her. She tried to determine how much Emma and Hilary would despise her for having a lesbian friend. Emma would be fine, she decided, but homophobic Hilary would excommunicate her.

Jaz thought she should break the silence. "Hope you're ready for camping tonight?"

Hilary and Emma muttered something in the backseats, not sounding over-enthusiastic.

"Yeah," said Lucy. "I didn't know what to bring though."

"Well, at least you've brought yourself," laughed Jaz.

The tour of Molepolole began as they entered the sizable village.

"That's the road we'll go along later to the campsite at the kloof. It's where the diamond cutting and polishing firm is based, they're big employers out here. Over there is a wonderful hardware shop, and that's the Kgotla." Jaz pointed a finger as she drove passed. Then she parked in front of a village store, for everyone to experience what was sold locally.

"I need to buy food for tonight," said Jaz to Lucy. "We'll need sweet corn, they call it maize over here, and meat." She put ten maize heads in her basket, added ten lean beef steaks and a long string of sausages. They carried on through the store, Jaz picked up a metal coffeepot in the hardware section. "White, green or brown coffee pot?"

"I'd choose the brown one, it looks rustic," said Lucy, pleased at being asked.

"Have we just come in here so that Jasmine can do her shopping," Hilary muttered to Emma.

Emma told her to shut up as she perused the cakes and biscuits, to buy as a gift for Bernard's friends.

Back outside, Jaz packed her foodstuffs in the cool box, and put the coffee pot into a metal trunk. They headed off again. At the mosque they turned right, leaving the main road, passing the secondary school and the college of further education.

Lucy took photographs of the exteriors for her travelogue. "It's a vast village," she said, intrigued at the range and colours of low-level buildings.

"Yeah, the diamond companies have been building houses for their employees, there's an older more traditional part if you go further out of town," Jaz replied, happier that the earlier tension was subsiding. "Now if you carry on up this road, you'll end up in the Kalahari Desert, but we won't be going that far." She did a U-turn.

Lucy listened to the information Jaz was sharing. Jaz's mouth was alive with words and her eyes searched for points of interest. To Lucy's amazement, she wondered if she'd enjoy kissing Jaz's lyrical lips. Gasping, she shifted her attention, taking a photograph out of the window.

Jaz turned her head, glancing at Lucy. "You okay?" she asked, unaware of Lucy's desires.

"Yeah fine," said a flustered Lucy.

"Here is the Livingstone Memorial Hospital, named after the missionary David Livingstone. He came to Botswana as part of the London Missionary Society disposition in eighteen hundred and something." Jaz parked the pickup, allowing that the party to explore. Hilary made notes and got a camera out of her bag, following Lucy around and taking photographs. Emma sat under a tree and watched them while she ate a biscuit.

Back in the pickup, Jaz headed toward the house that belonged to Bernard's friends, OJ and Melody. When they arrived, they saw Bernard standing by his car. Jaz parked next to him and he opened the rear door of the pickup, helping Emma step out. Hilary followed from the same door, crushing Bernard as she fell into him.

Jaz caught sight of the commotion through her mirror and giggled. Then she jumped out of Big Red, ran around the front and opened the passenger door for Lucy. "Time for lunch," she said.

Lucy took her hand to step out of the pickup, enjoying Jaz fussing over her. She smiled, "Thank you."

Jaz ploughed through the plate of food she'd concocted from Melody's delicious buffet and poured herself another beer. Step by step she went through her parachute routine while the others discussed the Mma Ramotswe' detective stories.

"Don't drink too much driver!" said Lucy, an eyebrow-raising above one eye.

Lucy's saucy look made Jaz's groins stir. "Sorry, keeping the parachute nerves at bay. Last one for now."

"You'll be fine." Lucy rubbed Jaz's hand. "You know Molepolole well."

"The Internet's a brilliant place for research." Jaz winked, and they both laughed.

Lucy realised that she was still touching Jaz and she quickly lifted her hand away, jokingly slapping Jaz's arm as she did so. "You cheat!"

"Don't tell the other two."

After dinner, OJ took Hilary, Emma, and Lucy on a tour of the garden. Bright colours emanated from the flowers and sensual aromas filled their nostrils. Waxbills and sparrows flitted in and out of the trees, and as they walked geckos ran in front of them tiptoeing along the hot sandy path.

"Jaz," said Bernard, distracting her from contemplating another beer. "I've been chatting with Emma and Hilary and they're not sure they want to go camping tonight, it's too basic for them!"

"Are they going back to Gaborone?" asked Jaz.

"Yes, I'd better take them back. I'll have a word with Lucy and see what she wants to do."

"Yeah, okay." Jaz opened the third beer in frustration.

Returning from the garden tour, Lucy noticed Jaz's fresh beer and saw that she looked upset. Bernard took Lucy to one side and explained the issue. Lucy told him she'd still enjoy going camping, although she was concerned about being without her friends.

Jaz cheered up when Bernard told her she still had one camping companion, and she joined Lucy under a tree. "Hilary and Emma aren't joining us tonight."

"Yeah, wussies. I think it's exciting." Lucy tried not to sound nervous.

"Good, I thought you might have wanted to go back to the hotel with them."

"No, I'm happy being with you," said Lucy, surprising herself again.

After saying their goodbyes, the pair of campers headed towards the kloof. The road started off as tarmac but became more uneven as they travelled further into the bush.

Jaz eased off the speed as Big Red bumped along, apologising every time she hit a pothole and swerving to avoid as many as she could. Lucy held on to the roof handle, smiling as confidently as she could. Jaz pointed out the cliff edge of Execution Rock, and they parked in a space next to the car Lucy recognised as the one which collected Jaz at the airport.

"Made it." Jaz wiped the sweat off her brow with the back of her hand.

"I'm nervous," said Lucy.

"You'll be fine," said Jaz, smiling at her and squeezing her hand. Then she jumped out of Big Red into the arms of Aileen.

"Hiya Jazzy, you okay?" said Aileen, hugging her.

"Yeah, had a tour of Molepolole and a lovely lunch. Come and meet Lucy."

Lucy was leaning on the bonnet. Aileen came over and gave her a hug, then took her to meet Jeremy. He stopped placing sticks on the fire and greeted Lucy, then gave her a quick tour of the campsite.

Jaz collected the food from the cool box and took it to the makeshift kitchen. Then she went over to Naledi and Frank's tent, giving them both a hug and telling them that Hilary and Emma weren't coming.

"No worries," said Frank.

Lucy watched Jaz and Frank hammering pegs into two tents which sat side by side. Assuming that one of them was hers Lucy relaxed; she had been nervous that she might have to share a tent with Jaz.

"Grab these," said Jaz as she handed Lucy the sleeping bags. Then she struggled from the pickup carrying Lucy's cabin case, her own rucksack, and two sleeping mats. Jaz deposited the items in the correct tents. "There, what do you think?" she asked Lucy as they surveyed the pair of four-foot-wide tents.

Lucy ventured inside the small blue tent and unrolled her sleeping bag onto the ground sheet, trying to convince herself that camping was a good idea.

"The temperature can drop at night, so I've brought you a pair of jogging trousers and a sweatshirt," said Jaz, handing them over to Lucy.

Lucy took the clothing and imagined being alone in a tent. "Will it get very dark?" she asked. "Are there lions?"

"No lions, but it will get dark. I've hung a light in the top there. You can have my head torch as well and I'm next door, scream and I'll be right with you."

"Don't be stupid," said Lucy, frowning.

"You'll be fine. Honest."

"Jaz," whispered Lucy.

"Yeah."

"Where do I go to the loo?"

"Oh yeah, toilet's in the tall tent over there. When you go take this loo roll and a plastic bag to put it in, you know, after you've used it." Jaz pointed to the items which she'd placed at the end of Lucy's tent.

They wandered over to the fire and found a space next to Aileen and Naledi. Jaz opened a bottle of beer and handed it to Lucy. "Lager brewed the German way, lovely stuff."

"Shouldn't you stay sober if you're jumping out of an aeroplane?" asked Lucy, realising she sounded as if she was talking to Wes.

"I need something to stop me worrying!" said Jaz. "Besides, I'm testing the theory of a parachute jump being a cure for a hangover!"

Aileen giggled. "So, Lucy, how's Bernard getting on with his girlfriends?" she asked, saving Jaz from a lecture on the perils of alcohol.

"Oh, it's funny, Hilary came over here expecting Bernard to propose and he's fallen for Emma," laughed Lucy.

"He's enjoying the attention," said Naledi.

While they chatted, Jaz got up to talk to Debbie and Gareth, turning the steaks as she walked past the fire.

"Oy! That's my job," shouted Jeremy.

"Well, get on with it then, not everybody likes well-done steaks!" said Jaz, laughing.

"Jaz brightens up everybody's day," said Naledi.

Lucy nodded and took a drink of beer, trying to avoid Naledi and Aileen's eyes.

"What does your husband think about you being on holiday without him?" asked Aileen.

Aileen's question surprised Lucy. "Oh, he's fine, busy working, he paid for my airline ticket so he can't be too worried."

Jaz wandered back and put her arm around Lucy's shoulders. "Steak or sausage?"

Aileen sneered at Jaz, who shrugged and went to get Lucy's food.

After eating, Jeremy played the concertina, and the campers sang along. Jaz recited a rude northern poem. Then Frank told traditional tales he'd learned from his grandparents.

At nine o'clock, half of the group wandered to their tents. It wasn't late, but it was dark, and they said the sun always woke them early.

Jaz, was drunkenly lying on the sand, staring at the stars.

"Aileen's nice," whispered Lucy as she sat next to her.

"Yeah, but..." Jaz sat up and whispered in Lucy's ear. "She's monitoring my behaviour."

"Oh dear, you'd better be careful," said Lucy, observing the night sky. There were stars everywhere. "That's an incredible sky."

Jaz pointed out the constellations. "It's unbelievable how enormous space is it makes my mind explode."

They both studied the enormity of twinkling darkness.

"Are you tired?" Jaz asked as her eyes moved from the Milky Way to Lucy's face.

"No, I'm fine." Lucy's shoulder touched Jaz sending a buzz through her body.

"You know, I can see why your husband, what's his name?" Jaz paused. "Wes, that's it, I can see why he married you."

"Why?" asked Lucy, watching the fire reflecting in Jaz's eyes.

"Well, because you're gorgeous, that's why," slurred Jaz. "And kind," she added as an afterthought.

"Oh," said Lucy, blushing and not sure how to respond. "Are you chatting me up or are you just being polite."

Jaz stared at Lucy, a puzzled look on her face.

"It's just that last night Hilary told me that you're a lesbian, and now I'm confused."

"Ugh," said Jaz. "I'm sorry, I've drunk too much, ignore me, that's the best thing to do." Jaz's eyes returned to watching the stars glistening in the sky.

"I suppose I should turn in," said Lucy, noticing that Jaz had stopped talking to her.

"I'll just sort the fire." Jaz got up and walked over to the fire where Jeremy handed her a fresh bottle of beer.

Aileen stood up and hugged Jaz. "Goodnight nuisance." She kissed her on the cheek, then walked over to Lucy. "Come on, let's get you safely to your tent."

"I've upset Jaz?" said Lucy.

"Don't worry, she'll be fine in the morning," said Aileen. "Make sure you zip up the mozzie net."

Lucy crept into the tent. She changed into Jaz's joggers and sweatshirt and lay in her sleeping bag. The ground was hard, and it took her a while to become comfortable. Finally, after tossing and turning for some time she dropped asleep.

Sometime later Lucy woke. It took her a while to work out where she was. When she heard rustling and chirping noises outside her tent, she buried her head in her sleeping bag. Fortunately, before she could scream for help, she fell back to sleep.

Chapter 8

It was early when Lucy woke. She smiled, pleased that she had survived the night. She snuggled into her sleeping bag and watched beads of condensation run along the tent's cotton lining. The zipper of the door lowered, and a head popped through the gap.

"Morning camper." Jaz's early morning cheer filled the tent.

"Morning," said Lucy, covering her mouth as she yawned.

"Breakfast is cooking, coffee or tea?"

"Coffee, please."

The head disappeared and Lucy unzipped her sleeping bag, shivering in the cool morning air. She changed into her clothes, watching the doorway in case Jaz reappeared, then crawled out of the tent. Staggering to her feet she saw Jeremy and Jaz sitting either side of the fire, one heating coffee in a metal kettle the other frying bacon, creating a delicious aroma.

The peacefulness of the campsite stunned Lucy, and she watched the sunlight drift up the stone cliff face that bordered the side of the pool. She stood dead still as a woodland kingfisher darted across the water, landing on a branch, and hiding himself away.

"Have you shaken your shoes in case a scorpion crawled into them?" shouted Jeremy.

Lucy didn't know if he was joking, but she sat on a rock and took her pumps off, shaking them wildly. Sand flew out, but no creatures. Neither Jeremy nor Jaz laughed at her, so satisfied she wasn't being set-up Lucy slipped her pumps back onto her feet.

Jaz squeezed onto the edge of Lucy's rock and they sat drinking coffee, watching dragon flies skim above the still water as the day awoke.

"Did you sleep alright?" asked Jaz.

"Yeah," said Lucy. She didn't want to say that the dark frightened her, the ground was lumpy, and the noises were creepy. "I'm sorry if what I said last night upset you."

"No, it's cool and best that you know. I'll take you back to your friends and keep out of your way. Bernard will take over the driving."

"Why?" asked Lucy, shocked by Jaz's reaction. "I didn't think you'd be so touchy about being a lesbian." Lucy stared at the side of Jaz's face. "I have got gay friends."

Aileen appeared, squinting in the sunlight, inky shadows under her eyes. "Morning," she groaned, as she perched precariously on a rock opposite Lucy and Jaz.

"I'll get you a coffee," said Jaz, standing and going over to the kettle.

"Oh boy, somebody's miserable," said Aileen, absorbing the tension as Jaz handed her a metal mug.

"A slight misunderstanding," said Lucy. "We'll sort it out later."

"Yeah, later." Jaz miserably sat next to Lucy.

Everyone came out of their tents, and Jeremy handed each of them a bacon roll and an apple. He was the perfect primary school teacher. "Now today is the big day," he preached. "The big jump is upon us and we must concentrate on raising money for the orphans. Let's stay positive and believe we can do this." He sounded as if he was trying to convince himself more than the others.

Aileen clapped her hands, cheering, and wishing each of them good luck. Lucy joined in, wolf whistling her agreement. Jaz's mood improved, and she leapt up whooping, gathering the other jumpers into a scrum hug where they chanted something exhilarating in Setswana and jumped into the air.

"Come on camp mate, time you put your tent away," Jaz said to Lucy.

"What right now?" said Lucy, yawning.

"Yeah, we need to arrive at the airport before nine o'clock."

Lucy packed her bag and threw it into the back of the pickup, then started pulling up tent pegs. "Are you sure everyone's happy with this parachuting experience?" she asked.

"We're fine, just a few nerves," said Jaz trying to look positive.

Lucy could see the apprehension in Jaz's eyes. "Well, you're very brave, and I'm proud of you."

"Thanks." A nervy smile crossed Jaz's face. "I can do this, can't I?"

"Sure, you can." Lucy gave Jaz a hug.

They didn't speak much on the drive to the airport. Jaz settled herself by playing loud rock music on the radio and singing.

When they arrived, the instructors took the parachutists into a hut where they organised their equipment. Aileen sat with Naledi in the car, sharing coffee from a flask. Lucy snoozed in the pickup, wearing Jaz's fleece on top of her own, keeping herself warm. Not wanting to destroy their friendship, she considered the best way to resolve Jaz's bitterness towards her over the gay issue.

Bernard arrived and tapped on the pickup window. "How are they doing?"

Lucy lowered the window. "They're in there and ready to do it!"

"I'll get the video camera set up, got to get a record of the event."

Lucy stepped out of the pickup and stood with Emma and Hilary.

"Here they come," someone shouted.

Out of the hanger came a group of people wearing bright yellow outfits with red parachute backpacks harnessed to them.

Lucy saw Jaz and waved before taking her photograph. "There she is, Bernard, get her on the video."

The parachutists piled into a rickety old plane. It took off and climbed upwards until it was a dot in the brilliant blue sky. Then the first yellow body dropped out and floated downward. The watchers gazed, not knowing who was falling through the air. Lucy crossed her fingers, said a silent prayer, then photographed the descending body.

One jumper drifted toward the acacia bushes. It was Jeremy, and he landed onto the sharp thorns. Aileen rushed over to help him. Frank landed safely on the grass by the runway. Gareth headed towards the cars and crash-landed on the bonnet of a Mazda. Then disaster, Debbie's parachute twisted itself into a tight whirl and she turned wildly in mid-air. She ejected the chute and emitted the safety chute, but not in time. She plummeted downward and crash-landed in a field. A first-aid team rushed over to her.

"Oh, don't let that be Jaz," gasped Lucy. "No, it's okay, here she comes."

Bernard filmed Debbie's disastrous crash and swung around to catch Jaz's parachute opening. She glided majestically downward and landed in a bundle on the tarmac. She stood, then dropped onto the floor. "Bloody ankle!" Jaz screamed, her parachute billowing on the floor as she undid the harness.

Lucy arrived and carefully took off Jaz's shoe. She did a non-medical assessment of the injury, determining that Jaz's foot remained connected to her leg, and there were no obvious bones poking out. "You've sprained your ankle."

"I think I bloody know that!" Jaz replied.

Lucy ignored Jaz's abrupt answer. "If we help could you hobble to the pickup and I'll take you to the hospital to get your ankle checked."

"Yeah, I guess so, but it hurts!"

"I know, but we'll get you sorted out," said Lucy, removing Jaz's headgear and stroking her hair into a decent style. She rested her arm across Jaz's shoulders and Jaz leaned into her, letting out a loud, painful groan.

Bernard arrived and with Lucy helped Jaz stand and limp over towards Big Red.

"Jaz are you okay?" asked Emma.

"I hurt my ankle," cried Jaz.

"Oh, poor you, here." Emma took a bottle of water and a chocolate bar from her handbag and handed them to Jaz.

"Thanks." Jaz smiled in gratitude. She needed painkillers, but chocolate was an excellent substitute.

A parachute trainer brought Jaz's rucksack over, handing it to Lucy.

"Thanks," said Lucy. "I'll drive Jaz to the hospital then on to her house." She put Jaz's shoe into the rucksack. "Bernard, I'll phone you later."

"Great, take it easy pumpkin," Bernard said to Jaz, rubbing her head.

Jaz scowled. "My keys are in the zipper pocket of my bag."

"Thanks, pumpkin," said Lucy, grinning as she started the pickup and steered it out of the airport.

Jaz directed her along the roads, then gave an excruciating wail as a sledgehammer blow of pain throbbed around her ankle.

Lucy's hand patted Jaz's leg. "Wait here," she said as she parked Big Red and entered the hospital. Lucy emerged with a wheelchair which Jaz sat in and was wheeled to reception and then into a cubicle.

"We should get your jumpsuit off," Lucy suggested. "I've got your clothes here."

"Yeah, guess so." Jaz took her arms out of the jumpsuit, revealing her white sports bra, and a tattoo on the top of her left arm. Lucy looked away as she handed over a white cotton shirt which Jaz put on, leaving it unbuttoned.

Lucy removed the shoe from Jaz's good foot, then Jaz stood holding onto Lucy's shoulders while she lowered the jumpsuit to the floor. Jaz sat, and Lucy pulled the outfit over Jaz's feet.

Lucy fed a pair of shorts over Jaz's feet, and Jaz repeated the standing and leaning pose while Lucy pulled them up around her waist, fastening the button and zip.

"Sorted, you're tidy now," said Lucy.

"Thanks," said Jaz, blushing.

"No probs."

The doctor arrived and sent Jaz for an X-ray. Then he reported that Jaz had sprained her ankle and prescribed pain killers. A nurse wrapped a bandage around Jaz's ankle and provided her with a pair of crutches.

By the time they drove out of the hospital they realised they were starving.

"Take-away?" suggested Lucy as she saw the Spicy Chicken Shack.

"Oh, brill idea,"

They sat in the car park eating Cajun chicken on pitta bread, sharing a bag of chips, and drinking cola.

"I haven't eaten this badly for years," said Lucy.

"I've got to admit I'm a regular here, not the best at cooking."

"That'll be why you've got a belly coming on you!"

"Cheeky," said Jaz as they looked at the tummy sticking out from under her shirt. "Just to check, you have got your driving license with you?"

"Yeah," said Lucy. "And Bernard told me he'd insured the pickup for anyone to drive."

"Good," sighed Jaz.

"Time to get you home and tucked up in bed," announced Lucy.

Jaz directed Lucy to the bungalow where she was staying.

"This is a delightful house," said Lucy as she approached.

"Yeah, it's Bernard's, but he prefers to live in his flat," said Jaz.

Lucy drove through the metal gateway into the drive, got out of Big Red and unlocked the front door, before helping Jaz clamber out of the pickup.

With her arms entwined around Lucy, Jaz limped into the house. Passing through the lounge and entering the bedroom. Jaz sat on the edge of the bed and removed her shoes.

Lucy shut the curtains. "Cup of tea?" she asked.

Jaz nodded as she raised her legs onto the bed and lay back, exhausted.

In the kitchen Lucy switched on the kettle, then wandered out to the pickup to fetch her cabin case and Jaz's rucksack. She rooted through the rucksack and found Jaz's old-fashioned mobile phone. Clicking her way through the phone's buttons, Lucy became irritated by how long it took to find a phone number. "Get yourself a touch screen," she muttered.

Eventually, Lucy was able to phone Bernard. "Yeah, she's okay, not broken, just sprained…She's gone to bed…I'll stay and make sure she's okay…Yeah, see you tomorrow. Bye." She wrote Bernard's phone number on a scrap of paper.

Looking around the lounge, Lucy saw how basic the furniture was, a sofa, two chairs, and a coffee table, with a bookshelf by the wall. Lucy found a CD player and pressed play. Paloma Faith warbled into the evening air.

Back in the kitchen, Lucy rummaged in the cupboards and found a packet of chocolate biscuits. She placed them on the tray with two cups of tea. Then went into the bedroom to find Jaz fast asleep and snoring.

Trying not to sing to the music, Lucy sat on the bed and stroked her fingers through Jaz's curly hair. "I wonder if I'd enjoy living in Botswana?" she said aloud. "Just stay here and tell Wes I wasn't coming home." She kissed Jaz on her forehead and left the bedroom, wandering into the room next door.

The room was being used as an art studio. Completed paintings leaned on the walls, and a half-finished painting of a village rested on the easel. On a table were squeezed tubes of paint, brushes, sketchbooks, objects, jars, everything an artist needed.

Lucy picked up a sketchbook and sat on the single bed. Flicking through it, she found a drawing of herself crying at the airport table. Further in the book was another sketch of her worriedly sitting in the bar waiting for Jaz. Lucy was in awe of Jaz's ability to capture her emotions in a few drawn lines. But being drawn without her knowledge upset her. She shut the book and went back to the lounge, checking on Jaz as she walked past the bedroom.

There was no television, so Lucy looked through Jaz's CD collection, replacing Paloma with a classical music album. Then she checked the bookcase. There were two books, a tourist guide to Botswana, and a tatty copy of a Cumbrian walking guide. She wasn't inspired to read either of them.

On the top of the bookcase an incense stick rested in its holder. Lucy opened a match box and lit the stick. She smelt the herbal aroma of sandalwood that embedded Jaz and her clothes. Feeling relaxed, she lay on the sofa and fell into a light doze.

An hour later the sound of movement in Jaz's room woke Lucy. She yawned and wandered into the bedroom. "Are you okay?" she asked.

Sitting on the side of the bed, Jaz jumped when she saw Lucy. "Sorry, I thought I was on my own," she said drowsily, wondering what Lucy was doing in her house. "I need the toilet." Jaz sounded as if she were a small helpless child.

Lucy helped Jaz stand and held her arm while she limped to the bathroom, waiting outside the door until Jaz was ready to go back to bed.

"You can have more pain killers now," said Lucy handing over two white tablets.

"Thanks," said Jaz. "Blooming ankles aching."

"Get yourself changed and back to sleep." Lucy passed Jaz a nightshirt, turning her back while Jaz removed her clothes and pulled the nightshirt over her head.

Jaz undid her shorts and jiggled them off her legs, leaving them in a heap on the floor. Lying down, she mumbled her thanks and fell back into a deep sleep.

Lucy pulled the quilt over Jaz and kissed her cheek. Then she picked up and folded the shorts, putting them with the other clothes on the chair. She left the bedroom door ajar and made her way into the guest room.

Chapter 9

When Jaz woke her head was mushy, and her ankle throbbed. She remembered the accident, visiting the hospital, Lucy looking after her, and a kiss. She threw a fleece over the top of her nightshirt, grabbed her crutches, and hobbled into the kitchen.

Lucy wolf-whistled Jaz's tanned legs, a bandage on one ankle and a tartan bed sock on the other.

"It's not funny, you know," said Jaz, perturbed.

"Sorry, sit outside, I'll bring breakfast."

Jaz limped out onto the patio and sat on one of the cushioned metal seats that surrounded the Victorian-style table.

Lucy brought out a tray stacked with pancakes. Jaz's mouth watered and she scooped the top pancake onto her plate, adding sugar from the bowl next to them.

"Glad the accident hasn't ruined your appetite." Lucy poured two cups of coffee and chopped slices of banana onto her pancake.

"No chance, if you don't eat you die." Jaz laughed. "Did you find the spare bed?"

"Yeah, I worked my way through the clutter of the guest room."

"Thank you for staying over and looking after me," said Jaz.

"Not a problem." Lucy smiled; she had enjoyed looking after Jaz. "It's a splendid garden," she said, soaking in the colours.

"Yeah, it'll be sad to leave it behind," Jaz said with a sigh.

"Oh, when are you leaving?"

"In two weeks, got to get back to my job."

Lucy sighed, upset that her dream of staying in Botswana with Jaz was no longer an option. "What do you do for work?"

"I'm a National Trust warden in the Lake District, looking after wildlife and footpaths, organising volunteers," said Jaz.

"Is that where you're from, the Lake District?"

"Yeah, I live in a farmhouse near Bassenthwaite Lake. It was the family home, but a fire trashed it last year, and my parents moved into a house in the next town," said Jaz. "The insurance paid to rebuild the farmhouse, and I'll move in when I get back. Just got to do the decorating."

"Sounds idyllic," said Lucy.

"Do you live near your parents?" asked Jaz.

"No, they were in a car crash thirty years ago, they both died." Lucy's throat choked with tears.

"Oh jeez, I'm sorry." Jaz patted Lucy's hand.

They both stopped talking and drank their coffee, neither knowing what to say next.

"Can I visit you in Bassenthwaite?" asked Lucy when she'd composed herself.

"That'd be wonderful," said Jaz, looking at Lucy over her coffee cup.

"Bernard said he'd come over this morning, come and visit his little pumpkin." Lucy laughed and squeezed Jaz's cheek.

"Get out of it," said Jaz, grinning.

A car horn beeped, and Bernard drove into the garden. "Hello sicky wicky," he shouted as he got out of the car and gave Jaz a hug.

"Coffee Bernard?" asked Lucy.

"Yes thanks," he said pulling over a chair.

Jaz caught Lucy's eyes as she poured the coffee and winked. "What's the update on the jump?" Jaz asked Bernard.

"Well, Jeremy got himself scratched from the acacia bushes," said Bernard, adding sugar to his coffee cup.

"I bet Aileen had fun pulling out the thorns," said Jaz, laughing.

"Frank did an excellent landing, but Gareth landed on his hire car, he told the rental company he'd hit a cow! Debbie came off worst, her parachute didn't open, and she crash-landed in the outer field, dislocated shoulder and fractured leg!"

"Bloody hell, not one of my best fund-raising ideas!" said Jaz, frowning.

"No, but you raised five thousand Pula," said Bernard.

"That's excellent," said Lucy.

"Brilliant, worth the pain," said Jaz, prouder of herself.

"I'm off to the airport this morning. The manager of the parachute club has asked to watch my video to try and work out what went wrong with Debbie's chute." Bernard put his coffee cup on the table. "Do you want to join me, Lucy? You can tell them what you saw."

"Okay, I can take Jaz's jumpsuit back." Lucy looked tenderly at Jaz. "Will you be alright while we pop out?"

"Yeah, I'll be fine, are you coming back here?" said Jaz, trying not to sound too needy.

"Sure, if that's alright with Bernard."

"No problem," said Bernard. He leaned over and kissed Jaz on the cheek. "Emma sent more chocolate." He pulled a bar of dark chocolate out of his jacket pocket and rubbed Jaz on the head. "I'll phone mummy and daddy later and explain that little Jasmine's had an accident."

"Don't you dare!" Jaz hit his bottom with a crutch. She picked up the last pancake and waved them off with a sugary hand.

Bernard's car trundled along the roads, and Lucy sat with Jaz's yellow jumpsuit folded on her knee.

"Do you know Emma well?" asked Bernard.

"Ah, so that's what you're after, inside information," said Lucy, smirking. "Well,

Emma used to work with me in the library, until she retired. Sadly, her husband died a few years ago and then her son moved to America."

"Oh, that's sad, she's lonely like myself," said Bernard. "Lucy, do you think Emma might go out with me?" he asked shyly.

"Yes, I think she would. If I were you, I'd start by inviting her to lunch."

"Good idea," said Bernard.

"While I've got the chance, I wanted to say that you shouldn't have told Hilary about Jaz being gay. Hilary's homophobic, she's already told me to keep out of Jaz's way," said Lucy.

"Oh damn, I didn't think it would be a problem, what with Hilary being your friend."

"Bernard, just because I'm spending time with Jaz doesn't mean I'm a lesbian or bi," said Lucy.

Bernard glanced at her. "Oh dear, you and Jaz are so close I thought you might be dating. I'm sorry," he said, parking outside the parachute club.

"It's okay," sighed Lucy, slamming the door as she got out of the car.

Jaz was fast asleep when Lucy returned. She tiptoed into the house and made two sandwiches and a pot of odd-smelling tea she found in a caddy.

Lucy placed everything on the outdoor table, then sat and relaxed. Green mesh netting covered the patio, keeping it cool and shaded. Out in the heat, dazzling Marico sunbirds hovered and dipped into the yellow trumpet headed flowers of the tree that stood by the garden wall. A hoopoe pecked its way across a sandy flowerbed, and red-faced mousebirds methodically checked the date tree for fruit.

"Bloody things those mousebirds, they always get the fruit before me!" said Jaz yawning.

Startled out of her thoughts, Lucy looked at Jaz who was watching her intently.

"You look upset," said Jaz.

"Oh, it's nothing, it's just that Bernard thought I was a lesbian." Lucy poured the tea and handed a cup to Jaz.

"Oh," said Jaz, staring silently into the brown liquid as if she was reading the leaves, wishing that Lucy was a gay, then she could ask her on a date. She took a sip of tea. "You found the rooibos tea."

"Pardon?"

"The rooibos tea, or red bush tea. It's a southern African tea made from the leaves of the rooibos plant. I remember Bernard saying Mma Ramotswe drinks it."

"You're right, she does." Lucy tasted the tea. "Oh, that's nice, refreshing."

"You can have with milk or it's nice with lemon."

"Have a sandwich, I made cheese and pickle," said Lucy.

"My favourite," said Jaz. "You can take the pickup after lunch; you'll need it to get back to the hotel."

"Thanks, that's nice of you." A sweaty waft drifted from Lucy's armpits. "I need to have a shower, I got grubby camping." Lucy finished her red bush tea and took the cups and plates into the kitchen. When she returned outside, she found Jaz trying to unload the pickup.

"Will you stop that," said Lucy. "Let me do it, you're supposed to be resting."

Stubbornly Jaz stopped and stood to one side, resting on the crutches, while Lucy unloaded and carried everything into the bungalow.

"Thanks," said Jaz, impressed at Lucy's strength, considering she looked somewhat delicate. Jaz wrapped her arms around Lucy, giving her a thank you for helping me hug.

Lucy could have stayed in that hug forever. "I'll come back and see you later," said Lucy as Jaz sat in her metal seat.

"No, have yourself a rest, maybe I'll see you tomorrow."

"Definitely, I'll come and cook dinner."

"Now that'll be excellent."

Lucy bent and kissed Jaz on the cheek. "Don't do too much."

Jaz blushed. "No, I'll behave."

"Okay, bye." Lucy got in the driver's seat and started the engine, waving as she left.

Chapter 10

To escape the heat Lucy, Emma and Hilary set off to Riverwalk shopping mall early in the morning, arriving just as the shops were opening. They found a large clothes shop which sold clothing for every occasion.

Emma headed for the shoes, needing an extra pair of sandals. Hilary bought a lacy black bra and matching pants. Lucy found two short-sleeved shirts, one in a pale green and the other in light denim blue. Then she chose a pair of beige trousers with lots of pockets and a green pair of trousers that zipped off at the knees, turning them into shorts. They were practical, stylish, and made from thin cotton, adding to their coolness.

Joining Emma in the shoe department, Lucy bought a pair of canvas walking shoes.

"That's outdoorsy," said Hilary, scanning Lucy's items. "We're going home on Sunday, surely you won't need them."

"And what you're buying is very saucy, who are you after?" asked Lucy.

Hilary rushed off to pay.

Next, they visited the supermarket. Emma headed straight to the cakes and biscuits. Lucy found curry powder, coconut cream, onion, rice, and a mango. She'd buy the chicken later, on the way to Jaz's bungalow.

When they returned to the hotel, Lucy pulled into a parking spot next to a waving Bernard. Emma got out, hugging him as she told him of her shopping trip. Then she asked him if he'd take her to the Provincial Hotel in town for lunch.

"That would be delightful," replied Bernard, smiling at Emma, and winking at Lucy.

Hilary looked at them in disgust and stormed into the hotel where she bumped into Ian who whisked her off to the bar.

"I'm dining out tonight, so I'll catch up with you tomorrow," said Lucy.

"Hope you have a pleasant evening," said Bernard leading Emma away.

In her room Lucy switched on her tablet, checking her emails. There was a message from Wes, and two bank statements, which once again she moved unopened into her banking folder.

She replied to Wes. *"Hi, visit still going well. Survived the camping, didn't realise how mucky it was. Off to a pottery tomorrow and a safari visit on Friday. Hope you are okay. Can we talk when I get home? See you soon, love Lucy."*

Lucy walked over to the pickup in the scorching sun, feeling cooler dressed in her new clothes. She perched on the driver's seat and unzipped the green trousers above her knees, turning them into shorts. Putting the legs on the back seat for later when the temperature dropped.

On the way to Jaz's bungalow Lucy stopped to buy chicken, cans of cola, and a bottle of wine. She found a phone shop and asked an assistant what tariffs were available, purchasing a touch screen phone and SIM card. Next door, in the newsagents, she bought an art magazine for Jaz. Then she popped into a chemist.

Back in the pickup, Lucy turned on her phone and typed Bernard's number into the contacts list. Then turning on the radio, she sang her way to Jaz's place.

When she heard Big Red at the gate, Jaz was sitting on a tree stump in the garden drawing the bungalow. Looking over it took her a few seconds to recognise Lucy. She was stunning, wearing only a touch of make-up, and dressed in cool green shorts and a denim blouse.

"How are you feeling?" Lucy asked as she emerged from the pickup.

"Good, thank you." Jaz tried not to smile too adoringly at the view of Lucy. "You look trendy."

"Thank you." Lucy did a twirl. "I'll put this food in the fridge."

Jaz tottered over to the patio on her crutches and sat on a seat by the table. Lucy returned with two cans of cola, a magazine, and a paper bag.

"For you." Lucy presented the magazine to Jaz.

Jaz flicked through the pages and thanked her as if it was the best present in the world.

"Cheers," said Lucy clinking cans with Jaz. "What have you been doing?"

"Just sketching and dozing." Jaz opened her can and took a long drink.

"I bought this." Lucy pulled an elastic tubular bandage out of the paper bag. "It might be more comfortable than the hospital bandage." She looked at the binding on Jaz's ankle, stained orange by the sand. "Let's see the damage." Lucy sat cross-legged on the tiled patio floor and unwound the dressing. The swollen ankle emerged in a rainbow of colours. "Wow, that's some sprain, can you move it?"

Jaz wiggled her foot; the pain made her grimace.

"I know what you need." Lucy disappeared into the house and returned with a towel filled with ice cubes, which she rested over Jaz's ankle.

"Oh, that's freezing." A shiver ran through Jaz's body.

"I thought you could have a shower today," said Lucy.

"Yeah, I stink." Jaz could smell her sweaty, dusty body, and had wanted a shower since the parachute jump. But she couldn't step in and out of the shower cubicle and was far too embarrassed to ask for help.

"Good, we'll get you cleaned when you've finished your drink," said Lucy. "Look, I bought a mobile phone."

"Do you want my number?"

"Well, yeah, okay," said Lucy, attempting to be coy.

Jaz got her dad's old Nokia phone from her pocket and tapped away to find her details. She handed the Nokia to Lucy, who entered her number into her phone. Lucy dialled and Jaz's phone rang.

"I won't answer, they can call back later." Jaz laughed at her joke.

"You know these modern phones have got touch-screens." Lucy showed Jaz her phone. "You can do the Internet and social media on it."

"Oh, I can't do that modern stuff, technology confuses me." Jaz paused while she had a drink. "Bernard phoned earlier, he was in a state, said he'd upset you."

"No, he didn't upset me, well I suppose he did. Don't get funny with me again, but I told him off for telling Hilary you were gay, she's such a gossip. I mean, she's warned me to watch myself around you."

"I told you, if it makes your life awkward, you don't have to hang around with me."

"I know." Lucy stopped talking, convincing herself that all she was doing was visiting and making lunch for her friend. "It's just that I need to see how you are and make sure you're eating," she said.

"Ah right."

"That's what friends do." Lucy looked at Jaz.

"Well, it's very good of you." Jaz wallowed in the brownness of Lucy's eyes. "And you don't mind me being a lesbian?"

"I'm not bothered if your gay or straight, it's who you are."

"Okay, I'll add you to my list of straight friends."

"And don't take advantage of me, or I'll set Hilary on to you." Lucy laughed nervously.

Jaz giggled, knowing precisely what her hands could do to Lucy if given the chance.

They paused as they finished their cola, watching the kites soaring above them, looking for prey.

"Your ice has melted." Lucy got up and removed the damp towel from Jaz's ankle. "Are you ready for your shower?"

Jaz stared at Lucy, humiliated that she needed help to have a shower.

"Come on, it'll be fine." She held out her arm for Jaz to lean on and led her into the bedroom. "Get yourself changed and I'll meet you in the bathroom."

Jaz sat on the bed, removed her clothes, put on her dressing-gown, and hobbled into the bathroom.

"I've put you a stool there with a clean towel and I'll get your clothes while you're washing," announced Lucy.

"Thanks, it's embarrassing. I can't balance to step in and out of the shower."

"That's why I'm here, pretend I'm a nurse helping you."

"Nope, that thought doesn't help me." Jaz smirked.

Lucy tutted. "Right, I'll turn my back and you can lean on my shoulder."

Lucy stood with her back to the shower. Jaz disrobed and lightly rested a hand on Lucy's shoulder while she stepped into the cubicle, then she pulled the curtain across and turned on the shower.

"Okay?" shouted Lucy over the noise of the spray.

"Yes, thanks."

Lucy entered Jaz's bedroom and found clean underwear in her untidy drawers. She got a beige shirt from the wardrobe, and her shorts from the back of the chair. Lucy took the clothing into the bathroom and put it on the cupboard top. "How are you doing?" she shouted.

"Just finished?" answered Jaz, turning off the shower, her head appearing from behind the curtain. "Turn your back then."

"You're so shy!" Lucy turned around.

Jaz's wet hand gripped Lucy's shoulder as she stepped out.

Lucy blinked and stared into the mirror, absorbed by Jaz's nakedness, her muscles and breasts dripping with water.

Jaz swiftly grabbed the towel that Lucy was holding aloft, wrapping it around herself and sitting on the stool. "Thanks," she said.

Lucy caught her breath at the surprising urge she had to turn and kiss Jaz. "Your clothes are here. I'll see you outside." Lucy rushed out of the bathroom and sat on the shaded patio drinking a glass of water. Desperately trying to cool the hot flush that was burning her cheeks.

"That's better," said Jaz as she came outside drying her hair.

"Sit here, I'll dry your feet, pass me the towel." Lucy gently wiped Jaz's sturdy country feet. Then she stretched the elastic tubular bandage over the injured ankle and slipped on Jaz's slippers. "Now, you have a rest while I make my stunning meal."

"But it's early yet," said Jaz, her tummy rumbling.

"I need to make it now and let it rest, it tastes better that way," said Lucy disappearing into the kitchen.

Making the chicken curry distracted Lucy from her affectionate urges. She heated the spices, stirred in the chopped onion and chicken pieces, then added stock, mango slices, and coconut cream. She left it on a low heat to simmer and returned to the patio with two glasses and a bottle of white wine. Accidentally waking Jaz when a glass tumbled onto the table. "Sorry, I'm so clumsy, glass of wine? Is this a tasty wine, it's from South Africa? I hope you enjoy a curry."

"Yes, to everything," said Jaz. "I haven't had a curry for ages."

"I love making curry, my mum taught me, she was born in Agra, that's in India."

"Oh, that's where the Taj Mahal lives," said Jaz. "Well, from the smell of the curry she must have been a marvellous teacher."

As they drank Jaz told Lucy stories of her art training and how useless she'd been at college. "Only got a third-class degree, my art was before it's time, or crap!"

"Well, I adore your work." Lucy moved her glass. "Top up my glass while I cook the rice."

"A small one for you, don't forget you're driving."

"Oh yeah, best to be safe." Lucy cursed the thought of having to drive back to the hotel. In the kitchen she waited for the pan of rice to boil, turning it to a simmer before returning outside to her small glass of wine. "I'll be serving dinner in twenty minutes." She took a sip of her drink. "Have you always been gay?"

"Born and bred. You always been straight?"

"Yeah."

"Always been with Wes?"

"Yup."

"And you're happy to be with Wes?" Jaz asked.

"To be honest, I'm not too sure whether me and Wes should stay together anymore." Lucy paused. "I need to check the rice."

Jaz looked at Lucy.

"What?" said Lucy.

"Nothing. I was just thinking."

"Well, don't."

Lucy went inside, coming out a while later with two plates of her curry and rice. "I didn't make it too spicy."

"Thanks." Jaz tucked into the meal. "Wow, this is perfect, may I kiss the chef?"

Lucy proffered her cheek and Jaz leaned over and gave her a tender kiss.

"You're such a charmer, don't flatter me too much, I might enjoy it!" said Lucy, feeling the urge to return Jaz's kiss. "Stop it."

"What do you want me to stop?" asked Jaz, a puzzled look on her face.

"Stop smiling."

"Oh, sorry." Jaz pulled a grim face. "Is that better?"

"Perfect."

"Weirdo."

It got cooler on the patio as the sun set. Lucy went to the pickup and zipped the legs onto her shorts. Meanwhile Jaz shuffled around inside the bungalow, grabbing two fleecy sweaters, and loading a CD into the player. She came back outside and sat on the patio seat.

Jaz handed Lucy a fleece. "That'll help keep you warm."

"Thank you." Lucy pulled it on and felt warmer inside and out. "Do you have anyone waiting for you back at home?" she asked, attempting to be subtle in her questioning of Jaz's lifestyle.

"No, she left me." Jaz sighed and tried not to sound too dejected by her failed relationship.

"Oh, that's sad." Lucy noticed that the answer had depressed Jaz and she took her hand. "What are you painting now?" Lucy asked, knowing Jaz enjoyed talking about art.

"Well, I thought I'd paint a picture of the bungalow to hang in my farmhouse, it should brighten me up on a dull Lake District day."

"It'll be lovely if you paint in the flowers and that stunning blue sky. I'll look forward to seeing it when I visit." She merged her fingers into Jaz's, relaxing as the music serenaded them.

Jaz looked longingly at Lucy's face, wanting to ask her to stay. But she was supposedly straight and married, it would be wrong. "I know this will spoil the evening," said Jaz. "But I suppose you should go back to the hotel soon? It gets freaky driving here at night."

Lucy looked at her watch. "Oh, it is late, I suppose I should head off now." Lucy wished she could stay. She removed her hand from Jaz's and stood.

"You can hang on to my fleece," said Jaz, getting up with her. "Don't want the chill getting to you."

"I'll keep it with the jogging suit I'm borrowing." Lucy got into Big Red and lowered the window.

"Thanks for the lovely afternoon and wonderful food," said Jaz.

"I've had a brilliant time," said Lucy, recollecting the shower scene. "I'll come and pick you up in the morning. You can direct me to Thamaga."

"Sure, I'll be up and ready." Jaz stood precariously holding onto the pickup door. She hadn't meant to, but she kissed Lucy on the cheek. "Oh, sorry." Jaz stepped back, twinging her ankle as she did so.

"No need to apologise. Goodnight," said Lucy.

Chapter 11

The trip to Thamaga didn't start well. Hilary insisted on sitting in the front seat with her map, guiding Lucy to Jaz's house. Lucy wasn't listening as she knew the way. When they arrived, Hilary refused to move.

Jaz handed her crutches to Emma and climbed into the back seats, greeting everyone as she did so. She caught Lucy's eye in the mirror and winked, deciding Lucy looked the part in her green shirt and beige trousers.

Lucy grinned back.

"Concentrate Lucy," instructed Hilary. "That way." She pointed a scrawny finger.

"Yeah boss," said Lucy.

"How's your ankle?" Emma asked Jaz.

"Oh, much better, but I'm fed up with using these crutches, and I'm missing not being able to drive."

Emma patted Jaz's hand.

Lucy sat silently at the front, turning the pickup when told.

"How's Bernard?" Jaz asked Emma.

"He's fine," Emma replied. "Did you ever meet his wife, Lorato?"

"Only once when they visited the UK, she was very nice, very gentle."

"Did they have children?" asked Emma.

"No, it's a sad story. When she was a teenager Lorato's uncle raped her and she became pregnant, she lost the baby and had to have a hysterectomy."

"That's awful," said Emma.

"Lorato trained as a nurse and moved to Gaborone. She met Bernard when a cow kicked his leg, and he had to go into hospital. He was heartbroken when she died of cancer three years ago."

"It's an awful thing cancer," Emma said sighing. "Lucy, wasn't it sad when Carly died."

Lucy looked in the mirror and nodded, choking on a tear, and swerving toward a ditch by the side of the road.

"She had breast cancer," Emma whispered to Jaz.

"Oh, that's sad," said Jaz.

"Lucy, Lucy, turn here," announced Hilary.

"Sorry, miles away," said Lucy parking outside the Botswelelo Centre pottery.

Hilary stepped out of the front seat and met Emma on the other side of the pickup. They introduced themselves to the lady who was standing outside the pottery.

Lucy walked around to Jaz's rear door and helped her climb out.

"Thanks," said Jaz, grabbing her satchel. "Hilary's a snobby bitch showing off to the cleaner."

"Don't forget your crutches." Lucy handed them to an irritated Jaz.

"Ugh, bloody things," said Jaz ramming them under her armpits.

Jaz shook hands with the cleaner and asked if the pottery director was available. She said she was, then took up her broom and carried on sweeping the terrace. Jaz introduced the group to Mma Moduli, the pottery manager, organiser, and director.

"I'll be outside drawing," said Jaz to Lucy.

"Okay, see you in a while," said Lucy.

Mma Moduli took the visitors through to the main pottery, where they met and talked to the workers, and studied their elegant creations.

Then they visited the shop. Emma purchased a teacup and saucer as present for Bernard, and Hilary found a small teapot for her red bush tea. Lucy bought a tall narrow pot that could hold Jaz's brushes. Then, in the corner, she saw a pot stacked with handmade wooden walking canes; she studied them and purchased one.

"Had a pleasant time?" asked Jaz.

"Yes, it was interesting, we had a good chat to the workers," said Emma.

"Excellent," said Jaz.

"Bought you a present." Lucy handed the walking stick to Jaz. "I thought you'd prefer it to your crutches."

"Oh no, you shouldn't have." Jaz admired the head of an eagle carved into the handle. "That's marvellous, thank you." Standing, she walked with the support of her new stick.

Lucy wanted to take Jaz's other hand, but she didn't think it was right, so she picked up Jaz's painting equipment and crutches, and carried them to the pickup. The gigantic smile from Jaz was the only thanks Lucy wanted.

In the pickup Emma passed Jaz a cup of milky red bush tea from her flask. Lucy looked at them enviously through the rear mirror, having forgotten to put bottles of water in the cool box.

"Here you go, Lucy, have a drink." Jaz passed the cup of tea forward.

"Thanks," said Lucy, concerned that Jaz was reading her mind.

"These sweltering days get the thirst, but it might rain tomorrow," said Jaz.

"Oh, how can you tell," asked Hilary. "Are there signs in the vegetation to consider?"

"No, I just read it on the Internet!"

Lucy spluttered on her tea.

Hilary tutted. "Enough nonsense, we're off to David Livingstone's house, this way."

"Okay captain." Lucy saluted and handed the cup back to Jaz. She turned Big Red around and travelled in the direction of Hilary's finger.

It was a wayward route that Hilary took them on, along rutted roads that Lucy bounced along before they joined up with the main road again.

"That way," said Hilary.

"I don't want to interfere," said Jaz. "But you turn left here and then right further along the road."

Hilary scowled and studied the map. "Left here, Lucy."

They found the turning on the right and Lucy parked next to two cars. Nearby, a guide was organising a tour of the site.

"Oh, excellent, we get a tour," said Emma, climbing out and going over to the party. Hilary joined her. They paid the guide and wandered off with the group.

"We'll just follow along at the back," Lucy shouted as she helped Jaz.

"Alone at last." Jaz leaned on her stick.

"Yeah, sorry if Hilary annoyed you, she's having an in-charge day."

"It's been entertaining watching the driver plan to kill the director!" Jaz used the eagle-headed stick to help her plod along, linking her other arm with Lucy's. They caught up with the tour at the stone outline of Livingstone's house.

"Not much left of this place," said Jaz. "Come over here, this part is spooky, it's where Livingstone's daughter is buried, a lion attacked and killed her."

Lucy didn't know whether to believe Jaz and she looked around warily, taking a hazy photograph of the eerie space.

"Livingstone and his workers had to fight the lion off, but it was too late. There are no lions here now," said Jaz, seeing Lucy's worried face. "Well, not that you can see."

They'd wandered away from the tour group and Jaz showed Lucy the chapel site. "It was a shame for his wife, following him around having loads of children, only for them to feed the local wildlife or die of disease."

Lucy nodded. "In those days women had to get married and have kids, it was such a patriarchal society."

"Even gay women had to marry, only a few made it through being themselves. I'll bore you with a lecture about them one day," said Jaz. "We should do a lesbian tour of Britain."

"Oh, how very quaint; I can't wait."

They strolled back to the pickup. "Want a piece of chocolate?" asked Jaz, bringing a bar from her pocket, and breaking off pieces for herself and Lucy. They lazily leaned on the pickup, munching the chocolate.

"Right," said a returning Hilary, now a Livingstone expert. "Time for lunch." She climbed into the front seat.

Jaz looked at Lucy and shrugged.

As a thank you for lending them the pickup, Emma bought Jaz lunch. After eating Jaz popped off her boots, pulled the tubular elastic bandage off her ankle and dangled her legs in the swimming pool. The heavenly cooling water eased the joint.

"I'd better sit with you, otherwise the management will ask you to leave," said Lucy, slipping off her own shoes and putting her feet in the pool. "Your ankle's looking good."

"Yeah, I can move my foot now, must have been your wonderful nursing skills," said Jaz glancing at Lucy. "I might try driving tomorrow. I need to get back into it to get ready for my lengthy drive up north next week."

"Well, be careful, you don't want to overstrain it." Lucy stared into the pool, driving, and caring for Jaz had given her the perfect excuse to see her. "Is it nice in the north of

Botswana?" she asked, resigned to the fact that Jaz didn't need her help anymore.

"Oh, it's more rural and there's a bigger variety of wildlife. You know if you weren't going home, I'd ask you to come with me."

"Come where?"

"Up north, dodo."

"Oh, that'd be special."

"It would be like *Carol*, going on a wayward drive together," said Jaz in a sultry voice.

"Who's Carol?"

"Have you not seen the film? No, you shouldn't watch it, read the book instead, it's based on *The Price of Salt* by Patricia Highsmith. I've got a copy at the bungalow, remind me to give it to you later."

"Oh okay, thanks."

Bernard arrived at the poolside, hugging Emma and rubbing Jaz's head, pushing her toward the swimming pool.

"Get off," Jaz shouted.

Ian arrived telling them he'd just got back from working in Serowe. He sat next to Hilary, and they discussed Livingstone and looked at Hilary's photographs. Lucy heard Ian invite Hilary to visit Livingstone's caves with him.

"I suppose I should get back home and carry on with my packing," said Jaz.

"I'll drive you," said Lucy.

"No, it's okay, I'll take Jaz," said Bernard. "Emma wanted to visit the old bungalow."

"Oh okay," said Lucy, smiling politely but feeling disappointed.

"Well, I'll see you on Friday for the safari," said Jaz, making strange hand signals to Lucy, saying she'd phone her at four o'clock.

After her swim Lucy lay on her wrap under a sunshade. Bernard and Emma returned, and sat by her.

"What a nice bungalow and such a lovely garden," said Emma. "Shall I get tea?"

Bernard nodded. "Yes, please."

"You've made Emma happy," Lucy said to Bernard.

"Yes," he said. "Lucy, Jaz has talked of you for most of the afternoon, how you've helped her, and she's flashing her walking cane around as if it's made of gold. I mean, it's lovely that you care so much, but please tell her you're not romantically interested. I don't want her getting hurt again."

Bernard's words flustered Lucy. "Oh right, yes, I'll tell her."

"Good." Bernard sighed, relieved at having got through an awkward conversation.

Lucy's head ached, she checked her watch, a quarter to four. "I think I'll have a rest," she said to Bernard and Emma.

"Please tell her," Bernard whispered, and Lucy nodded.

Just as she reached her room Lucy's phone rang. She stared at it, allowing it to ring several times before answering.

"Hi." Jaz's voice echoed through the ear-piece.

"Hiya," replied Lucy.

Jaz intercepted Lucy's sad tone. "Oh dear, what's wrong?"

"Well, I need to tell you I shouldn't meet up with you anymore."

"Why?"

"Because you fancy me."

"Oh, Uncle Bernard has been talking to you."

"Yeah, how did you know?"

"He's overprotective and doesn't want anyone to upset me."

"Well, I don't want to hurt you."

"Does it matter if I fancy you? I realise you're straight and married. I just thought we were friends."

"Well no, I mean yes, oh I don't know what I mean anymore."

"I don't know, the grown-ups have treated us as naughty teenagers today."

"I know it's been ridiculous."

"If you don't see me, how am I going to get my pickup back?"

Lucy giggled. "I'll meet you with a chaperone."

Jaz laughed. "Yeah, escorted by Hilary, with Emma and Bernard backing her up from the rear."

"Why does our friendship have to make life awkward?" asked Lucy.

"Don't worry about it," said Jaz. "On Friday I'll take you to Mokolodi for the safari tour, and afterward we'll never see each other again." Jaz paused. "If that's what you want."

"I suppose," was Lucy's grim reply. "Oh, I'm so confused. I don't understand my feelings anymore."

"I think we need to talk," said Jaz. "Sneak out and we'll take this conversation to the lake."

"But what will the others think."

"Oh, sod them." Other people's interference in her life was annoying Jaz. "Surely at your age they can't tell you what to do!"

"What do you mean at my age? I'm only forty-nine," said Lucy, laughing. "And yes, I suppose I can do what I want."

"Good, I'll see you in an hour."

Lucy took a shower and put on a light dress. Taking Jaz's fleece to wear later, she slipped out of the hotel's side door, jumped into Big Red, and drove away.

At the bungalow Jaz was waiting by the gate, confidently leaning on her stick. "Well hello girlfriend," she said getting into the front seat.

"Shut up and be serious," said Lucy, scowling.

"Sorry," said Jaz directing Lucy to the takeaway, and then on to the lake.

They sat staring at the water, eating burgers and sucking cola through straws.

"Do you want to tell me what's upsetting you?" asked Jaz.

"It's just that people keep telling me that because you fancy me, I shouldn't be friends with you."

"But we are friends, so they're too late, and I'll not go any further than fancy you from a distance. You'll be like a work of art; I can look but not touch."

Lucy studied Jaz. "When I was younger, I had a friend."

"Carly?"

"Yeah, she was my best friend, we were at school together and grew close."

"Oh!"

"But our families weren't open to our relationship and my dad made me go out with Wes who worked at the post office with him."

"It upset Carly, but I thought me being with Wes made life easier for us both, and I suggested she should get a boyfriend."

"I don't suppose that went down well," said Jaz.

"No, we had an argument, and we didn't speak for years."

"So, you married Wes?" asked Jaz.

"He said he'd take care of me, and I trusted him."

"And you got a job?"

"Yeah, in the same library as Carly."

"Oh dear," said Jaz.

"We went out everywhere together until the breast cancer took her away from me." Lucy started weeping.

Jaz handed her a tissue and wrapped her arms around her, stroking her hair until she was calmer. "So, to summarise," said Jaz, trying to make sense of everything. "You married Wes, but then started going out with the girl you'd had a relationship with when you were younger."

"Yeah, but me and Carly did nothing physical. Anyway, Carly enjoyed playing the field on Manchester's Canal Street." Lucy sobbed and she turned her head, looking into Jaz's concerned eyes. "But now I'm having feelings for you."

"Is that good?" asked Jaz.

Resting in Jaz's arms Lucy felt her heart beating wildly, she so wanted to kiss her. "Jaz, can I...."

"What?" asked Jaz as she caressed Lucy's arm, her head wallowing in Lucy's perfume, she was finding it difficult to just be Lucy's friend.

"Nothing." Lucy settled her head onto Jaz's shoulder. "I've never been able to talk so openly."

They relaxed in their hug, both wary of what to do next. Eventually they decided it was getting late, and they should head back. Lucy started the engine and drove Jaz home.

"So, you'll come over tomorrow, after breakfast," said Jaz when they arrived at the bungalow gate.

"Definitely." Lucy got the Thamaga pot out of her bag and handed it to Jaz. "I bought this for your paint brushes."

"Thank you, it's stunning." Jaz held it as if it were a work of art.

Lucy had another passionate urge to kiss Jaz's lips. "Okay, best be off," she said. "I'll see you tomorrow."

"Yeah, bye." Jaz stepped out of Big Red. "Ke a go rata."

Lucy waved as she drove off, wondering what Jaz had said.

When she reached her room Lucy remembered the book, she'd have enjoyed reading it as she fell asleep. She sent Jaz a text. *"Forgot to get the book."*
A message came back. *"Oops, get it tomorrow x."*
Lucy replied. *"Okay, don't forget, goodnight x."*
"Goodnight, sleep well xxx."

Chapter 12

Lucy left the hotel early in morning, and nobody saw her drive away.

It was pouring with rain. Enormous drops fell from the dark grey sky, bouncing off the bonnet and rolling down the windscreen. The rain drenched Lucy's flowery dress when she stopped at the bakery to purchase two breakfast baguettes.

At seven o'clock the rain ceased, leaving a light morning mist hanging in the air.

Lucy knocked on the bungalow door. It took a while for Jaz to answer. Her eyes were half closed, and she yawned.

"Ready for your breakfast?" asked Lucy, standing on the doorstep in soggy clothes, water running through her hair.

"Oh, err, breakfast, great." Jaz shivered in her rainbow patterned t-shirt and thin shorts. "You'd better come in, you're soaked. I'll just put more clothes on." Jaz disappeared into the bedroom.

Lucy went through to the kitchen, carrying the damp paper bag of baguettes. "You said it would rain," shouted Lucy.

"Yeah, the parched ground needed it." Jaz came into the kitchen wearing a fleece over her t-shirt, fluffy tartan woollen socks and carrying a dressing gown. "I tell you it's weird having your clothes packed away. I'm having to multi-task my clothing. Here change into this till your dress dries." She handed the dressing gown to Lucy and leaned on the doorjamb as Lucy squeezed by, heading for the bathroom.

"I'm sorry, did I wake you?" said Lucy, hanging her dress on the washing line above the bath, then strolling back to Jaz drying her hair with a towel.

"Well yeah, you woke me, but it's okay, it was a pleasant surprise." The smell of Lucy's perfume intoxicated Jaz's nose, and the thought of Lucy being naked under the dressing gown bewitched her.

"It's just that I couldn't sleep, thoughts kept rolling around in my head and nothing made any sense." Lucy sat opposite Jaz and sipped her coffee. "I kept trying to work out if I loved Carly."

"I'm sorry, my talking therapy might not have been the best thing to do." Jaz opened her baguette and squeezed tomato sauce onto the innards.

"No, it was good to talk."

"I'm not the best person to discuss love with, I thought I knew what it was, but I was wrong. All I know is it fucking hurts," said Jaz biting through the bread, sauce running down her chin.

"You're right," sighed Lucy. "I guess I'll hurt Wes when I leave him."

"Wow, that's major. Is that what will make you happy?" Jaz wiped away the red ooze with the back of her hand.

"Yeah, I don't love him anymore. I…" Lucy paused, afraid of saying the wrong thing. "It won't be easy, will it, leaving him?"

"No, it'll be hard, but you'll both survive," said Jaz. "There's always someone else, you've just got to find them." Jaz was desperate to take Lucy to bed and kiss her entire body, but her brain told her to behave. So, she continued to spill out the philosophical wisdom she'd read in a book years ago after her so-called loving partner had abandoned her. "You see in the life span of the universe our lives are very short and we waste time worrying about what we should or shouldn't do. I mean, we could be dead tomorrow. So, you must be practical and sort things out so you can enjoy each day to its fullest potential. Carpe Deum."

Lucy stared at Jaz in admiration of how deep and meaningful she could be at this time of the morning. "That's what you do, I spend the night worrying and you just sit there and come up with magical words of wisdom. I wish I had such clarity and conviction."

Jaz leaned over and, without thinking, she wiped a crumb from the side of Lucy's mouth. "Tell you what, I'm meeting up with Naledi and Aileen this morning for coffee and cake at the garden centre, why don't you join us?"

"That'll be fun," said Lucy, excited to spend a day with Jaz.

"I'd best have a shower, no need for any help today," Jaz said. "Why don't you have a nap, you look knackered."

Lucy followed Jaz into the bedroom and lay on the still warm bed, resting her head on the soft pillows.

Jaz got her clothes as Lucy closed her eyes.

After her shower Jaz sat in the chair sketching Lucy sleeping. She smoothed charcoal over the paper to create the wavy folds of the dressing gown and drew deeper lines to show Lucy's hair falling across her face. Then she swept lighter wafts of charcoal to illustrate the curve of her breast, which was seductively presenting itself. Jaz added subtle white lines of chalk to areas where the morning light, which was creeping through the window, highlighted Lucy's body. As she looked at the finished picture Jaz thought it could be one of her best drawings yet.

Jaz took the drawing into the garden and sprayed it with fixative. She rolled it up and put it in a tube with her other drawings. Next Jaz phoned Aileen to tell her not to pick her up because Lucy was driving her to the restaurant. Aileen made her tutting sound and Jaz told her to be quiet.

Jaz sat on the edge of the bed and gently stroked Lucy's face.

"Have I slept for long?" said a sleepy Lucy.

"A couple of hours. We'll go when you're ready."

"Okay, I'll just have a wash," said Lucy, heading for the bathroom. She washed her hair, brushing it through with Jaz's unkempt hairbrush. Then applied a touch of make-up, from the small set she kept in her handbag, and put on her now dry dress. She observed herself in the mirror and decided she was presentable.

"Gorgeous," said Jaz as Lucy wandered into the lounge.

"Pardon?"

"It's gorgeous outside now," stuttered Jaz. "Look the sun's shining."

Aileen and Naledi greeted Jaz with their usual hugs. Naledi was a week bigger around her baby bump, which made her back ache as she walked along. Lucy and Aileen took an arm each and helped Naledi wobble along the flowered path. Jaz limped behind using her coveted new walking stick, appreciating Lucy's fetching backside.

They ate their cake and discussed if Bernard would get together with Emma. Naledi said Debbie was now out of hospital and lying bored at home. Jaz showed off her ankle, which was now an odd yellowish colour, praising Lucy for helping it heal.

Aileen tutted again, and Jaz's good foot gave her a kick.

They discussed Jaz's journey to the north of Botswana. She told them her plans, and they threw in other ideas, which Jaz noted in her sketchbook.

"It'll be quiet here next week," Naledi said to Aileen.

"I know, we can have a sensible conversation for once!" said Aileen laughing. "Lucy, it's a pity you're going home so soon, you could have joined the explorer on her safari trail."

Jaz stared at Aileen and grimaced.

"I've got an idea," said Aileen in glee. "Change your ticket, you can do it on-line nowadays. We'd be happier if Jaz wasn't alone."

"Splendid idea." Naledi winced as the baby kicked.

"Well, I don't know," said Lucy. "You see ..."

Jaz jumped into the conversation. "Lucy's got to go back to work."

"Oh, stuff that, email them and say you're stuck out here with an unpronounceable disease!" said Aileen. "What flight are you on Jaz?"

Jaz told Aileen her flight details, and she wrote them on a scrap of paper. "There you are everything noted for you." She passed the paper to Lucy and grinned at Jaz, who frowned back. "Now tonight," continued Aileen. "We're having a braai to wish Jaz good luck on her journey and say farewell to Lucy, that's if she's going home. I expect everyone to be there, including Frank and the little one. Seven o'clock. Jeremy's cooking so we're in safe hands."

After another coffee, they wandered back to the car park. Hugging and looking forward to seeing each other later.

"Shall I drive?" Jaz was eager to get back behind the wheel.

"Yeah, if you're sure your ankle can take it," said Lucy.

Jaz got up into the driver's seat. "Big Red, I've missed you." She kissed the steering wheel and carefully drove out of the car park. Pulling her face in pain each time she pressed the clutch pedal.

"Aileen likes to plan things, doesn't she?" said Lucy.

Jaz laughed. "Yeah, I guess she's spontaneous. What do you want to do now?"

Lucy shrugged. "Well, we could attempt the mini safari park, driving around there should test your ankle."

Jaz painfully completed the mini safari tour and then took Lucy to the sports bar, buying them a beer each.

"We didn't see much?" said Lucy, sighing as she looked through her animal book. "Only a bush rabbit and a sparrow."

"You'll see much more on Friday at Mokolodi Safari Park," said Jaz. "What's the time now?"

"Four o'clock."

"Do you need to change your clothes for Aileen's party?"

"No, I was hoping to stay away from the hotel today, my so-called friends are stressing me."

"A game of pool then," said Jaz.

"I've never played pool." Lucy stared at the green table as Jaz set up the balls.

"No problem. I'll take the first shot, then I'll show you how to hold the cue." Jaz struck off, and the balls flew around the table. "Which ball next?"

"This red one here," answered Lucy, her finger resting on a ball.

"Okay, well you hit that red one with the white ball using this cue," directed Jaz. "So, you rest the pointy end of the cue on your left hand, between your thumb and index finger."

Lucy did as Jaz instructed her.

"Then you hold the other end of the cue with your right hand." Jaz stood behind Lucy helping her hold the cue. Jaz's hands wrapped around Lucy's body, and she breathed warmly onto Lucy's neck. "Rest your left hand on the table, aim the white ball at the red ball, pull the cue back and hit it."

They did the shot together. The white ball hit the red one perfectly, and it rolled into the pocket. Lucy shrieked, not knowing if it was potting the ball that excited her or having Jaz hold her close.

"Okay, you get another go," said Jaz. "You've got to pot the red balls now, don't pot the black one till the end."

Lucy pointed to another red ball. "Right, we'll go for that one next." Feeling giddy in Jaz's arms she missed the pot. "Your turn now, I guess."

Jaz potted her yellow balls and then the black, winning the first game. She made a few deliberate mistakes in the next game so that Lucy could win.

After another beer and two games, it was a draw.

"Best stop now, don't want any falling out." Jaz lay the cue on the table.

They were early, but they headed over to Aileen's house. Lucy was driving again, as Jaz's ankle ached.

The braai was lit when they arrived. Jeremy was arranging meat on the grill, and Aileen was placing bowls of salad on a table. She waved at them as they arrived. "The beers are in the cool box," she shouted.

"Thanks." Jaz got out two beers, handing them to Lucy while she limped into the kitchen to get a bottle opener. "Why were you trying to get Lucy to change her ticket?"

Jaz said to Aileen across the kitchen table.

"Well, why not she's spellbound by you?"

"What do you mean? Where's the bottle opener?"

"I can see it in her eyes, a love-struck puppy if ever I saw one. I'm surprised you haven't noticed. It's here."

"Well, no." Jaz took the opener from Aileen's hand.

"Liar, you'd throw yourself off a cliff if she asked you to."

"Alright, yeah, well I might fancy her, but I mean she's married."

"Oh rubbish, people change," said Aileen, opening a large bag of crisps. "One romantic move and she's yours!"

"Don't be ridiculous," hissed Jaz.

They continued to bicker over the table and only stopped when Lucy came into the kitchen.

"Is everything okay?" Lucy asked.

"Oh yeah, fine," said Jaz. "I've got the opener."

"Lucy, could you take these out with you, please?" asked Aileen, passing her a basket of bread and a bowl of crisps.

Lucy placed them on the outside table as Jaz opened the two bottles of beer.

"Cheers." Jaz looked into Lucy's shimmering eyes.

Lucy sat herself next to Naledi and watched Jaz chatting to her arty friends.

"It's hot this evening," said Naledi, her face gleaning with a sheen of perspiration.

"Here." Lucy passed Naledi a glass of water.

"Thanks, I felt different when I had my little boy, Kgosie." Naledi took a drink. "Have you got children?"

Lucy's throat tightened, and she wept.

"Oh, I'm sorry," said Naledi, leaning forward and hugging Lucy.

Jaz saw Lucy's distress and rushed over to her. "What's wrong?"

"We were talking baby talk, and Lucy got upset," Naledi whispered.

"Oh!" Jaz took Lucy's plate of food from her knee.

"Get her a drink," said Naledi.

"Yeah, okay." Jaz came back with a glass of wine.

"I meant water!" Naledi hissed.

Lucy was wiping her eyes with a tissue. "No, it's okay, I'm fine. Wine is wonderful. Thank you."

Frank cheered Lucy with a joke and Kgosie sat on her knee, showing her the picture he'd drawn. "It's the party," he told her, pointing out who was who. "That's you with me on your knee."

Lucy smiled and gave him a cuddle, then told him a story of a teddy bear's party she went to once. He fell asleep before the end of the story and sat slumbering on Lucy's knee until Frank and Naledi took him home.

Jaz sat in Naledi's empty seat and passed Lucy a fresh glass of wine. "Are you alright now?" she asked, concerned over Lucy's tears but not wanting to push for reasons.

"Yeah, sorry, I don't know what came over me."

"Can't have you crying at a party." Jaz held Lucy's hand and squeezed it tight.

"I think I've drunk too much!"

"Looks that way, time I took you home."

Lucy continued to hold Jaz's hand, stood, and said goodnight to Aileen and Jeremy.

Jaz helped her climb unsteadily into the pickup, fastening the seatbelt around her waist, then driving away whistling to tunes on the radio.

When they reached the Grand Sereto car park Lucy jumped out of Big Red, ran into the hotel and waltzed through the lounge. Jaz tried to keep up with her, apologising to anyone they met.

In the lift, Lucy's arms clung around Jaz's shoulders and she breathed into the erotic recess behind Jaz's ear.

Jaz led Lucy to her room, desperately trying not to get turned on by her advances.

Lucy kicked off her shoes and ran to the toilet, while Jaz turned the sheets and poured a glass of chilled water from the water jug. Lucy came out of the bathroom, sat on the bed, and complained that she felt ill.

"Drink this it'll help," said Jaz handing Lucy the glass.

"Thanks." Lucy hiccupped as she downed the water.

Jaz unzipped Lucy's dress.

When Lucy stood, the dress dropped to the floor. Lucy's arms were back around Jaz's neck, her lips kissing Jaz's throat.

Jaz undid and removed Lucy's bra. *"Fucking hell,"* she muttered, staring, and blinking at Lucy's luscious breasts. She quickly threw a nightshirt over Lucy's head and smoothed it over her body.

Lucy sat and swung her legs onto the bed, her head plunging onto the pillow.

Jaz walked around the bed, sitting on the other side, and leaning on the headboard.

Lucy rolled over, resting her head on Jaz's shoulder, kissing her cheek.

"Oh boy," said Jaz, knowing it would be wrong to fall for Lucy's drunken attentions.

"Jaz?"

"Yeah."

"There's something I didn't tell you last night."

"Oh, what was that?"

"I had a baby." Lucy snuggled on Jaz's breast for comfort. "It was a long time ago."

"Oh!" Jaz stroked Lucy's shoulder. "Wes's baby?"

"Yeah, he was travelling in Australia. I didn't think he'd come back to me." Lucy was sobbing. "A couple adopted her."

Jaz lifted Lucy's head and looked into her eyes. "I'm so sorry."

"I never told Wes, you're the only person who knows." Lucy's head dropped back to the pillow, and she fell asleep.

Jaz sighed and closed her eyes for a few seconds.

Chapter 13

The sun was rising when Jaz woke. "Shit, not supposed to be here," she muttered, slipping her arm from around Lucy's shoulders. Jaz rested Lucy's head on the pillows, and pulled the quilt over her shoulders, then leaned over and kissed her sleeping lips. "See you later trouble."

As she opened her eyes Lucy realised that someone had slept next to her. "Hello," she said aloud. No-one answered. She was alone.

By the door she saw a piece of paper lying on the floor. She staggered out of bed and gingerly walked over. Leaning on the furniture she bent and picked up the note.

"Gone to Lobatse hope to see you later, love Emma."

In the bathroom, Lucy looked in the mirror at her pale, drawn face. She found a stomach powder in her bath bag, emptied the packet into a glass, added water and drank the sour lemon liquid. Exhausted, she returned to bed.

Lucy vaguely remembered the journey home and cringed when she recalled snuggling up to Jaz. Lucy bundled her head into the pillow and groaned when she recollected that she'd told Jaz about her baby. She decided she needed a massage to help her relax.

Lying on the massage bed, aromatherapy smells filled the air and a masseur pummelled Lucy's back and legs.

Lucy's mind contemplated what love was. Suddenly, she was hit by a Sapphic blow, her eyes opened wide and she stared at the grey-tiled floor. A voice in her head told her she was in love with Jaz.

Staring at the mobile phone, and building up her courage, Lucy found Jaz's number and tapped the call button.

Jaz answered straight away. "Good morning, darling."

"Hello," said Lucy's weary voice.

"How are you feeling?" Jaz tried to sound concerned.

"Shit!"

"Good."

"What do you mean good?"

"Well, you were rubbish in bed, and I don't think I'm into you anymore."

At Lucy's end of the line there was a long, painful silence.

Jaz howled with laughter. "Only joking, honest. I just got you to bed, had a brief nap, and then I came home."

"You bitch! Are you sure I didn't embarrass myself?"

"Wow, you're full of vulgar language this morning, no, you were fine."

"Sorry, thank you for looking after me," said Lucy.

"My pleasure."

There was a pause. "What are you doing now?" asked Lucy.

"I'm packing my boxes. The Gotogo Package Company are coming this afternoon to take them away and ship them home."

"Is there much to send?"

"Art stuff, paintings and clothes, and this precious pot someone gave me." Jaz rotated the ceramic jar in her hand.

"I'm trying to sober up," said Lucy, yawning. "Can I take you somewhere for dinner this evening, as an apology for being drunk and disorderly."

"Okay. I'll come over at six."

"Great, see you later."

"Yeah, see you," said Jaz.

"Right, bye."

"Bye."

Lucy sat in a darkened corner of the lounge and switched on her tablet to check her emails. There was a message from Wes telling her he was well and hoping she was okay. She sent a reply with the arrival times of her flight home.

Then Lucy got a sheet of paper from reception and wrote a letter to Bernard. She put it in an envelope and labelled it with Bernard's name care of Emma Manu. She left it at reception and ordered a taxi to take her first to the supermarket, and then to Jaz's bungalow.

Lucy stood at Jaz's gate, and took a deep breath. Hesitantly she walked along the path and tiptoed into the lounge through the open front door.

"Fucking hell!" Jaz jumped back, the box she was carrying wobbled in her hands. "You scared the fucking life out of me."

"Sorry, let me help." Lucy put her shopping bag on the chair and grabbed the other half of the box, helping Jaz place it on the floor.

"I thought I was seeing you tonight." Jaz touched Lucy's shoulder and kissed her cheek.

"Well, the others have gone to Lobatse, and I was at a loose end. I should have let you know I was coming. I brought food."

"In that case, you'd better stay. I'll just finish stacking these boxes outside. They're being collected at two o'clock."

"No problem, I'll sort out lunch." Lucy laid out houmous, carrot sticks, falafel, and pitta bread. Then poured two glasses of lemonade.

"I didn't realise I'd gathered so much stuff," said Jaz sitting at the table, piling her plate high with food. "What no beer," she grinned.

"Me and beer don't get on."

"It could have been the wine?" Jaz's eyes gazed at Lucy, her hands yearning to touch her face, and repeat this morning's kiss.

"No, it was definitely the beer." Lucy chewed a carrot stick. "I've been busy this morning. I wrote a letter to Bernard."

"Oh, interesting, what did you write?"

"I told him I was your friend and I…" Lucy stopped talking, not confident enough to finish her sentence. "Well, I wanted to…" continued Lucy.

A horn of the Gotogo Package Company van beeped.

Jaz looked at the gate. "Tell me later," she said. "I've just got to sort this, is that okay?"

Lucy nodded her head and sighed.

With most of her belongings gone, Jaz like a lost soul meandered around the empty bungalow.

Lucy put her arm around her waist. "Come outside, have another glass of lemonade."

"I'm sad now," said Jaz as the two of them sat and drank.

"Well, you can look forward to your safari tour."

"Yeah, I suppose so," Jaz sighed, not sure she'd enjoy being on her own, having spent so much time with Lucy. "What did you want to say earlier," asked Jaz. "You know, just before the van arrived?"

"Oh, nothing important," said Lucy. "I was just wondering if you'll be alright travelling on your own?" Lucy was trying to decide if Jaz would mind her taking on board Aileen's idea and changing her flight to join Jaz on her travels.

"I'll be okay, there's always something to keep me occupied and other travellers to meet."

"Good," said a disappointed Lucy.

They sat and watched a hoopoe wander in and out of the long grass, pecking at the floor.

"Dinners not until six, what do two people do on a sunny afternoon?" asked Jaz, her eyes looking expressively at Lucy, knowing exactly what she'd do if she had the chance.

"Well, we could go shopping, but I've done that today." Lucy looked away from Jaz's eyes.

"They might have a nap," purred Jaz. "Only a suggestion, I've got a spare bedroom now."

Lucy raised an eyebrow in response. "No. I'm wide awake, thank you. If I was at home, I'd read a book."

"Oh yes, the book, wait here." Jaz dashed into the bungalow and returned with a paperback, pads, pens, and paints. "Here," said Jaz handing the tatty book to Lucy. "You read, and I'll sit here and paint your portrait, it doesn't matter if you move, I'll work around you."

"Pardon?" said Lucy.

"What?"

"Well, I didn't hear you ask if you could paint me."

"Oh damn, Lucy, please could I paint you?"

"Yes, I suppose you can," said Lucy, grinning.

"Thank you."

So that was the afternoon sorted. Lucy became absorbed in the reading *The Price of Salt* and mumbled odd phrases out loud throughout her reading. "That's a brilliant description of a fifty-year-old stuck working through exhaustion and fear. Have you ever been to America?"

"No."

"Me neither." Lucy continued to read. "The way they inadvertently meet is charming, similar to me and you."

"Yeah." Jaz wasn't listening, she was too busy drawing Lucy from various angles. Finally, she chose her preferred position and drew Lucy's portrait onto watercolour paper.

Lucy suddenly stopped reading. The fact that Carol had a baby girl caused jolts of pain in Lucy's heart. She put the book on the table and stared at the garden wall; she needed to pull herself together. "Cup of tea?"

"That'd be lovely. I'll work on the landscape while you're away."

When she returned from the kitchen, Lucy passed Jaz a lemony red bush tea and sat back on her seat. Her eyes drifted back to the novel.

Jaz stared at Lucy before mixing her paints and washing them onto the paper. It was a serious, puzzled Lucy that Jaz kept seeing, lost in her own thoughts. "There you go, finished."

"No, you can't be, I'm only a third of the way through, let me get to the end of this chapter."

Jaz relaxed, stretching her shoulders and arms, while she watched Lucy read.

"There, finished chapter nine," said Lucy.

"It looks as if you're enjoying it?"

"I am, the thought of two emotional women falling in love and discovering themselves, is enthralling."

"Things get intense in parts, don't they?"

"Yeah." Lucy looked longingly at Jaz and sighed. "Let's see this portrait then."

Jaz propped the picture against the wall.

"Oh, it's lovely." Lucy looked at the lines and colours.

"You're so vain."

"No, not me, I mean the painting. You've got me looking very distant though."

"Well, that's where I saw you, a million miles away."

Lucy couldn't deny that right now her unexpected feelings for Jaz made her feel as if she was living on another planet.

"Are you hungry yet?" asked Jaz. "Do you fancy trying a fondue? There's a restaurant in town I've never been to, it'll be retro."

They enjoyed the meal, dipping pieces of chicken and lamb into hot oil and watching it fry. When cooked, they pulled out the sizzling meat and dipped it into the garlic mayonnaise.

"Did you want to discuss your baby?" whispered Jaz.

Lucy sighed. "I'm sorry I bothered you with that."

"No, it didn't bother me, it's special that you have somebody out there, your own little person."

"She won't be little now, she'll be thirty."

"I've seen people looking for their adopted family on the TV."

"Yeah, but they've got to be looking, she might not know she's adopted."

"You could send her a letter through the adoption agency," suggested Jaz. "And maybe you should tell Wes."

"You might be right. I'm sure it won't hurt him too much, telling him he has a baby somewhere in the world and then asking for a divorce."

"Oh yeah, never thought of that." Jaz paused. "So, you're going to divorce him?"

"It'll be for the best. It's obvious to me that we don't love each other, he can fall in love with someone else." Lucy sipped her water. "Look can we discuss something else?"

Jaz paused while she thought of a suitable topic of conversation. "Do you read lesbian books in your book club?"

"No, it's a very straight group!"

"You should read *The Fingersmith* by Sarah Waters, that's a classic, and you could try *Tipping the Velvet* if you were brave enough," said Jaz, winking.

"Oh, interesting title," said Lucy.

"It was made into a television series," said Jaz. "Have you noticed how characters look different and the story changes when they turn books into films?"

"It's alright as long as they stay to the principal theme of the story," said Lucy.

"I don't know, it irritates me, and I end up telling everyone the story in the book."

"Wow, I bet you're annoying to be with at the cinema!"

They both laughed and smiled adoringly at each other.

Pudding involved sharing marshmallows and fruit pieces dipped in melted chocolate. Lucy flirtatiously fed strawberries to Jaz and wiped chocolate from her chin. While Jaz constantly told herself that she could not to kiss Lucy's chocolate covered lips.

Jaz studied Lucy as she parked Big Red in the Grand Sereto car park. "I guess you're sober enough to get yourself to your room tonight."

"Was I embarrassing?" said Lucy.

"No, but you waltzed through the foyer as if you were Ginger Rogers."

"Oh shit!"

Jaz leaned over and kissed Lucy on the cheek. Lucy turned her head at the same time and their lips met, holding them together for longer than either of them expected.

Lucy pulled away; her relaxed moist lips still parted. "Goodnight," she stuttered, staring at Jaz's mouth and then her eyes, wondering if she'd kiss her again.

Jaz's smile beamed across her face. She sat back in her seat, surprised by Lucy's sudden move on her. "Goodnight, I'll see you tomorrow."

"Yeah, tomorrow." Lucy ran her fingers over her lips as she left the pickup.

Jaz watched Lucy walk into the hotel, then merrily beeped Big Red's horn as she drove away.

Chapter 14

Lucy lay in bed considering the events of the previous night. Every time she closed her eyes, she could taste Jaz's lips on hers, the experience had enthralled her. But Lucy knew that if news of her kissing another person, especially a woman, reached Wes his response would be merciless.

Lucy skipped breakfast and waited in the car park. She needing to tell Jaz that she was a married woman and was unavailable. As Jaz pulled up beside her Lucy tapped on the passenger window.

"Good morning," purred Jaz.

"I couldn't sleep last night and it's your fault," said Lucy.

"What have I done to upset you?" asked Jaz, a grin spreading across her face.

"You kissed me, that's what." Lucy stood scowling at her.

"I think you'll find it was you who kissed me!"

"No, it was definitely your lips on mine."

"Well, I beg to disagree. I kissed your cheek, you turned your head and kissed me stunningly on the lips. What's the problem? I remember you snogging my neck to distraction the other night, and I didn't complain."

Lucy paused. "The practicalities aren't important; we shouldn't have done it."

"Why?" asked Jaz, surprised at Lucy's response to what Jaz thought had been a tender moment. "Are you being homophobic again?"

"No, it's because…because…I'm married."

"I thought you were divorcing him," said Jaz, irritated by Lucy's words.

"I am, eventually."

"Oh, I see! You've kissed a woman and now you've decided it's not your thing." Jaz sighed. "Okay, I'll forget about you kissing me if you promise not to do it again."

"What?" gasped Lucy.

Jaz waved at Hilary and Emma, as they came out of the hotel.

"We need to discuss this later," hissed Lucy.

"If you say so," said Jaz glaring at Lucy, before turning to Hilary and Emma. "Ready for safari you two? Got your cameras and bottles of water?"

"Yes," said Hilary, nodding her head.

"Hilary, would you care to sit at the front?" said Jaz, refusing to look at Lucy.

"Oh, that'd be fantastic Jasmine, thank you." Hilary climbed into the front seat, filling the dashboard with her artefacts.

Lucy squinted in the sunlight and glared at Jaz, discontentedly she got into the back seat. When Lucy saw Jaz's distressed green eyes glance at her through the rear-view mirror, she stuck out her tongue and stared out of the side window.

Jaz drove slowly around Mokolodi safari park. First, because they were off-road and Jaz was looking after Big Red's suspension, and second, because it was the best way to see the animals and birds.

The first animals they saw were muddy grey Warthogs, who dashed across the track with their piglets. Then a group of ostriches walked by, staring at Lucy, as if Jaz had discussed the entire issue of the kiss with them. Lucy started taking photographs, trying to catch images of the creatures as they dived in and out of sight.

Jaz stopped the pickup in a shaded space, and the tourists got out to observe the wild animals nibbling the grasses on the plain.

Jaz poured cups of coffee from her flask and handed one to Lucy. "You've taken lots of photos?" she said.

"Yes," said Lucy, flicking through the pictures on her camera, avoiding looking at Jaz.

"Did you get the greater kudu and impala?" Jaz pointed over to them, her other hand touching Lucy's shoulder.

"Yes, I did." Lucy walked away, refusing to get into a conversation.

Jaz showed Hilary and Emma how to focus the binoculars, so they could have a closer look at the animals. Then she explained how the brown and ochre colours of each beast acted as camouflage.

Back in the pickup they drove to a group of rondavel huts, which the safari park had built with money donated by Alexander McCall Smith. Jaz parked by a hut so that the group could take photographs and explore the tiny village. Lucy took a selfie, standing smiling in front of the traditional rondavel.

"You can stay in the accommodation as if you were living in a rural village setting. Up near the restaurant there are huts which overlook the waterhole," Jaz shouted, trying to get Lucy's interest.

"That would be a marvellous place to stay," said Emma.

"Much too basic for me," announced Hilary.

Lucy said nothing and carried on taking her photographs. She constantly asked Jaz to stop the pickup so she could jump out and take close-up photos of what she saw. Golden orb spiders sewing their long webs across tracks and then perching on the edge waiting to catch bugs. Dung beetles walking backward, pushing animal poop along the floor, the mound getting larger as it rolled along gathering dirt. Termite mounds, built from African red soil, growing upward from the ground. Giant termites crawling over them, finding their way in and out of the cavernous structures. Mystified, Lucy watched the endless wanderings of each creature.

"Watch the lions don't get you!" shouted Jaz, chuckling as Lucy jumped back into the pickup.

"There aren't any are there!" Lucy slapped Jaz hard on the shoulder. "Stop irritating me!"

"Lover's tiff," Hilary mouthed to Emma.

Jaz drove on, then she quickly stopped the pickup, jarring Lucy in her seat, making her scowl even more. Jaz pointed to a white rhino standing in a clearing of trees tending her calf. The group gasped at the sight and Jaz passed around the binoculars. They sat for a while watching the rhinos eat, until the mother wandered into the trees, followed by her baby.

Continuing onward they drove passed two elephants being walked by their Indian guides.

"Asian elephants," said Jaz. "They're being used to help with the workload as they are easier to train than African elephants."

They entered an enclosed run and got out of the pickup. A warden greeted them and took them through to a grassy pen where they met a stunning yellow, black-spotted, cheetah. The cheetah rolled on the ground, wanting them to rub his tummy.

Lucy ecstatically sat on the sandy floor stroking his soft fur.

"Photograph?" Jaz reached over for Lucy to pass her the camera.

"Thank you."

"You're welcome." Jaz pointed the camera at Lucy and her cheetah friend.

Leaving the cheetah compound, they headed towards the restaurant where Bernard was waiting for them.

"Had an enjoyable time?" asked Bernard.

"Oh, it was wonderful, we've just been cuddling a cheetah." Emma took Bernard by the arm.

"Fantastic," said Hilary, resigned to the fact that she had lost Bernard to Emma.

"Late lunch?" said Jaz as she helped Lucy step out of the pickup.

"Sorry," said Lucy. Her tantrum surrounding the kiss was pathetic now that Jaz had allowed her to witness such natural splendour.

"It's alright." Jaz's mind winced, she'd enjoyed last night's kiss so much that given the opportunity she'd kiss Lucy forever. But now she knew the kiss had been a mistake and to save her sanity was grateful that Lucy was going home in a couple of days.

When she'd finished eating a tasty ostrich burger, Lucy swished a mouthful of white wine around her mouth. The flavours of gooseberries and herbs burst onto her tongue, bringing a smile to her face. She flicked through her photos, deleting the blurred ones and those that contained half an animal.

"You sod," she shouted at Jaz. "You photo bombed my selfie. I don't think I like you anymore." Lucy glared at Jaz's laughing mouth.

"No, admit it, you love me," whispered Jaz seductively into Lucy's ear.

The words and the warm air of Jaz's breath made Lucy blush.

Bernard told Hilary and Emma that he was taking them to visit the Oodi weavers' shop, where they could buy handmade gifts to take home.

"That sounds interesting," said Lucy.

"Oh," said Bernard, anxiously. "I can only take Emma and Hilary."

Lucy frowned, wrinkles forming across her forehead. "Why?" she asked.

"Got to go," said Bernard, standing and rushing Hilary and Emma to the car.

Lucy was left alone with Jaz. "Is something going on here?" she asked.

"Did you want to go with them? I can catch them up."

"No. I guess I can put up with you for a few hours."

"I suppose I should tell you Bernard's plan," said Jaz. "He's taking Hilary and Emma back to the hotel after their shopping trip, then I've got to phone him and tell him there's a water leak at the bungalow. Bernard and Emma will go over there and spend the evening together. Nice, isn't it?"

"But won't we be there?"

"No," said Jaz. "I suppose I know what the answer will be, Bernard asked me to invite you to stay overnight in a rondavel, one of those that overlook the waterhole. But it's okay, we're having a bad day, so I'll take you back to the hotel and kip at Aileen's."

"Oh, I see." Lucy drank her wine. "Well, I guess it'd be nice to stay."

"The waterhole is a magnificent sight; you'll see lots of animals and birds."

"But I haven't brought my night things with me."

"Well, I packed two pairs of pyjamas, and Bernard bought you a new toothbrush." Jaz produced a toothbrush from the side pocket of her trousers and held it aloft.

Lucy found it impossible to be angry with the woman sat opposite her casting spells with a toothbrush.

Lucy sat on the veranda looking at the dirty brown waterhole. Delicate night waterlilies floated atop, rough tussocks of reeds grew around the edge and short thorny trees jutted out of the bank.

Jaz brought over two plates of marinated steak and buttery maize she'd cooked on the barbecue.

A night heron stood stock still in the shallows, watching Jaz and Lucy eat in silence. He soon became bored and dived into the water to find a fishy meal.

Jaz phoned Bernard as planned, then she and Lucy gazed the darkness, listening to jackals howling inharmoniously in the distance.

"I wanted to say I'm not homophobic," said Lucy, her voice breaking the haunting atmosphere.

Jaz sighed. "I know, it's just that you annoyed me."

"Can we be friends again?" Lucy rubbed Jaz's arm.

"Yeah, I was missing you."

"You want another beer?" Lucy pulled a bottle out of the cool box and popped the lid.

"Oh, if I must." Jaz smiled as Lucy passed her the bottle.

"Can I ask you a question?"

Jaz glanced at Lucy and shrugged. "I suppose."

"Bernard mentioned that he didn't want to see you upset again. Did something go wrong?" asked Lucy.

Jaz gave Lucy a shy look. "Oh, my story's not very interesting."

"It's interesting to me. I want to know you better."

Jaz stared up at the stars. "I was another woman who led me on before she left me."

"Don't tell me, she ran off with a flash young woman."

Jaz looked sadly at Lucy. "Well no, she wasn't very flash, or young."

"Oh, shit, I'm sorry, I was stupid to say that." Lucy took Jaz's hand. "As you taught me, it helps to share your story."

"I'm not very good at talking about myself, you know how painful the past can be."

"I know, but there's only me and the jackals listening to you."

"Well, I was with Helen for ten years and six years ago she had a brain haemorrhage. She survived but became tired and confused. It was hard looking after her and getting her through her depression." Jaz stopped for a moment and drank, emptying her bottle.

Lucy topped her own glass with wine and handed Jaz another beer. Their eyes met as she passed it over, and Lucy smiled.

"Helen joined a religious group, and Fiona, the pastor, used to visit her several times a week." Jaz had a swig of beer. "One weekend the group went on a camping holiday."

"That was nice for Helen," said Lucy.

"Not nice for me though. I got home from work one day and the house was silent. I found a note on the table from Helen. She'd left me and moved in with Fiona."

"No way," gasped Lucy bursting out laughing.

"What's so funny?" asked Jaz, stunned by Lucy's reaction.

"I thought Helen would die, not disappear with a woman of God!"

"It was the most tragic thing that ever happened to me!" pined Jaz.

"I know!" Lucy patted Jaz's hand. "But it sounds funny, doesn't it?"

"I guess," said Jaz, trying not to smile. "It hurt so much. I couldn't work out how a religious person could steal another woman's partner? She had no conscience. I was heartbroken, and I thought, no more women for me, thank you!"

Lucy looked thoughtfully at Jaz. "Let's hope that feeling doesn't last forever."

Lucy's words and the cool surrounding air made Jaz shiver. Then she noticed the constellations disappearing. "I think it's going to, yes, it's raining." Jaz pulled Lucy out into the rain which lashed onto them, the large drops of water soaking through their clothes. Jaz started her weird dancing and splashed through the puddles.

There was a terrific flash of lightning followed by a roaring, tympanic roll of thunder. Lucy screamed and ran up the steps onto the veranda, closely followed by Jaz.

"I hate storms," Lucy whimpered, as she pushed herself into Jaz's arms.

"Oh boy, look, let's get inside, it'll be safer." Jaz held Lucy close as they went into the rondavel and sat on the sofa. Lucy screwed her eyes shut and snuggled into Jaz's breasts.

Jaz watched the storm through the square window. The lightning flared through the sky and the thunder rumbled chaotically. Eventually the thunderous roars became more distant from the lightning flashes and faded into a quiet drum roll as the storm passed.

"There you go, it's over," Jaz whispered into Lucy's ear.

Lucy lifted her head. "Sorry, storms scare me."

Jaz stroked Lucy's rain-soaked hair and leaned forward, her lips glancing Lucy's.

Lucy gently pulled away. "We should get dry, change into our pyjamas and drink hot chocolate," she said, standing and switching on the kettle.

"Yeah great." Jaz tried not to sound too dejected.

In her bedroom, Lucy dried herself with a fresh white towel. Then put on the over-sized pyjamas she was borrowing from Jaz, rolling up the legs and the sleeves. Returning to the kitchen she made two hot chocolates.

A dry and changed Jaz, came back into the lounge. "I'll get the biscuits," she said.

They plonked themselves onto the sofa. Snuggling together, drinking, and dunking biscuits into the chocolaty foam. Lucy rested her head on Jaz's shoulder as she dreamed of first being cuddled by a cheetah and then by Jaz.

Lucy confused Jaz. One minute she was pushing her away, the next she couldn't keep her hands off her. Jaz didn't think she'd ever understand women. "Ah well, time for bed," said Jaz, yawning.

"Yeah, I suppose." Lucy picked up the cups and rinsed them under the taps, leaving them on the side to dry.

"Will you be alright on your own in your room? There might be another storm."

"I'll be fine." Lucy tried to sound confident as she wandered over to her bedroom door.

"I'm only across the lounge if you need me. Wake me up if you're scared," said Jaz, following her.

"Thanks, but I'm sure I'll be alright." Lucy opened the door.

"Okay, well goodnight then."

"Goodnight." Her heart beating loudly Lucy closed the door.

Jaz knocked.

"Yes?" said Lucy, opening the door a smidgen and seeing Jaz's grinning face.

"You still okay?"

"I'm fine, go to bed." Lucy smiled as she closed her door and leaned on it. She heard Jaz wander to her room and her door click shut. Lucy prayed for another storm, hoping that Jaz would run to her room and hold her. But the storm stayed away.

Chapter 15

Lucy opened her eyes and yawned. She heard a chair being dragged across the veranda. Finding a patterned blanket folded on the back of the chair, Lucy wrapped it around her body and pulled yesterday's socks onto her feet.

Outside, a dressed Jaz was sitting with her feet resting on the veranda railing, watching the sun rise over the low hills. Wildebeest and impala ate and drank by the waterhole. A spoonbill stood daydreaming, its legs disappearing into the dirty water, and Egyptian geese and white-faced ducks swam in and out of the reeds.

"Isn't it stunning?" Jaz smiled up at Lucy.

"Lovely." Lucy dropped onto the seat next to Jaz and leaned her head on Jaz's comfortable shoulder recalling the dream she'd had where Jaz had kissed her.

"Coffee?" Jaz topped up her mug and passed it to Lucy.

"Thanks."

Jaz soaked up the closeness that had developed between the two of them. "Did you sleep well?"

"Yes, nice comfy bed, a few freaky noises though."

"It's those jackals, you never know what they're planning!"

"Did you sleep alright?" asked Lucy, trying to make sure Jaz wasn't too upset about her backing away from last night's kiss.

"Oh yeah, sure, I was asleep as soon as my head hit the pillow."

They sat and watched a group of warthogs arrive at the waterhole and roll in the damp mud.

"Do you want breakfast now? Then we can go on an early morning tour, it'll be nice to drive in the coolness," said Jaz.

"We could take it with us and stop at your picnic site."

"Excellent idea. I'll make a flask of coffee and get oat biscuits and fruit."

"Best get dressed," said a weary Lucy.

Lucy leaned on Big Red's passenger window, soaking in the scenery. She had to tell Jaz to stop whistling tunes since she was spoiling the songs of the birds that were flying in and out of the trees. Jaz made a squawking sound and Lucy slapped her.

They stopped for breakfast in the same grassy spot as yesterday. Serenely they sat in the pickup cab, eating biscuits, and drinking *Camp* coffee. The orange sun rose in the sky, creating a dawn of delicate purples and yellows, and impala and zebra ate grasses on the plain.

"I hope you've enjoyed your holiday," said Jaz.

Lucy remembered that she was travelling home tomorrow. "Oh yes, it's been wonderful, you know I...." Lucy still needed to ask Jaz if she could stay and go on safari with her, but she froze. "I've loved it."

"Good, I'm glad," said Jaz, driving back toward the rondavel.

A yellow-billed hornbill hopped across the track. Jaz made an emergency stop and Lucy bumped her head on the side window.

"Shit, sorry," said Jaz.

"Bloody hell, that hurt." Lucy rubbed her forehead.

"Let me see." Jaz studied the bump and kissed it, then her lips moved toward Lucy's.

Lucy welcomely responded to the pressure of Jaz's lips, but then her arms pressed Jaz away. "I can't..." she said, instantly regretting her words.

"I'm sorry," said Jaz. "I just can't control myself." Her hands returned to the steering wheel. "I'd best get you back to the hotel so you can get yourself packed."

As they left the safari park Lucy leaned through the window photographing everything around her, wanting to remember it forever. Then she glanced at Jaz, wishing she'd let her continue her kiss.

When they reached the hotel, they sat in the pickup, neither of them knowing what to say.

"When you get home, you can phone me whenever you want," said Jaz. "I'll always be there for you."

"That's lovely to know." Lucy chewed her lip. "Thanks for telling me about Helen, I hope it helped to talk."

"Yeah, it was good to get it off my chest."

"Do you want to stay for brunch?" asked Lucy

"No thanks, I'd better get home, have a shower, and finish packing for my trip."

Lucy looked at Jaz's face. "I'd best say goodbye, thank you for a lovely time."

"Oh, you're not rid of me just yet! Bernard has arranged for us to go to an Irish Ceilidh tonight, there's a band, dancing, and stuff," said Jaz.

"That's great, so I'll see you later." A sense of relief rushed through Lucy.

"Yeah, I'll pick you up at six." Jaz struggled to sound chirpy.

"Where's your smile?" Lucy stroked Jaz's cheek.

"Lost it in the bush," said Jaz, still upset about Lucy resisting her ardour, she couldn't even look her in the eye. "You'd better get yourself ready."

Lucy stepped down from the pickup.

Jaz put Big Red into gear and pulled away, stopping before the car park exit and considered turning around. She thought better of it and carried on driving.

Lucy watched Jaz leave, lost in a moment of remorse. A car beeped its horn at her, bringing her back to reality.

Going into her room Lucy stared at herself in the mirror. "You are being ridiculous," she muttered. "If you fancy Jaz you should tell her and give it a go. Stop worrying about what Wes thinks."

Lucy grabbed her tablet and wrote Wes an email. *"Hi Wes, going to extend my holiday for a few more days if that's okay with you. Been invited to travel up north and go on safari, won't be able to message you while I'm away, there's no signal. Lucy."*

Then she logged onto the airline website. She took Aileen's piece of paper from her purse, and instead of checking in for tomorrow's flight, she changed her schedule to match that of Jaz. It cost a few hundred pounds, but she didn't care, all she had to do now was tell Jaz she had a travel companion.

Outside at the pool bar, Lucy saw Emma and waved.

"Fancy a coffee," said Emma.

"Why not?"

Emma ordered two lattes. "Lucy, what do you think of Bernard?"

"He's lovely, and he thinks you're wonderful."

"Good, I'm glad because he's asked me to go out with him."

"Oh, that's marvellous. I'm so happy, and Jaz will be too."

"It's a wonderful thing to meet someone and make an instant connection."

"Well, I've got news. I won't be flying home with you tomorrow," said Lucy.

"Are you going travelling?" asked Emma.

"Well, I'm hoping to go on safari."

"With Jaz?"

"If she agrees."

"That's lovely, you'll see so much."

Bernard arrived. "Hello both." He kissed Emma on the cheek. "You ready to go?"

"Yes, we'll see you later Lucy," said Emma.

"Yeah, bye," said Lucy ordering herself a white wine and soda. She took a deep breath and phoned Jaz. The phone rang and went to voicemail. Lucy hung up and rang again. Still no answer. She thought it would be rude to leave a message, she'd have to talk to her later. She got *The Price of Salt* out of her bag and started reading.

When Jaz arrived at six o'clock Lucy was sitting at the bar.

"Have you had a pleasant afternoon?" said Jaz, smiling and admiring Lucy's flowery dress, devouring the familiar air of perfume that surrounded her.

Lucy was pleased that Jaz's smile had returned. "Just a rest and a drink."

"Excellent. Bernard has taken Emma to the Ceilidh, so I'm here to collect you and Hilary."

"Oh, Hilary's gone with Ian."

"So, it's just you and me again." Jaz gazed into Lucy's seductive eyes.

"Yeah, I'm sorry to lumber myself on you."

"No, it's not a problem, I love spending time with you. Sorry if I was glum earlier."

Lucy took Jaz's hand. "Jaz, I've had a muddled mind over the past few days, but things are getting more comprehensible for me now."

"That's good," said Jaz.

"Jaz…I was wondering…I wanted to ask..."

"Can you ask me later?" asked Jaz. "We'll be late if we don't get going."

Jaz kept hold of Lucy's hand and walked out to the pickup, then drove toward the venue. She looked over at Lucy. "It's been fun showing you around and getting to know you."

"Well, I've enjoyed being with you. I...err." Lucy paused. "Well, it's just that..." Lucy sighed at her inability to create a pertinent sentence.

"Still stuck for words." Jaz patted Lucy's hand. "I know I shouldn't fancy you, but I do and that's my problem. I'm sorry I got carried away a few times, you know, with the kissing. I don't want to traumatise you."

"Thanks, I'll bear that in mind," said Lucy. "I err...I enjoyed your kisses."

"You did?" said Jaz glancing at Lucy, who was staring at her feet.

When they arrived, Jaz linked Lucy's arm through hers and led her into the shindig where they sat around a wooden table, and Bernard bought a round of drinks.

A fiddler began to play, then a flautist and barren joined the tune. After a few phrases, Bernard escorted Emma to the dancefloor, followed by Hilary and Ian. Lucy sat tapping her feet to the music, wishing she and Jaz could dance.

Jaz chuckled. "They are the oddest couple; he must appreciate the older woman."

"Same as you," said Lucy winking at Jaz.

Jaz regarded Lucy's body. "I guess he's right, elderly ladies are ravishingly desirable."

Lucy's hand rested on Jaz's knee. "Jaz, I wanted to ask..." Lucy didn't finish the sentence as Ian came over and asked her to dance while Hilary had a rest. Lucy glanced at the frowning Jaz before joining Ian on the dancefloor.

Jaz watched them twirling around in a jig as she swigged her beer. "Off to the loo," she said to Hilary, wandering to the bar and disappearing into the darkness.

Two dances later, Lucy returned to her wine. "Have you seen Jaz?" she asked Hilary.

"Oh, Jasmine visited the toilet a while ago."

Lucy waited, but Jaz didn't return. She tried to phone her, but there was no answer.

"I'll check the bar," said Bernard. He came back with a tray of drinks, but no Jaz.

"She might be in the pickup," suggested Emma. "She didn't look her happy self this afternoon."

"You saw Jaz earlier?" asked Lucy.

"Yes, me and Bernard popped over to visit her this afternoon," said Emma.

As the others returned to their dancing Lucy wandered over to the car park. Jaz wasn't in the pickup. Lucy stared into the darkness toward the lake where she thought Jaz might seek salvation. In the distance, Lucy viewed a tiny orange flicker.

Lucy switched on her phone's torch app and walked towards the orange dot. As she got closer, she saw Jaz sitting on a rock staring into the watery depths. Lucy stopped and sent a quick text to Bernard to say they'd found each other.

"Didn't think you smoked?" said Lucy, sitting next to Jaz.

"I thought it might help me feel more content, but it tastes disgusting!" Jaz mashed out the cigarette on a rock.

"You okay?"

"No," sighed Jaz. "I watched you dancing with that bloke, and I wanted to dance with you. I get pissed off with straight social restraints."

"Well, you can dance with me now." Lucy stood and grabbed Jaz's hand in hers. "Listen it's a slow one, please will you dance with me?"

Jaz stood and Lucy put her arms around her neck, resting her head on Jaz's shoulder.

"Jaz," whispered Lucy.

"Yeah," said Jaz dreamily.

"I'm not going home tomorrow."

"I know."

"Emma?"

"I was so upset she wanted to make me smile."

"Oh," said Lucy, the wind knocked out of her sails. "Well, I was wondering if I could come on safari with you."

"Absolutely, that would be amazing."

"Thank you." Lucy placed her hands on either side of Jaz's face and placed her lips on Jaz's lips. Music played and water lapped beside them.

Their first kiss was short. Lucy's lips dried out with nerves. They stopped for a moment and looked into each other's eyes before Jaz's lips moved back to Lucy's.

Lucy's lips relaxed and worked their way around Jaz's mouth, their tongues tentatively touching.

They both stopped for a breath.

"Are you okay with this?" asked Jaz, checking that Lucy was not regretting this moment.

"Perfect."

They kissed more passionately, and their tongues danced in synchronisation.

It was after midnight when Lucy and Jaz returned to the dance floor. Holding hands and separating as they approached their table where they sat and watched the band pack to leave.

"Time, I went back to the hotel," said Lucy.

"Are you sure that's where you want to go?" Jaz suggestively held Lucy's hand.

"I think it's for the best," said Lucy. "Kissing and cuddling is my limit right now."

"Many lesbians sleep together on their first date," said Jaz.

"Well, this woman has principles."

"Ah, shame," said Jaz, cheekily as she got into the pickup and drove back to the hotel with Lucy's hand resting on her leg.

Jaz parked the pickup at the edge of the car park, and kissed Lucy once more, her hands discovering Lucy's bodily curves.

"Goodnight," said Lucy. "I'll see you in the morning."

"Definitely, is ten o'clock alright?"

"Perfect."

They kissed again, and Lucy entered the hotel on her own. Jaz waited for a while in the car park, but much against her hopes Lucy didn't come rushing back out full of lustful passion.

Chapter 16

Lucy sat in the hotel restaurant drinking a milky coffee.

"So, you're not coming home with us," said Hilary, storming in and sitting by her side.

"No, staying to go on safari," replied Lucy.

"I see." Hilary spoke in an accusatory tone, as if she were talking to a schoolchild who had cheated in an exam. "What does Wes think?"

"I've let him know and he's fine." Lucy didn't care what Wes thought, it was her choice.

"Oh, and this one here," Hilary pointed at Emma. "Has stolen my boyfriend."

"He was never your boyfriend, he was your pen-friend," said Emma.

"Near enough the same thing." Hilary hissed.

Emma ignored Hilary's sarcasm. "Anyway, you've got another boyfriend now."

Hilary stared at Emma. "Ian's only a friend."

Emma grinned. "A friend who stays over, at your age that makes you a leopard."

"A cougar," said Lucy, giggling. "It makes her a cougar."

Emma giggled. "Bernard and I are spending the day together," said Emma standing and giving Lucy an enormous hug. "We'll meet up with you and Jaz in a few weeks, when Bernard joins me in Manchester."

"That'll be wonderful." Lucy kissed Emma on the cheek.

Bernard was standing at the door waving. "See you tomorrow," he shouted to Lucy.

Lucy didn't know of any plans, but waved back. "Sure, tomorrow."

Hilary looked disgusted. "I'm off to find Ian, he's taking me to the airport."

"Okay, have a safe journey home." Lucy gave Hilary's starched body a hug and Hilary marched away.

Lucy went up to her room to fetch her suitcases. She checked the cupboards, drawers and bathroom, for anything she might have forgotten. "Bye room," she said as she shut the door behind her.

After she'd checked out of her room and paid her bills, she left her cases in the baggage room, and wandered out to the poolside bar, ordering a pot of bush tea for two.

As usual, Jaz was on time. "Morning." Jaz kissed Lucy on the cheek.

"Morning. Cup of tea?" Lucy poured the rich russet liquid into a white china cup and added a slice of lemon.

"That'd be lovely." Jaz sat next to her.

"Did you sleep alright on your own?" asked Lucy.

"Yeah, and I had marvellous dreams." Jaz winked at Lucy.

They sat and looked at each other while they drank their tea, neither knowing how to play the next step. Jaz was still working out the rules of courting, which she decided included being polite.

Lucy tapped Jaz's hand, feeling her soft skin. "So, what are we up to today?"

"Do you want to see Hilary and Emma off at the airport?"

"No, we've said our goodbyes here."

"Okay, we'll take your cases to the bungalow and pack for the trip. This afternoon we need to visit the camping shop to buy a few extra things."

"Excellent, I can find myself a new pair of boots," said Lucy.

"Great. So where are your bags?"

"In the baggage room."

"You ready to go then?"

Lucy nodded her head and stood.

"Are you sure you want to join me?" asked Jaz.

Lucy looked into Jaz's eyes. "I'm sure."

Jaz carried Lucy's two suitcases into the bungalow. She kicked the door closed and Lucy wrapped her arms around her neck and kissed her.

"I've been waiting the whole morning to do that," sighed Lucy, once the embrace came to a natural pause.

"Wow." Jaz dropped the luggage on the floor, took Lucy in her arms, and returned the kiss.

"Time for more tea," said Lucy, thinking if she didn't do something, they'd cling together for the entire day.

"Yeah, tea, splendid idea." Jaz released her, feeling as if she'd escaped and might never return. "Are you taking both cases?" she asked as Lucy disappeared into the kitchen.

"No, just the cabin case."

"Look I've got a spare canvas bag here that your gear will fit into. It'll save your Gucci case from getting damaged. Things get messy in the back of the pickup."

"Yeah, fine."

"We'll take your suitcases and the stuff I'm not taking with us to Bernard's in the morning."

"Can't we leave it here?" asked Lucy, bringing in the tea.

"No, it'll be safer at Bernard's." Jaz sat on the lounge floor with a notebook, staring at the items lying in front of her. "I've put everything for cooking in that metal trunk, a bag of charcoal here for the campsite braai. We've got to remember to get the ice blocks for the cool box out of the freezer. And my art equipment is in that bag." Jaz ticked the items off her list. "Have you brought a waterproof jacket?"

"No, I'll add it to my shopping list." Lucy wrote *jacket*, in mid-air.

"I hope you're taking this seriously."

Lucy nodded her head as she giggled.

"I've got a box of tinned food, T-bags, coffee, bread, biscuits, we'll buy more on the way," said Jaz.

Lucy tried not to yawn. She got up and kneeled behind Jaz, massaging her shoulders and studying the scribbled writing in the notebook. "I didn't know we'd need so much stuff to go camping." She moved Jaz's hair to one side and kissed her neck.

Jaz tried not to let Lucy distract her. "I've borrowed a bigger tent from Naledi and Frank, with an awning, so we can sit inside, get away from the bugs."

"Good, bugs and me aren't friends." Lucy kissed Jaz's neck again.

Jaz sighed. "Then we've got a trunk with tools, candles, torches, spare batteries, mozzie repellent, sun cream, tin opener, bottle opener, etcetera, etcetera!" She leaned her head back and kissed Lucy's lips. "We just need to sort out the sleeping arrangements."

"Oh!" said Lucy, her arms going limp on Jaz's shoulders.

"Well, it's just that you'll need a sleeping bag and a mattress, unless you want to get a double set."

Jaz's words embarrassed Lucy. "No, best stick to single. I'll buy those because I'm the intruder, so to speak."

"Righto, *courting set* for sleeping!" Jaz added Lucy's items to the list. "So, the table is over there, two chairs, a water carrier, buckets and bowls for washing self, clothes and pots. I think we've got everything."

"Have you got a first aid kit?"

"In the pickup."

"Matches."

"Bloody hell the matches, well done." Jaz jumped out of Lucy's arms, ran into the kitchen and came back with a box of matches. She knelt and put them in the metal cooking trunk.

Lucy lay on the floor laughing. "You're just crazy."

"Did you call me a crazy lady?" Jaz crawled over and straggled Lucy, leaning and kissing her.

Lucy surprised Jaz by flipping her over, ending up on top, and holding Jaz by her wrists.

"Fucking hell," said Jaz in shock.

"Self-defence, never know when you need it."

"I surrender," sighed Jaz.

Lucy let go of Jaz's wrists and lay on top of her, kissing her soft lips.

"Hey up, steady on," said Jaz. "Best go shopping, before we get carried away and the shop shuts."

"Oh, I suppose so, I enjoy shopping more than kissing." Lucy laughed.

The store was enormous. Lucy headed for clothes, finding herself two t-shirts, a red one and a green one.

"Don't go for red, it'll attract the mosquitoes," said Jaz.

Lucy sighed and swapped it for a beige one. Then chose a matching pair of shorts, a tawny fleece and a blue waterproof jacket. Selecting a pair of boots was more difficult.

Jaz suggested buying a pair that fitted but allowed Lucy's feet to swell in the heat. "If you can afford them, I'd buy these." She handed Lucy a pair of suede boots. "They're waterproof with good soles, and ideal for the Lake District."

"Okay, they're nice." Lucy tried them. "They fit lovely."

"You'll need a hat." Jaz plucked a beige sun hat off a stand and put it in the trolley. "Right then, camping department."

"Oy, wait for me." Lucy pulled off the boots and slipped on her pumps, then grabbed a new pair of sandals from a sales rack.

They found Lucy a colourful sleeping bag with a small sewn-in pillow and a self-inflating mattress.

"Right, that should be everything," said Jaz.

As Jaz paid, Lucy added several bars of chocolate to the trolley.

Back at the bungalow Jaz loaded the camping gear into the opened rear of the pickup. She pulled closed the pickup's corrugated shutter and locked it with a sturdy padlock.

"I've left room on the rear passenger seats for our bags of clothes, coats, art gear and cool box." Jaz's stomach rumbled as she sat on the patio seat. "I'm starving now."

"I'll make something," said Lucy.

"No, we'll go out."

"No, I've got to earn my living." Lucy disappeared into the kitchen and studied the cupboards and fridge. She returned to the patio half an hour later with two plates of macaroni cheese.

After eating the last mouthful Jaz patted her tummy. "Delicious," she said. "You're definitely a keeper." She took the empty plates into the kitchen then spread a map of Botswana over the lounge floor. "Do you want to see where we're going?"

Lucy poured herself a glass of wine and passed Jaz an open a bottle of beer. Then she sat next to Jaz watching her mark the route with a highlighter pen.

"We can make changes if you see any other places you want to visit. It depends on how tired we get and the state of the roads."

"Will I be driving as well?" asked Lucy.

"I was hoping you could, the distances are long."

"Okay, but you can do the off-road driving, it's freaky."

"Sure, no probs." Jaz chinked her beer bottle against Lucy's wine glass. "The open road beckons."

Lucy stood and switched on the CD, songs from the eighties filled the room. Lucy grabbed Jaz and smooched across the floor.

"Watch the map," said Jaz.

Lucy fell on the sofa giggling as she watched Jaz impressively fold the map and put it in her satchel.

"There everything's sorted," they both said in unison.

"Did you make a wish?" asked Lucy.

"A what, when?" said Jaz lounging next to Lucy.

"If you say the same words at the same time, you're supposed to make a wish," explained Lucy.

"Oh."

"It's too late now because we've both spoken."

"Blimey that's complicated. I could have made a few wishes," said Jaz, nuzzling Lucy's lips as she reclined on the cushions.

"What's the time?" asked Lucy.

"Ten o'clock."

"Bedtime I suppose."

Jaz sensed Lucy's qualms. "You have my bed; I'll sleep in the guest room."

"No, I'm the guest, and I've seen the state of your bed."

"Cheeky."

"It's only until I..."

"Until you lose control and ravage me." Jaz laughed, grabbing Lucy around the waist.

"Stop it." Lucy slapped Jaz lightly and then kissed her. "I've got to get used to this, you know."

"I know, sorry." Jaz kissed her goodnight.

Chapter 17

A loud beeping shook Jaz out of her dreams. She rolled over, grabbed her phone and turned off the alarm. Jumping out of bed, she went into the kitchen, warmed two croissants in the oven and made a pot of tea.

Jaz tapped on the guest room door and crept inside, deciding Lucy was lovely even when fast asleep. Gently, she nudged Lucy's shoulder as she placed the tray on the bedside table.

"Wakey, wakey," Jaz whispered as she sat at the end of the bed.

Lucy's sleepy eyes looked at Jaz. "Ugh, what's the time?"

"Six o'clock, we've got a long day ahead." Jaz kissed her as an apology. "Breakfast?"

"Um, lovely." Lucy sat up, sipped her tea and nibbled a croissant. "Ooh look at that." Jaz turned. "Oh, a gecko, he's cute."

"Yeah, he's sweet. It's snakes I hate, they're horrible."

"I'm afraid we might see snakes on our travels. It's the mamba you've got to beware of; he'll slide around you." Jaz put her cup and plate on the cupboard and slid her arms around Lucy's body. "Then just when you're unprepared, he'll bite." She nibbled Lucy's neck.

"Get off snaky." Lucy slapped Jaz's arms, which were sensuously wandering around her body.

"Oops, he's gone." Jaz kissed Lucy's soft mouth, happy to receive a passionate response.

After finishing breakfast, Lucy slid out of bed and entered the bathroom. Jaz took the dishes into the kitchen and washed them.

"Aargh you sod," Lucy screamed.

"What's wrong."

"Look!" Lucy stormed out of the bathroom and showed Jaz the red mark on her neck. "I've had to put foundation over it."

"It's fine, you can hardly see it," said Jaz, trying not to giggle as she filled the cool box. She carried the box outside and placed it on Big Red's rear seat, then stared at Lucy as she brought over two pillows.

"I need comfort, and I've got you one."

Jaz sighed as she locked the bungalow's front door and padlocked the metal door gate. "Right, first stop Bernard's." She got into Big Red and switched on the engine.

At Bernard's flat Lucy trundled over her two cases. Jaz carried Bernard's laptop and a black bin liner, which contained a clean set of clothes and the few things she wasn't taking camping.

"Morning uncle," said Jaz, wandering through the open front door.

"Morning pumpkin." Bernard kissed Jaz on the cheek. "Morning Lucy. It's a lovely day for travelling."

"Morning Bernard."

"Here's your laptop uncle, thanks for lending it to me."

"No problem, put your bags in the spare room. Tea?" asked Bernard.

"No thanks, Jaz has got a schedule." Lucy laughed.

"Where are you going first?"

"Straight up to Francistown, stopping at Palapye for lunch," said Jaz.

"Good, good. Well, you know to be careful, watch the roads, terrible traffic nowadays."

"Yup, right off we go." Jaz manoeuvred Lucy toward the door.

"Oh, wait a minute." Bernard opened a cupboard and returned with a wrapped box, which he handed to Lucy. "Thank you for looking after my troublesome niece."

"I don't need anything for doing that," said Lucy blushing.

"Well, it's only a small present. Open it later."

"Well okay, thank you," said Lucy.

"Bon voyage," said Bernard.

Jaz gave him a massive hug. "Love you uncle."

"Love you too, now go away." Bernard sniffed away a tear as he shut the door behind them.

Jaz took Lucy's hand, and they wandered to the pickup.

"How far are we going today?" asked Lucy.

"Two hundred and seventy miles near enough," said Jaz.

"Wow, that's further than a return journey from Manchester to Keswick."

"How do you know that?"

"I was just exploring distances on the Internet," said a bashful Lucy.

Jaz grinned and rubbed Lucy's thigh. "If I drive to Palapye, we can stop there for lunch. After that you could drive the couple of hours to Francistown."

"Marvellous. Do you know the way?"

"Oh aye, only one road and we're on it now."

"Good." Lucy studied Jaz's profile with its mindful brow, green eyes, largish nose, and kissable mouth.

"Are you staring at my nose, my dad told me it's Roman the same as his."

"It's prominent, but it suits you." Lucy kissed Jaz's cheek and tapped her fingers on the box that rested on her knee.

"So, what did uncle buy you?" asked Jaz, glancing at the parcel.

"Looks as if it's a box of chocolates."

"Oh, I fancy a chocolate."

Lucy undid the wrapping paper. "Blimey!"

"What is it?"

"A camera." Lucy removed it from the box. "A big camera with a zoom lens."

"Bloody hell, you're a lucky one, and there's me thinking I was worthless."

"No, I must give it back, he can't give me this."

"Too late, we're not back till next Tuesday."

"I take it you knew about this."

"Are you accusing me and uncle of colluding?"

"You're both very naughty, and it was a pleasure looking after you."

"You'd best thank Bernard."

Lucy sent Bernard a text. He replied saying that anyone who could spend so much time with Jaz and stay sane deserved it.

"It looks difficult to use." Lucy held the camera and slotted in the battery and SD card.

"You turn it on there." Jaz pointed to a switch. "Put it on *auto* using that dial, then point and shoot."

Lucy pointed the camera at Jaz. "I can't see anything."

"Take the lens cap off."

"Oh yeah, that's better." She took Jaz's photograph. "Oh, that was straightforward, and it focuses itself." Lucy started taking photos of people wandering along the side of the road. "This is so cool. I can zoom closer than with my smaller camera."

"Great, we can have decent animal photos from our safari."

Lucy put the camera on her knee and got her mp3 player from her handbag, plugging it into the USB slot on Big Red's radio. "What do you fancy?"

Jaz glanced at Lucy, wondering if that was one of her chat up lines.

"What music do you want?" Lucy asked.

"Oh, what you got?"

"Erasure, Madonna, Abba...."

"Very eighties! Have you got Whitney Houston?"

"Yep, here we go." Lucy pressed play and Whitney started singing.

"Cool." Jaz took a drink from her water bottle. "Got any biscuits?"

"We've only been travelling for a while and you're hungry!"

"Got to keep my energy up, never know when I'll need it."

"Why?"

Jaz winked at her and grinned.

Lucy slapped her as she passed a digestive. "Right, time for the questionnaire."

"The what?"

"Since we're sharing a tent, I need to know you better."

"Oh, err okay, fair enough."

Lucy took a folded piece of paper from her bag, found a pen and leaned on the camera box.

"Right question one, your full name?"

"Can I phone a friend?" Jaz asked. "No okay, Jasmine Eleanor Page."

"That's such a lovely name," said Lucy, admiring it as she wrote it on the page. "Question two what's your star sign?"

"Hang on, you haven't told me your full name."

"Oh okay." Lucy wrote her name.

"You must say it. I can't read while I'm driving."

"Lucy Hilda Cobble."

Jaz snorted and took a quick drink of water. "Sorry, I got a fly in my throat."

"Don't laugh. It's a horrible name. I don't mind Lucy, but Hilda and Cobble are awful."

"Well, you can change Cobble back to your maiden name. What was that?"

"Pratt."

"Oh! Who was Hilda?"

"My grandmother and she was horrible to me."

"Shall we stick with Lucy," suggested Jaz compassionately. "Do you think the questionnaire's a good idea, look you're upset already."

"No, it's fine. I know the answer to the next one, your star sign is Scorpio."

"How do you know that?"

"Tattoo," said Lucy, tapping the top of Jaz's left arm.

"Oh yeah, clever. What are you?"

"Guess."

"Oh no, I'm hopeless at guessing games."

"No go on, have a guess."

Jaz scoured her memory of the star signs of past loves, friends, and family. She glanced at Lucy as she considered each sign.

"You're taking ages, there's only twelve to choose from," said Lucy.

"Right, okay, I've got two possibilities."

"Which one are you going to choose?"

"Pisces."

"How did you come up with that?"

"Am I right, please tell me I'm right."

"Okay, you're right, it's a shit questionnaire." Lucy screwed up the paper and threw it onto the back seats.

"Yeah, I'm right." Jaz peeped the horn.

"How long till lunch?" Lucy asked moodily.

Jaz looked at the dashboard clock. "Not far now, these big slow trucks are a pain though." Jaz had overtaken a few of the lumbering trucks that crept along the road. "This road's bloody frightening."

Whitney stopped singing, and Lucy put on a Texas album.

Jaz whooped. "I'm glad you like Texas, they're my favourite group, and Sharlene's just gorgeous. Have you seen them live?"

Lucy shook her head. "I've never been to a pop music concert."

"You live in Manchester, you must have been to something, even if it's only Take That."

"I used to go to classical concerts and the theatre with Carly, but it's no fun going on your own."

"We could go to a concert together?"

"Yeah, that'll be nice."

They sang along to the singles as they journeyed on. Jaz made up the words when she couldn't remember what they should be.

"I thought you said you were their biggest fan?" said Lucy, laughing.

"Well, it's not my fault they keep getting the words wrong. Here we are, Palapye, lunchtime."

Inside the service station, they tucked into a beef and squash stew.

"Yikes." Lucy pointed to the corner of the room.

Jaz looked around to see a long white snake slithering along the edge of the wall. She took Lucy's shaking hand. "It's alright, he's a house snake, eating up the yucky insects, bugs and mice. It's like a cat, but less furry."

Lucy stared at the snake.

"Oy, look at me." Jaz waved her hand in front of Lucy's eyes. "It won't hurt you."

"Are you sure?"

"Absolutely, but finish your dinner in case it fancies that."

Lucy looked away from the snake and a man standing in the car park stared at her through the window, elephantiasis twisting and deforming his face. He turned away and sat himself on the floor, begging from people entering the cafe.

When they'd finished eating, Lucy ordered a cup of tea and took it outside, handing it to the man with a ten Pula note. He took both and smiled.

"You're an exceptional person," said Jaz, smiling tenderly at Lucy.

Lucy blushed. "My turn to drive," she said.

Jaz handed over the keys. "The camp site is in the grounds of the Marang Hotel, and as visitors we're allowed to use the hotel's facilities. If you stop just before Francistown, I'll take over the driving."

"Okey dokey." Lucy started the engine and joined the main road. "I was wondering, do you have libraries in the Lake District?"

"There's one in Keswick. Why?"

"I was wondering where I could work if I lived closer to you."

Jaz choked on her sweet.

"Are you okay?" asked Lucy.

"Yeah fine." Jaz was exhilarated that Lucy might move to be near her.

They didn't talk much for the rest of the journey, losing themselves in their daydreams. Lucy listened to the classical repertoire on her mp3. Jaz put her head back and fell asleep, opening her eyes occasionally to see where they were and ask Lucy if she was okay, before falling into a deep sleep.

Jaz woke with a start when Lucy slammed the pickup door extra hard. "Where are we?"

"The hotel campsite. I just followed the signs for the Marang Hotel," said Lucy. "I've booked us in for one night, is that right?"

"Yeah great."

Lucy drove around the campsite and pulled up underneath a shady tree.

"What's the time, Looby Lu?"

"Time you got a watch!" Lucy threw her empty water bottle at Jaz. "I hate that name, they used to tease me with it at school."

"Sorry babe. Lucy, have you got the time?"

"Oh, now you're being too charming," said Lucy. "It's five o'clock."

"Blimey, I'll never get it right, first I'm rude then I'm too nice," moaned Jaz.

Lucy kissed her. "My princess charming."

"Ugh, now I'll throw up." Jaz pulled a face as she unlocked Big Red's rear shutter. She found and removed the tent, spread out the blue outer shell, and gave Lucy a folded plastic pole. "Okay, so you unfold your pole, and you slide it through that slit there." Jaz unfolded her pole and pushed it through the slot nearest to her.

"Right." Lucy copied Jaz, finding the opening and feeding the pole through, immediately it became stuck and folded back on itself. The canopy billowed upwards as Lucy fought with her task. She fell on the ground in fits of laughter.

"Tell you what you hold this side and I'll feed your pole." Jaz tried to stay calm as she slid Lucy's pole into place. Then she worked her way around the tent, knocking in tent pegs. "Lucy Cobble, I expect to see a better performance in tent erection tomorrow." Jaz laughed while Lucy giggled.

Jaz buttoned the inner tent into the outer tent. Lucy brought over the two mattresses, which Jaz laid side by side. Turning the switch on each she watched them inflate.

Jaz lay on her bed. "Care to join me?"

"Why not?" Lucy threw the sleeping bags on top of Jaz and crawled inside with the pillows. "This is reasonably comfortable." She rolled onto her side and kissed Jaz. "Sorry I'm so useless."

"You'll get the hang of it." Jaz enjoyed their affectionate embrace.

Emerging from the tent a while later, Jaz handed Lucy two folding chairs from the back of the pickup. Then brought over the cooker and cool box.

"Eggs, bacon, and bread, is that okay?"

"Sounds perfect." Lucy handed Jaz the bottle of beer she'd opened for her, and poured herself a glass of wine, then she slumped into her seat. "Cheers."

After devouring her sandwich, covered with tomato sauce and smeared with egg yolk, Jaz took the bowl of dishes and pans to the dish-washing sinks.

Lucy tidied and sorted things inside the tent. Then, sitting on the back seat of Big Red, she put her camera into its box, hiding it under some coats.

While Lucy was busying herself, a small black car, with a toy skeleton wobbling on the dashboard, drove slowly passed the camping pitch. Lucy sat still, hiding behind the driver's seat, looking to see who was driving the car. "Bloody hell, it's Ian," she whispered to herself. "What's he doing here?"

She let him drive by, ensuring he was out of sight before she exited the pickup and ran into the awning. Lucy pulled the zipper shut and waited anxiously for Jaz.

Jaz whistled an indecipherable tune as she approached the tent.

"I'm in the awning, too many bugs!" said Lucy. "I'll open you a beer."

"Thank you," said Jaz, coming into the awning and sitting next to Lucy.

"Guess what?" said Lucy.

"What?"

"Ian drove passed our tent."

"Is that odd?" asked Jaz, not sure whether it was a problem.

"Well, he's not here camping, and he didn't mention he was coming up this way."

"Maybe Hilary told him where we'd gone and he's got some work on, so he came to say hello."

"In that case he'd have stopped."

"Yeah, I suppose." Jaz had a drink. "You sound wary of him?"

"I suppose he's alright, he's good to talk to, and he dances better than you."

"Bet he doesn't kiss as good as me," said Jaz with a grin.

"I've yet to find out."

"Oh." Jaz's smile fell from her face.

"And I'm not going to because I'm only ever snogging you." Lucy leaned over and kissed Jaz's beery mouth. "Besides, he's been kissing Hilary."

At bedtime Lucy changed inside the tent, while Jaz changed in the awning, piling her clothes onto a chair.

"Can I come in?" asked Jaz through the cotton doorway.

"Yeah," answered Lucy.

Jaz crawled onto her mattress with two bottles of water, passing one to Lucy. She leaned forward and zipped the outer cotton doors and mozzie net closed. Then fell backward onto her bed and slipped into her sleeping bag. "There nice and cosy."

Lucy snuggled into her sleeping bag. "Do you want some lip gel?" She brought out an arm holding a small tub of strawberry Vaseline. "Keeps the lips moist."

"Oh, okay, nothing better than moist lips." Jaz grinned as she took a finger full and rubbed it on her lips.

Lucy prodded her in the stomach. "Don't be rude."

"Me rude, never. Yum, it tastes nice." She turned off the torch and gave Lucy a passionate goodnight kiss.

Lucy rolled over and reversed, nuzzling into Jaz, who wrapped her arm around Lucy's waist, pulling herself close to Lucy's body.

Chapter 18

Lucy woke with her arm resting across Jaz's chest. Jaz rolled toward her, shivering in the damp chill of the tent, snuggling up to Lucy's body.

"I'll have a coffee please," whispered Lucy.

"What?" Jaz forced her eyes open.

"When you put the kettle on, I'll have a coffee."

"Oh okay, give me a minute." Jaz yawned and dozed off again.

"Come on, I'm thirsty." Lucy rolled on top of Jaz, kissing her awake.

"Well, that's done it, I can't make coffee now." Jaz smiled, enjoying the extra warmth of Lucy's body against hers.

"Get up lazy bones or I'll tickle you awake."

First, it was Jaz's neck Lucy tickled, then she moved to her armpits and stomach. Jaz wriggled but remained where she was. Lucy moved her hand to one of Jaz's knees and grabbed it.

"No," Jaz screamed, pushing Lucy away.

"Okay, calm down."

"I can't cope with my knees being touched." Jaz fell back onto the mattress.

"I'm sorry." Lucy laughed and stroked Jaz's face.

"Feel free to touch anything else, though," said Jaz as she slid out of her sleeping bag, waggling her backside as she went into the awning. She filled the kettle and put it on the cooker. Then she partially unzipped the outer canopy and studied the misty damp weather, disappointed, but reassured, knowing that it'd dry up later. She returned to Lucy with two mugs of coffee and raisin pastry twists. "Your breakfast, my lady."

"Thank you."

They ate and drank, sharing the peacefulness of the morning, and soaking up the tender intimacy of the tent. Jaz broke the silence when she suggested that as soon as they'd dressed, they pack everything away and set off to the camp at Nata Lodge. "It's only two hours away."

"What's at Nata?" asked Lucy.

"A surprise."

"Oh, that's nice, I enjoy surprises." Lucy drained her coffee cup. "There's a gym in the hotel, do you think I can use it before we leave?"

"I suppose so," said Jaz. "I'll have a shower while you're in there, because I stink."

"Great." Lucy dug in her bag for her workout gear. "The gym that is, not you stinking," said Lucy, sitting and waiting.

Jaz was leaning on her bed finishing her coffee. She watched Lucy rummaging and then wondered why she was sitting so still. "Oh, sorry." Jaz realised that she'd have to go out into the awning so Lucy could get changed. "I'll get my stuff together for a shower."

Lucy baffled Jaz; she'd seen Lucy ninety percent naked. They'd slept in the tent together and kissed a million times. Yet she still had to leave Lucy alone for her to get dressed and undressed.

"Thanks," said Lucy. "I won't be a minute."

Lucy wandered to the hotel reception desk and asked permission to use the gym. The receptionist was very polite and pointed her in the right direction. An hour later Lucy came back to the tent feeling fit, showered and wearing her cream shorts and light green blouse.

Jaz had taken the tent apart and packed everything into the pickup, before going for a shower. Now she was cooking bacon on the stove. She stopped turning the rashers as she watched the striking image of Lucy walking towards her. Jasmine, her brain said, calm yourself and carry on with the cooking. "Thought I'd make tea and bacon butties to keep us going." Jaz held out a sandwich.

"Great, just what I need after a workout, a greasy bacon sandwich."

"Oh sorry. I'll have yours and get you an apple."

"No way." Lucy grabbed the sandwich. "It looks delicious."

"Tomato or brown sauce?" Jaz asked the ultimate bacon butty question.

"It's got to be tomato."

"Excellent answer, because that's the only sauce we've got. I hate brown sauce, yuk."

"So that's no brown sauce and no knee grabbing," said Lucy, winking and biting into her sandwich. Suddenly she stopped chewing and drifted into a trance, statically sitting and staring into the distance.

"Lucy, what are you looking at? Lucy, Lucy!" shouted Jaz, turning her head to see a diamond head swaying from side to side in the long grass. "Bloody hell!" She moved in front of Lucy and tapped her cheek. "Lucy, look at me."

Lucy blinked. "Oh, sorry, I was watching something."

"Yeah, another snake, I'm afraid."

"Jeez, not another one!" gasped Lucy in shock.

"It's okay, a spitting cobra this time; they can only spit six feet, and he's further away than that."

"Oh, for goodness sake." Lucy hugged Jaz, keeping her eyes shut.

"Come on, swap seats, you can't see him from over here."

Staying in their hug, Lucy stood, span around, sat in Jaz's seat, and hurriedly finished eating her sandwich.

"You alright now?" said Jaz to the quivering Lucy.

"Yeah, that one was horrible. I think they're following me."

"Come on, let's make a move."

"Brilliant idea." Lucy jumped into Big Red to escape the hideous cobra.

Jaz threw everything into the rear and drove out of camp. "Let's find the road to

Maun."

"Pity we didn't see any of the shops in Francistown," said Lucy.

"Well, we're coming back this way, we can pop in then. If we'd have had the time, I'd have taken you to visit the Victoria Falls."

"That's a shame, maybe next year."

Jaz looked over at Lucy, amazed that she'd suggested they'd still be together in a year's time.

"We could come over for my fiftieth birthday."

"Sounds wonderful," said Jaz.

"I was wondering, when I was on the exercise bike, did you ever see Helen again after she'd left?"

"She visited one day for a chat. We had a drink and ended up sleeping together. She asked if she could come back to me and I told her no because I didn't trust her anymore."

"Oh, do you want to, you know, hear from her."

"Well yes and no, it's difficult, when you've loved someone it's hard to be friends." Jaz wallowed in the pain of Helen leaving her, and worried what would happen to her relationship with Lucy when she returned home to Wes.

"I'm sorry she hurt you." Lucy put a CD into the player and gazed through the window at the bleak sandy plains, listening to Cher singing that she needed someone to take away the heartache.

"That was good timing," said Jaz as they arrived at the campsite and the CD ended.

They followed the same routine as yesterday, with Lucy more confident at putting up the tent. By three o'clock they sat in their chairs relaxing with beer and wine.

"What's for tea today, chef?" asked Lucy.

"I thought we'd have sausage roll and salad before we go out, and I'll barbecue the steaks and maize when we come back."

"Where are we going?"

"Well, you'll need your camera, and wear your trousers and fleece."

"Yeah but where are we going?" Lucy got up and sat on Jaz's knee, putting her hands around Jaz's neck, pretending to squeeze.

"Okay, I surrender, we're going on a tour of the bird sanctuary."

"Ooh, that's wonderful." Lucy gave Jaz a quick kiss. "I'll get changed." She dived into the tent and Jaz laughed at her excited reaction.

Lucy came back out in fresh clothes and holding her camera. "Right ready."

"Well, wait awhile, we're not leaving for an hour. Let's eat first."

Jaz took Lucy's hand, and they wandered over to the reception hut where they climbed into the open back of a tour truck.

"This is so exciting," said Lucy, continuing to hold Jaz's hand.

The truck trundled along the road and turned into the bird sanctuary, travelling slowly to give everyone a chance to see the bird-life. Lucy snapped away at the flocks of ostriches, and Jaz pointed out a mustering of storks in the distance.

When the truck stopped, everybody climbed out and walked over the dry sea bed towards a long pink mass.

"They're flamingos," gasped Lucy, taking hundreds of pictures with her camera.

Jaz picked flamingo feathers from the floor and took in their elegance. "They're known as a flamboyance of flamingos."

"Look pelicans," said Lucy pointing over the sand. "Is there a group name for them?"

"Yeah, they're called a squadron." Jaz made some sketches, drawing a few simple lines and shapes, and making notes of colours before Lucy moved her onward.

It was nearing twilight and the two travellers sat on a rock, Jaz's arm wrapped around Lucy's waist.

"This is the most amazing treat." Lucy rested her head on Jaz's shoulder. "Thank you."

"There's something better to come," said Jaz as they wandered back to the truck.

Lucy looked suspiciously at Jaz.

"What?" asked Jaz.

"Don't get any saucy ideas," whispered Lucy in Jaz's ear.

"No, I mean on the tour there's more to see. Fancy calling me saucy, you're the saucy one."

"I'm not," said Lucy, tapping Jaz's bottom. "I'm only being friendly."

"Just friendly, is it? Well, I hope you're not this familiar with all your friends." Jaz grinned as she helped Lucy climb into the back of the truck and they set off again.

The truck drove for a short distance before stopping and turning off its headlights. Everyone sat in the darkness.

"What's happening?" whispered Lucy.

"Watch over there." Jaz pointed outward across the landscape.

Up from the ground came a light that grew brighter and larger as it rose from the surface of the pan. The pure white hemisphere growing into the largest full moon they'd ever seen.

"That's amazing," said Lucy looking at Jaz's face, which glowed in the moonlight.

The view of the moon filled their minds when they lay kissing in the tent, feeling each other's bodies through their clothes.

Lucy stopped when she realised, she was on the verge of losing control. "Jaz."

"What?"

"We must stop."

"Got to stop." Jaz devoured Lucy's neck.

"Yeah, we're going too far."

"Too far, got to stop," muttered Jaz, rolling away. "Sorry."

"No, don't be sorry, it's my fault. I'm not ready yet." Lucy mopped Jaz's sweaty brow with her towel. "I think the moon's gone to your head?"

"No, it's definitely you. I can't blame the moon." Jaz flopped onto the mattress and sighed.

Lucy blushed, disappeared out of the tent and walked to the toilet block, realising that making love to Jaz scared her. She didn't know what to do, she might do it wrong, then Jaz would hate her.

Out in the awning Jaz splashed her face with cool water, trying to calm her feelings. She lit the braai and put on the steaks. Dabbing butter onto the maize and wrapping each piece in foil, she placed them either side of the steak. "Hungry now?" Jaz asked Lucy when she returned. "How do you like your steak?"

"Medium rare, please," said Lucy, nervily filling her wineglass and opening a beer for Jaz. "This looks delicious," she said, taking the food Jaz passed her.

"Thank you," said Jaz. "Lucy?"

"Yeah."

"No, it doesn't matter."

"What?" Lucy held Jaz's hand.

"Well, I just wondered if...." Jaz was nervous, she preferred having sex than discussing it, and she became flustered. "Well, I know that we're courting, as you explained, but I didn't know if we might sleep together, you know..."

"You mean make love?"

"Yeah, that." Lucy was so grown up regarding this stuff, thought Jaz as she blew across the top of her beer bottle, making an irritating howling noise.

Lucy let go of Jaz's hand and went quiet, creating an uncomfortable silence. "Well," she said eventually. "I'd like to be sure we we're both committed to our relationship before we go any further."

"That's fair enough." Jaz considered what Lucy had said and drank more beer to calm the uneasiness she was feeling.

"It's not just physical, it's mental. I'm worried that things might change if we have sex. What if it does nothing for me, we'll fall out, it'll ruin our relationship?"

"Yeah, that could be a worry," said Jaz.

"And if we're making love, I need to know that you love me. I don't know if you do, you've never said."

"Oh," said Jaz, going red with embarrassment.

Then, if it was possible to have an even more awkward silence, they both fell into it.

"I think I'll get off to bed," said Lucy. "I'll see you in a while?"

"Yeah, I won't be long, I'll just finish my beer."

Safe in the inner tent, Lucy dressed in her pyjamas and got into her sleeping bag. She wanted to hide from the scenario and her uncomfortable conversation with Jaz. Lucy wished she could hide forever, hoping to make Jaz forget about wanting sex. A panic attack was taking over her body.

Tired from considering her feelings for Lucy, Jaz changed into her pyjamas and entered the inner tent. She saw Lucy huddled in the corner staring at the tent doorway, clasping her sleeping bag tightly around her, rocking backwards and forwards.

"What's wrong? Not another snake." Jaz looked around the tent. "Are you okay?" Jaz asked, crawling towards Lucy.

Lucy tightened her body and reversed into the canvas.

"Oh jeez, it's okay." Jaz backed away. "I'll stay here, it's alright."

"Are you angry?" Lucy whispered.

"No," said Jaz, puzzled by Lucy's plight.

"You won't hurt me?"

"Oh, good grief no, I'd never harm you." Shocked, tears welled in Jaz's eyes, unconsciously she wiped them away.

"I'm sorry." Lucy appeared to unwind and her head fell onto her knees. "I thought I might have annoyed you."

Jaz reached her hand towards Lucy. "Look its fine. I'll go back into the awning, you relax. It's okay." A worried Jaz backed out, taking the travel blanket with her, zipping the tent doors closed as she left. She didn't know what to do, she'd only been going to bed, and now she'd terrified Lucy.

Tears flooded Jaz's cheeks as she wrapped the blanket around her body and tried to get comfortable in the chair. It was impossible to find a position where she could sleep, so she opened Big Red and climbed across the rear seats, stretching out, before falling asleep.

Chapter 19

Early in the morning a clicking noise woke Jaz. Her face was jammed against the velveteen fabric of the back of the seats, and the cramped position she'd fallen asleep in had seized her bones.

"I'm sorry," said a quiet voice from the front passenger seat.

Jaz rolled over and opened her eyes. It was so dark she couldn't see a thing. She turned on the interior light, and her eyes adjusted as she looked over, making out the outline of Lucy's head. She pushed herself upwards and back, leaning on the rear door. "Hi, are you okay?"

Lucy's red eyes looked at Jaz through the windscreen mirror. "I didn't mean for you to sleep out here."

"No, I'm fine. I couldn't get comfortable in the awning."

"I err...I," stammered Lucy.

"I didn't mean to scare you earlier," said Jaz. "I'll not touch you, honest. It's just I thought you... well it doesn't matter, I was wrong."

Lucy looked at Jaz through the mirror. "No, it's me. It...it well...the alcohol and I thought I'd made you angry...it scared me...I thought...well, I thought..." Lucy cried big tears.

Jaz reached over and stroked Lucy's cheek. "It's alright, please don't cry."

"He used to hit me when he drank too much, he'd hit me and force me to sleep with him." Lucy's head fell into her hands and she sobbed.

Jaz climbed out of the pickup and she opened Lucy's door, taking her in her arms she led her back into the tent. Jaz lay in silence holding Lucy, rocking her gently, until she drifted into an uneasy sleep.

Jaz woke a few hours later. She quietly exited the tent and went to take a shower.

As Jaz eased her aches, she contemplated what Lucy had told her, then her temper exploded. "Evil bastard," she screamed, hitting out at the water falling from the shower-head. "I'll fucking kill him."

Back at the tent Jaz's anger remained, though she tried desperately to keep calm for Lucy's sake. She dropped the kettle onto the stove, clanged the mugs onto the table, and almost ripped the zipper off its runner when she opened the inner tent door. "Cuppa." She handed Lucy a mug of tea, trying to stop her hand from shaking.

"Thanks." Lucy sat up and took the tea, her eyes pink and swollen.

Jaz looked at Lucy's furrowed brow and wobbling bottom lip and put her arm around her.

"Do you hate me," spluttered Lucy.

"Oh, for goodness sake, no." Jaz stroked Lucy's head. "But I'll kill that fucking bastard?"

"No, you can't, he'll hurt you. Please don't go near him," pleaded Lucy.

"But he's abused you. He's fucking... fucking evil...for fuck's sake." Jaz hit the side of the tent. "We'll report him to the police, get him charged."

"No, we've got to leave it. I don't want to churn everything up. They might find out about the baby and they'll blame me. It's too frightening." Lucy cried even more.

Jaz held Lucy tighter. "Please don't go back to him. What if he attacks you again?"

"He's done nothing horrible since he stopped drinking. I'll be alright, honest."

"I suppose you know him best." Jaz let go of Lucy and drank her tea. "Why don't you have a shower, wash those tears away." Jaz suggested, her emotions now under more control.

"You won't leave me?" stammered Lucy.

"I'd never abandon the woman I love?" Jaz said as she tenderly kissed Lucy's cheek and watched her leave, cursing Wes as she thumped her pillow into a puffed-up ball.

Lucy sat trimming her toenails and delicately painting them with cherry red nail varnish.

"Did you want to go out today or do you prefer to stay around the camp," asked Jaz compassionately.

"It'd be nice to go somewhere. What have you got in mind?"

"Well, we're on the edge of the Makgadikagdi safari park."

"Marvellous, I'd enjoy going on safari. How long will we be out?"

"Most of the day, it's a sizeable place, and I was hoping to paint a picture if that's alright."

"Sure, that'll be nice, I enjoy watching you painting. I just need these to dry." Lucy raised her legs and wriggled her toes.

Jaz pottered around, packing what she thought might be essential into the back of Big Red.

Lucy put on her socks and boots, grabbed her camera and jumped into the passenger seat. "Ready," she said.

"I've put your long trousers and fleece on the back seat with mine in case it gets cooler."

"I'm sure they're thrilled to be together."

"Have you got your hat?" Jaz asked. "You'll need it in the bush."

"Yeah, it's here somewhere." Lucy had tried to hide the hat as she thought it was horrid. Though, it wasn't as terrible as Jaz's, with its dangling corks, she looked as if she was an outback wanderer.

"Where is it?" Jaz searched around the cab. "What's it doing stuffed under your seat?"

"Oh, that's good, you've found it." Lucy tried to sound relieved.

"You'll be glad of it when we're on the salt pan."

"It's not very urban safari is it."

"It's just a hat, it keeps the sun off, stops sunstroke, keeps the bugs away. We're not off to a fashion show. Put it on your head."

Lucy looked in the passenger mirror and put on the hat, adjusting it to a fashionable angle.

"There you go, utterly gorgeous." Jaz dipped her head under the brim of Lucy's hat. "Is it still alright to kiss you?"

"Yeah, I told you it's me with the infinite list of problems. I guess I just need time." Jaz kissed her cheek. "And I'll be right here to support you."

Lucy blushed and tried not to cry again, messing with her camera bag as Jaz drove out of the campsite.

At the main gate Jaz paid the Makgadikagdi Salt Pan entry fee and talked to the warden about the best tracks to follow in a two-wheel-drive vehicle. Studying the map together, they planned a route that avoided the soft ground, and Jaz marked it onto the map with a highlighter pen.

In the pickup Jaz explained the plan to Lucy. "The warden said the sun has parched the ground but we should still stay on the main tracks. We need to avoid any dark ground because that's where the water is lying underneath the salt covering. And most of the animals are over here." Jaz pointed to a spot on the map next to the Boteti River.

"Okay." Lucy held onto the map.

"Right which way?" Jaz asked.

"What?"

"Well, you've got the map."

"Oh, okay."

"Weren't you in the Guides?"

"No, I attended Brownies once, we watched the Good Samaritan puppet show."

"Could he read a map?"

"No, he stuck to the road." Lucy laughed a bright chuckling laugh and turned the map around to show herself the starting point. "Right, that way," she pointed to the right and Jaz drove forward along a dusty trail.

"You're good at map reading," said Jaz.

"Well, it's the same as working in the library, recording details and searching for information."

It was lunchtime and Jaz parked under a Baobab tree. The landscape was light yellow ochre with smaller dots of darker orange, and dotted with stubbly trees. "This looks an excellent stopping point," she said.

"I think it's the most amazing place I've ever been," said Lucy, awestruck. "This is a weird-looking tree." Lucy placed two chairs under the Baobab.

"Yeah, it grows with this thick trunk to allow it to hold moisture." Jaz set the cooker on the ground and filled the kettle with water. Then she removed her paint box and drawing pen from her satchel, and rested her watercolour pad next to her seat.

Big Red's tailgate rested at a ninety-degree angle and Lucy placed the food and plates onto it. She could set up a travelling cafe in the Lake District, she thought as she swatted away the flies. Lucy handed Jaz a plate of cheese, ham, bread, and salad, then sat next to her.

"Lovely." Jaz made a sandwich with everything on it.

They sat and ate, waiting for any living creature to appear. The odd bright coloured hornbill landed, hopped and then flew away. Insects buzzed around and termites wandered to and from their mound. In the distance clouds of dust rose from the ground.

"It's eerily silent," said Lucy.

"The animals are sleeping; only mad dogs and artistic women are out today." Jaz laughed and picked up her pad. She sketched an outline and painted the dominant colours.

Lucy made tea and put Jaz's mug next to her.

"Thanks," said Jaz, distracted by her painting.

"Try not to dip your brush into it." Lucy kissed the back of Jaz's head and sat in her chair. She took photos of the tree branches and leaves above her, the blue sky glowing through the greenery. Then she stood, stretched her legs, and wandered around the tree, snapping abstract pictures of the bark. A short distance away Lucy noticed something moving on the ground. It was a tortoise, ambling cautiously across the hot floor, heading for shade. Lucy took a photograph of its decorative shell. Wandering on, Lucy found hoof prints embedded in the floor, going in many directions. She photographed the divots and thought if she had plaster of Paris, she could have made casts.

Lucy turned and made her way back to the Baobab. When she arrived, the site was empty. Jaz had abandoned her in the bleak, empty desert. She fell to the ground and sobbed.

Jaz made a few marks on her painting and leaned it on the tree trunk, sitting back to study it. "There, finished." Lucy didn't respond and Jaz looked over at Lucy's empty chair and then at the empty pickup. "Lucy, Lucy," Jaz shouted as loud as she could. "Lucy." Silence.

Jaz stood and looked around, seeing no-one. She threw everything into the back of the pickup and drove into open ground. Then she reached up to the storage compartment above the front seats, finding Lucy's hat and the binoculars. Standing outside the pickup, Jaz peered through the lenses, scanning the salt pan.

The only thing she saw that might be human was a compact bundle of green and beige hunched under a Baobab tree about two hundred metres away.

Jaz drove toward the supposed person. When she arrived, she found Lucy helplessly crying on the dusty ground. "What the hell are you doing here. You haven't even got your bloody hat on!" screeched Jaz.

Lucy looked at Jaz. "Where were you?" she cried.

"Nowhere, I've been sitting under our tree over there." Jaz pointed into the near distance.

"Oh no, I'm so stupid, I'm under the wrong tree," said Lucy, rubbing her confused and dizzy head.

"Yeah," said Jaz, exasperated. "Lucky you weren't too far away. Have a drink."

Lucy took the bottle that Jaz offered her and drank wildly.

Jaz splashed water on Lucy's face and put her hat on her head. "Come on, get in the pickup, I'll turn up the air conditioning."

Lucy took hold of Jaz's proffered hand and raised herself. She felt sick as she climbed into Big Red.

Jaz thought Lucy shouldn't carry on with their trip. "We'll go back to the tent?"

"No, I want to keep going." Lucy worried that Jaz might never talk to her again if she returned to the tent.

"Okay, well don't traipse off again, the lions are watching you."

"You didn't tell me that earlier."

"Well, I didn't think you'd wander off on your own."

Lucy went quiet for a while as she realised how dangerous the situation could have become. "Did you finish your painting," she asked Jaz, trying to change the conversation.

"Yeah, it's in the back somewhere. I don't know what state it's in, I had to rush off and find my dodo!"

Lucy was silent and stared at the map. Then she looked through the window and studied the surroundings, pointing out the route as they approached turnings in the track.

It was quite a distance to the Boteti River, but when they arrived the view was spectacular. Herds of zebra, springbok, and gemsbok gathered around the riverside pools, drinking and eating the barren grasses.

Jaz pulled into a shaded viewing spot and they sat in Big Red watching the sight in front of them. Lucy took hundreds of photos and Jaz drew, trying to capture the atmosphere.

"Thank you for bringing me here." Lucy reached over and kissed Jaz's cheek.

"It's alright."

Lucy stroked her hand over Jaz's thigh, moving it along the inside of her leg and leaving it resting on her groin.

Jaz took a breath and swallowed hard, her sexual core throbbing.

As the sun lowered, they left the river and travelled out of the safari park. Jaz suddenly stopped the pickup in its tracks. There in front staring at them was an enormous elephant.

"Wow," said Lucy. "He's magnificent."

Jaz turned off the engine. "We'll wait here until he moves."

"He's enjoying whatever he's eating off that tree," Lucy whispered.

"It's a Mopane tree, they eat the sweet leaves." Jaz got two bottles of water off the back seat and handed one to Lucy. "Might as well have a drink."

"And chocolate." Lucy got a bar from her bag.

"Are you hoarding chocolate?"

"For emergencies."

"Well, we've had a few of them so far," lamented Jaz.

They sat and studied the elephant. Lucy tried to decide what mood he was in while Jaz sketched his outline and then added finer details. Lucy looked at her watch, hoping he would move before it got dark.

The elephant snorted at them, turned and wandered off the track, disappearing into the bush.

"Give him a few minutes in case he comes back," said Jaz. "Don't want to upset him."

It was dark by the time they got back to the tent. They sat with a cola each, contemplating the day and watching guinea fowl scurry around their camping pitch.

"Shall we eat in the restaurant, celebrate a lovely day," said Lucy.

"That'll be nice, but can we afford it?"

"I'll treat you for saving me from the salt pan."

"Oh, don't, that could have been a disaster, lucky I had my binoculars."

"Okay, I got confused, stop reminding me. Please, can we eat?" said Lucy, pulling Jaz out of her seat.

They sat and ate burgers, chatting about the day, and filling in Lucy's safari book. Then they wandered back to the tent, Lucy holding Jaz's hand.

"Hot chocolate?" said Jaz as they went into the awning.

"Lovely."

They sat next to each other staring at Jaz's picture, which was scratched and dusted with sand.

"I'm sorry I ruined your painting," said Lucy.

"It's okay, I might rub more sand into it and add a few more scratches." Jaz leaned over and kissed Lucy's cheek. "My artistic inspiration."

Chapter 20

Lucy woke with her face nestled on Jaz's neck. Without waking Jaz, Lucy gently left the tent and entered the coolness of the awning. She made tea and found two stale Danish pastries in the cool box.

"Chai sahiba," she whispered, kissing Jaz on the cheek.

"What? Oh, tea, thank you." Jaz yawned as Lucy passed her a mug. She'd slept well, having fallen asleep happy that Lucy was holding her and their sexual tension had lifted for a while.

"You okay?" asked Lucy. "I'm sorry about me being an emotional wreck, and that I wandered off yesterday, and I ruined your painting. And thank you for not abandoning me."

"Blimey, you're sorry for lots of things. But my painting is inspirational, and sadly for you, I'd never leave you! Can I have a pastry?"

"There you go, that's the last one, we need to go shopping."

Jaz bit into it and crumbs flew from her mouth as she spoke. "Lucy, you know how you've had a few struggles, I wondered if you might want to work them through with a therapist."

Lucy sipped her tea. "Yeah, I suppose that could be useful."

"I have a friend at home, she's a respectable psychotherapist." Jaz put her arm across Lucy's back and pulled her towards her.

"Okay," sighed Lucy. "Will you come with me?"

"Absolutely."

"Thank you." Lucy looked into Jaz's genuine eyes and rested her head on her shoulder.

By ten o'clock they'd breakfasted, packed.

"Off we go to Maun, it's only three hours away, we'll be there for lunch," said Jaz setting off, turning right out of the camp, and driving passed the bird sanctuary entrance. "There's a flamingo feather in here somewhere."

"Yeah, I put it up here." Lucy reached her hand into the storage compartment above the dashboard. "I can't believe it's so pink." She tickled the end of Jaz's nose with the feather.

"Oy get off." Jaz let out a loud sneeze and swerved across the empty road.

"Oops sorry."

"You tickling maniac."

"What surprises have you got planned for this part of the trip?" asked Lucy.

"Well, tomorrow we're doing the proper safari."

"I thought we'd just done it?"

"No that was practice, we haven't seen lions yet."

"Oh boy!" Lucy still wasn't sure she wanted to see lions.

"What vehicular entertainment have you got sorted for us, maestro?"

"Well, we could listen to my opera album," said Lucy.

"Oh, bloody hell, that'll be new to me."

Lucy found the tunes on her mp3 and pressed play.

Jaz listened. "Oh, I know this one, it's from the football world cup."

"Yes, Nessun Dorma by Puccini, from the opera Turandot. I've got it as my ring-tone at home."

Jaz whistled along, struggling with the top notes.

"I'm sorry to have to interrupt your whistles, but we need to make a shopping list." Lucy got her notepad out of her bag. "Pastries, milk, ham, cheese, salad, bread, and water."

"Couple of steaks for tea, and something for tomorrow night," added Jaz.

Lucy wrote everything down, tore the page from the notebook and put it in her pocket.

Jaz studied the burned sides of the road. "They've had an enormous fire here. It started there and travelled across the highway and covered the salt pan." Jaz pointed the route of the fire.

"It must have been dangerous."

"Oh yeah, the wildfires out here are crazy." Jaz paused as she looked at the recovering landscape.

"You've never driven through one, have you?"

"No, that'd be madness."

"Yeah, you'd have to be flaming mad to drive through a fire." Lucy laughed at her joke and started humming the next tune.

"This is a pleasant song," said Jaz.

"It's from La Boheme, by Puccini again. Rodolfo, an artist, falls in love with Mimi, but she dies of TB."

"Oh, that's sad."

"Composers base many operas on love, pain, and trust," said Lucy. "I could take you to an opera one day?"

"Ooh, I don't know, they're posh places these operas, I'd have to dress up."

"You can wear what you want, but it's nice to dress fancy sometimes."

"Well okay, tell you what, you take me to the opera and I'll take you to a pop concert."

"Perfect, that's two dates," said Lucy.

They looked at each other and smiled.

Lucy looked at the distant buildings ahead of them. "Is that Maun?" she asked.

"Yep." Jaz suddenly swerved up a side road, her keen eyes had seen a mound covered in a swarm of movement. As they got closer Jaz slowed. "Just look at that."

Lucy looked over. On the ground was the carcass of an impala covered with grey vultures, ripping and tearing at the animal's flesh.

"That's amazing, it's morbid reality." Lucy grabbed her camera and photographed the gruesome birds.

"I love their hunched necks and stubby feet," said Jaz, watching the vultures spread their wings and fight each other for every piece of meat. "Oh, now I'm hungry." Jaz's tummy rumbled. "Time for our lunch, let's leave them to theirs." She reversed, trying not to disturb the vultures, turning Big Red around and heading back to the main road.

Lucy flicked through the photos. "Remarkable," she kept saying.

A mile along the road, they came across the Cool Blue Cafe. "This'll do for lunch."

Inside the corrugated tin shack, they ate a tasty meal of salads, roasted squash and pulled beef with pickles and bread.

The next stop was the supermarket where they purchased everything on Lucy's list, with Jaz adding beer, wine, and chocolate.

Driving into the campsite, they followed their much-improved tent erecting routine. And with everything organised in double quick time Jaz lay exhausted on the bed.

Outside, Lucy cooked sausages, putting them into bread rolls and covering them with ketchup. She stared into the tent, watching Jaz dozing, not wanting to disturb her.

Jaz opened her eyes, grinning at Lucy. "What are you staring at?"

"Don't know, the labels dropped off!" Lucy giggled. "There's a beer out here and hot-dogs if you're hungry." Lucy had easily worked out Jaz's weaknesses.

"I'm sorry I fell asleep and you had to cook," said Jaz, stretching and yawning.

"It's okay, I should have driven for a while, given you a break."

"No, it's fine, I'm sorted now." Jaz crawled from the tent, sat in a seat and tucked into a hot-dog.

"There was a notice in the toilet block advertising a bar not far away, next to the Thamalakane River, we could wander over later for a drink," suggested Lucy.

"Sounds as if you're asking me on a date."

"Well, I suppose I might be."

"Okay, I'd love to have a drink by the river with you."

"Good. I'll finish eating, then have a shower and get ready." Lucy drank her wine.

While Lucy was away Jaz studied her creased, sweaty clothes, and checked her bag for something tidier to wear. She changed into a less creased t-shirt and a cleaner pair of trousers. Jaz felt even more daunted when Lucy came back to the tent wearing her flower-patterned dress. Lucy flaunted her tanned legs and arms, wore a light touch of makeup and further enticed Jaz with her mesmerizing fragrance.

"You are gorgeous," Jaz said out loud.

"Thank you," said Lucy. "Are you ready?"

"Yeah, but I couldn't find much to wear." Jaz's clothing limitations embarrassed her.

"You look wonderful, very outward bound." Lucy ran her hand around Jaz's T-shirt, straightening the creases, her hands brushing Jaz's breasts. She took Jaz's arm, and they walked to the bar.

"It's been a long time since I was on a date," said Jaz. "Hope I can remember what to do."

"I'm sure you're a natural at keeping a woman entertained," said Lucy, winking.

They sat side by side overlooking the Thamalakane River. Jaz bought pink gin cocktails, with a miniature paper umbrella sticking out from each glass.

"Cheers me dear," said Jaz glancing at Lucy who was staring at the slow-moving flow of the water. "The barman said that if we're lucky, we might see a hippo, they occasionally appear."

"Hippos are cute aren't they, with their wide friendly mouths." Lucy mimicked a hippo face.

"Well yeah, but they can run at thirty miles an hour and knock over a pickup if they're in a bad mood."

"Oh, that's not so nice." Lucy's stare returned to the river, and she watched fish jumping and creating ripples.

The sun set and Jaz's arm rested across Lucy's relaxed shoulders.

"No hippos today," said Lucy.

"I promise you a hippo or two tomorrow."

"Are you sure?"

Jaz held Lucy's hand. "Definitely, but I'm afraid we have to wake up at five o'clock in the morning ready to leave at six," said Jaz.

"Bloody hell, early night tonight then."

"Yup, early night required."

They walked back to the campsite, Lucy's arm through Jaz's.

"I just wanted to say I've enjoyed being out with you tonight," muttered Jaz.

"Why thank you," said Lucy. "And you are a wonderful date." She held Jaz's arm tighter and pulled herself into Jaz's side.

Back at the tent Jaz went through the usual changing for bed rigmarole. Lucy disappeared into the inner tent and Jaz put on her pyjamas in the awning. This time there was a slight exception as Lucy came into the awning and asked Jaz if she'd unzip her dress.

"If we didn't have to wake so early, this could be extremely seductive." Jaz undid Lucy's zip, noticing the fine bones of her spine dotted with tiny beads of perspiration. The aroma of perfume invaded Jaz's nose, it was too alluring, she kissed the back of Lucy's neck. "Oh shit, I'm sorry." Jaz guided Lucy's trembling body back into the inner tent. Then splashed her face with cool water to calm herself.

When Jaz entered the tent, Lucy was sitting in her sleeping bag hugging her knees.

"You alright?" asked Jaz, worried that Lucy might become upset again.

"Yeah fine."

Jaz looked at Lucy and realised her shoulders were bare.

"Will you come here?" pleaded Lucy.

"Why what's the matter?" Jaz watched Lucy unzip her sleeping bag.

As she leaned forward Jaz saw that Lucy was naked. Lucy put her hands around Jaz's head and passionately kissed her lips, pulling her further into the tent, her hands reaching under Jaz's vest and stroking her soft skin. "Please sleep with me," Lucy murmured.

"Are you sure?" Jaz was cautious of how emotionally vulnerable Lucy was.

"Absolutely." Lucy removed Jaz's vest and delicately touched Jaz's nipples, gently licking one, feeling it harden under her tongue. She then met Jaz's lips.

As they kissed Jaz slipped off her pyjama shorts and further opened Lucy's sleeping bag, revealing more of Lucy's figure. Jaz's hands ran around the side of Lucy's breast and over her hip, sweeping across her soft dark hairs.

Lucy arched her back and pressed herself onto Jaz's fingers, which were resting firmly on her lower lips.

Jaz's lips travelled around Lucy as she tenderly kissed each part of Lucy's body. She stopped for a few seconds at Lucy's nipples, where her lips sucked and nibbled. Then Jaz excitedly moved lower, her lips sinking into Lucy's juicy tenderness, her tongue circling and teasing Lucy's clit. Jaz tried to be gentle and careful, not wanting to overwhelm Lucy, but she was so excited about loving someone, she got carried away. And as Lucy widened her legs, her delicious juices flooded onto Jaz's flicking tongue.

"Fuck," Lucy cried as she joyously pulsated on Jaz's mouth.

Jaz lingered in the wetness, her lips bathing longingly in Lucy's spa, before they moved up Lucy's body to her mouth.

Lucy pushed Jaz onto her back, straggling herself across Jaz's hips. She bent and kissed Jaz's nipple, firmly this time, more confident with her touch, then she bit Jaz's neck.

"Ouch," moaned Jaz.

"My revenge love bite!"

Jaz grinned through the stinging.

Lucy's hands forcefully placed themselves between Jaz's thighs, rubbing her with immature control.

Jaz groaned. "Your nails are long."

"Sorry." Lucy replaced her fingers with her thigh onto which Jaz rubbed her throbbing pussy.

For them both, the entire experience was more than a sexual act; it was an overwhelming demonstration of love.

Chapter 21

The alarm on Jaz's phone beeped at five o'clock in the morning. Jaz untangled herself from the mound of sleeping bags, travel blanket and clothes. She leaned over and kissed Lucy's cheek. "Morning."

"Um," mumbled Lucy, nakedly wrapped in her bedding.

"Got to wake up now."

Lucy rolled over and met Jaz's lips with hers. "Do we have to?"

"Yeah, the hippos are waiting."

"Can't they wait longer?"

"Afraid not, hippo time's very strict." She started to dress and Lucy ran her finger along Jaz's back, kissing the inward curve of her spine. Jaz shuddered and tried to detach herself from Lucy's attentions. "Come on slow coach, we can't miss the bus."

"Can we come back to this later?" asked Lucy.

Jaz grinned and nodded.

Lucy dressed and pulled on her fleece before going over to the pickup to get her camera, the binoculars and Jaz's art satchel. Then she made two cups of coffee.

Jaz drank hers as she put together survival bags for the day. "Right, you've got a torch, sun cream, mozzie spray, water, and emergency chocolate. I've put in loo roll, because it'll be a long day, and don't forget your hat." Jaz plonked it on Lucy's head.

"You're so romantic." Lucy smirked and met Jaz's lips for a long romantic kiss.

A specially adapted four-wheel drive land cruiser stood at camp reception, beside it two tourists sorted their bags as they waited to board.

Lucy approached the older, grey haired woman. "Good morning," she said. "I'm Lucy and this is Jaz."

Jaz tried to balance her bag and shake hands with the woman.

"Oh hi, my name's Jodi," said the woman in a high-pitched Canadian voice. "And that's Heidi," she said pointing at the other woman.

Heidi finished tying her straight black hair into a ponytail and shook hands with them both.

Khumo and Tshepo, the safari guides, greeted them, with Tshepo giving each of them a bottle of water. Dineo, the driver, introduced himself, and started the land cruiser's engine.

Heidi helped Jodi climb into the rear of the truck, and Lucy and Jaz sat behind them. Lucy rested her head on Jaz's shoulder, trying to stay awake but failing and drifting off to sleep.

Jodi looked around at them both.

"She's tired," Jaz explained.

Jodi winked at Jaz. "It's the hot weather, makes it difficult to sleep." Jodi whispered something to Heidi as they admired the rising sun.

The land cruiser travelled for a while before pulling into a lay-by next to the front gates of the safari park. Tshepo announced that it was time for breakfast.

"Lucy." Jaz tickled Lucy's nose. "Got to wake you again."

Lucy opened her eyes and smiled at Jaz; then looked around at the surrounding spectacular landscape. "Have I missed it?"

"No, we haven't started yet. It's breakfast time."

Lucy got out of the truck, and Jaz and Heidi helped arthritic Jodi to disembark. Sitting in the chairs provided by the guides, they were each given a milky bowl of bran flakes.

Jaz studied the roughage and laughed. "Blimey, this'll get us going,"

Tshepo handed everyone a tin mug of coffee and a rusk biscuit.

"I love these, do you remember when you were little and your mum gave you a rusk, these are the same but for adults." Jaz dipped her rusk in her coffee and munched on the outcome.

Lucy vaguely recalled her mother feeding her a rusk soaked in warm milk. She smiled openly at Jaz for giving her that memory back.

Jaz smiled back, wanting to kiss Lucy's tender lips.

Tshepo welcomed them to Moremi Safari Park, giving them an outline of where they were going, and listing the animals they might see. He said that Dineo would drive steadily and make regular stops so that everyone could see the animals and take photographs. Lunch was to be at one o'clock, with a toilet stop.

"It'll be buckets," whispered Jaz. "Posh."

Tshepo told them he and Khumo would scour the grassland for wildlife and point out what they saw, but for safety everyone must stay in the truck.

"Got that Lucy my lovely, no wandering," said Jaz.

Lucy scowled at Jaz who dipped her last piece of rusk into Lucy's coffee, then stuffed the soggy rusk into Lucy's mouth.

They stood by the truck for Khumo to take a photographic portrait, using Lucy's camera, then they piled into the back for their magical journey.

Their first siting was a tower of long-necked giraffes, eating the sap green leaves from the trees, their heads framed by the blue sky. Lucy photographed their faces as they chewed from side to side, then she widened the lens angle to get a shot of a whole giraffe.

"Look there's a calf." Jaz pointed to a tiny giraffe, wobbling on his long legs.

"He's staying by his mum." sighed Lucy.

Jaz sketched the giraffe outlines and made notes of colours. Then she drew a cartoon of two giraffes standing back to back, their necks curved around making a heart shape as they kissed. Jaz drew a big x on the picture, ripped the page out of her sketchbook, folded it and, without her seeing, popped it into Lucy's day bag.

They trundled passed zebra and wildebeest, and Tshepo pointed out herds of antelopes and gemsbok, which Lucy and Heidi photographed.

The truck pulled into an open spot next to a pool of sandy brown water. On the opposite bank a gang of buffalo were eating and wading in the shallows, oxpeckers sitting on their backs.

"Do you know the difference between a buffalo and a bison?" asked Jaz.

"No." Lucy awaited Jaz's knowledgeable answer.

"Well, you can't wash your hands in a buffalo."

It took Lucy a moment, then she raised her eyebrow and slapped Jaz's arm. "Stupid."

"Yeah but it's funny isn't it."

Tshepo announced that it was lunchtime and surveyed the site, asking Dineo to park by a nearby tree. Khumo placed seats in the shade and set up the toilet in an isolated place.

"Good," said Jaz. "I'm bursting."

Lucy looked at her.

"Well follow me, but you must pretend there's a door, and don't listen."

For lunch they tucked into cheese, chilled meats, salad, and bread. Jaz placed her empty plate on the floor and drew the picnicking group. Something moved in the water, attracting her attention. She put her sketchbook away and nudged Lucy. "Look over there." Jaz handed Lucy the binoculars.

Lucy looked to where Jaz pointed. From the pool two huge nostrils appeared, followed by two gigantic eyes. "Oh, a hippo," shrieked Lucy, giving Jaz the binoculars back and picking up her camera, the nose disappeared. "Aw, he's gone."

"Keep an eye out, he'll be back," said Jaz.

Lucy's excitement bewildered Jodi and Heidi.

"She loves hippos," explained Jaz.

"Oh cool," said Jodi.

"We'll drive to a better viewpoint." Tshepo directed Dineo along the side of the pool.

Much to Lucy's delight, hippos floated in the water and lay on the river bank, and a hippo calf lounged on his mother's back.

Jaz loved seeing Lucy happy and relaxed, and was glad she'd drawn her a few times, as it made sketching her taking photographs of the hippos much easier.

The truck rolled along, following the edge of the pools. A parade of elephants marched along on the opposite side. Dineo stopped the truck, and everyone sat watching the elephants dipping their trunks in the water, drinking and showering themselves. A mother elephant sprayed her calf with water and rubbed its head with her trunk.

A satisfied smile on her face, Lucy held Jaz's hand, and listened to Jaz give each elephant a name.

"So, we've seen buffalos and elephants," said Jaz. "And we saw the rhino at Mokolodi, so out of the big five that just leaves the lion and the leopard."

"They'll be frightening." Lucy pulled herself closer to Jaz.

"Oh, definitely," said Jaz, holding Lucy tight. "But I'll keep you safe."

They drove along, following the tracks of earlier vehicles, heading toward a more open plain. Where they saw hartebeest and gazelles, and spotting storks, egrets, ibis, hamerkops, and more ostriches.

The land cruiser stopped and Tshepo and Khumo climbed out. They wandered into the landscape, Tshepo carrying a long stick, and Khumo gripping a rifle. The group in the truck sat still, listening to the rustle of the grasses.

When the guides returned, they pointed ahead and the truck drove forward. Around a slight bend, a pride of female lions walked along the track. A pack of cubs ran in and out of the adult's legs, viciously fighting each other. One jumped on top of another, knocking him on his back. A mother lion slapped the back of his head with her ungainly paw, then picked him up by the neck with her huge teeth.

"Oh, wow." Tears gathered in Jaz's eyes.

Lucy photographed the beige bundles of fur and ferocity.

The truck followed the wandering lions until one lioness stopped and turned around, staring straight into Lucy's lens. The lioness growled, her long sharp teeth showing her annoyance. She swung her gang into the bush; where they disappeared.

"That was fantastic," squeaked Jodi.

"Wonderful," agreed Lucy as the truck headed out of the park.

"No leopards today." Jaz sighed and took a drink of water.

"Maybe next time," said Lucy kissing Jaz's cheek, then digging in her bag for her water bottle. "What's this?" Lucy pulled out a piece of paper. "Oh, you big softy, that's very sweet." She folded the picture, put it in her blouse pocket and rubbed Jaz's thigh.

Back at the campsite, everybody climbed out of the truck. They thanked the guides for the safari, and Jodi gave them a large tip. The couples said goodnight to each other and split up, wandering to their separate tent pitches.

"Jodi and Heidi are nice," said Lucy.

"Yeah, they appear to be okay." Jaz was never sure of anybody at first meeting.

"Heidi gave me her email so we can exchange photos."

"That's nice," muttered Jaz. "Right time for tea, I'll get the steaks cooking."

"I'll sort salad and bread," said Lucy.

"What a team," said Jaz, stacking the charcoal on the braai and lighting the fire-lighters, watching the flames heat the coal. When the flames had settled and the coals were grey and hot, she placed the steaks on the grill.

Lucy chopped salad and sliced the bread, laying it on the plates where Jaz placed the medium rare steaks.

"Thank you for a wonderful day," said Jaz, handing Lucy a glass of wine followed by a kiss.

"Thank you for my hippos," said Lucy chewing a piece of tender meat. "Do you think we'll ever see a leopard?"

"It'll be difficult, they're so quiet and cautious."

Lucy picked up her camera and looked at the photograph of the staring lion. "The lions were amazing, just look at that face, she's terrifying."

"She's got dinner in her eyes," said Jaz, lunging toward Lucy, roaring.

Lucy curled up into a ball as Jaz grabbed her legs and nuzzled her knee.

"Oh, err excuse me," said a voice.

Jaz fell backward onto the floor while Lucy unfurled her legs and made herself tidy.

"Oh, hi Heidi," said Lucy.

"Heidi, hi." Jaz tried not to laugh as she scrambled back into her seat. "Drink?"

"No thanks," said Heidi. "Jodi, and I were wondering if you would like to come on a boat trip with us tomorrow, we're going up the river."

"We'd love too, what time?" asked Lucy.

"Four o'clock," said Heidi.

"Thank you for the invitation," said Jaz.

"I'll let you get on with your lion hunt." Heidi smirked as she wandered away.

Jaz's face reddened.

Lucy collapsed in laughter, spilling wine over her blouse. "Bloody hell, I've drenched myself. Oh, and my picture has got wet." She pulled the soggy giraffe drawing out of her pocket.

"Give it here, the pen's waterproof so it should be okay." Jaz took the drawing and spread it on the awning floor, putting a rock on top to hold it flat while it dried. "Best take that off," she pointed at Lucy's blouse.

Lucy went into the inner tent, followed by her lioness, who zipped the cotton door closed.

"Where are you going?" asked Lucy.

"Thought you might need a hand."

"What if Heidi comes back?"

"Well, she can join in this time!"

"Tart."

"Raargh," said Jaz, smothering the topless Lucy.

Chapter 22

When she woke Jaz heard raindrops hitting the canvas and found herself alone. "Hello," she said.

"Morning," said Lucy from the awning, clinking a spoon on the side of a teacup as she stirred in the milk. "It's fresh outside, been raining," she said re-entering the tent and passing Jaz her tea and a custard cream.

Jaz sat up. "That's good, the river needed filling for our boat trip. Hope it gets clearer though," said Jaz, eating and drinking at the same time.

Lucy watched Jaz's disgusting eating habits.

"What?" Jaz sprayed Lucy with crumbs.

"Wait till I meet your parents; I'll be discussing your table manners with them."

"We always eat this way. When I was younger, we'd sit in the cave fighting over food."

"I can believe that."

"What's the time?" asked Jaz.

"Half-past nine."

"Oh, heck." Jaz finished her drink.

"What's wrong?"

"Well, it's the last surprise I've arranged for our trip."

"Oh, not another one." Lucy enjoyed surprises, but today she could have just stayed in bed.

"Come on, we've got an hour to get ready." Jaz dressed, kissed Lucy and went off to the toilet block.

Lucy drained her mug and dressed. In the awning she removed the stone from Jaz's giraffe drawing, folded the page and placed it in her camera bag.

Jaz rushed back into the tent. "Come on, speed yourself up, you won't want to miss it."

"I might not want to go."

"But you don't know where you're going." Jaz pulled a sad face. "Come on shipshape, Bristol fashion, chop-chop."

"Yes madam, coming madam."

"And I'll see you later to sort out your subordination." Jaz grinned as the clouds cleared and the sun shone.

"I'm sorry, just tired."

"That's okay. Is your camera charged?"

"Yep, it should be okay," said Lucy. "Should I wear boots or sandals?"

"I'm going for boots."

"Okay." Lucy pulled on her boots and climbed into Big Red.

As they drove along the lane, they spotted Jodi and Heidi walking back from a local cafe. Jodi waved and Heidi glared.

Lucy returned the wave. "Can we stop and say hello?"

"I suppose so," said Jaz reluctantly slowing and stopping by Jodi's side.

"Where are you off to today?" asked Jodi.

"Oh, I never know, this one likes to surprise me." Lucy waved her head to a grinning Jaz.

"Lucky you, well enjoy, we'll see you later and you can update us," said Jodi.

"Yeah, we'll see you just before four," said Lucy.

They set off again.

"Do you think Heidi ever smiles?" asked Jaz.

"She's very serious," agreed Lucy.

"She thinks you'll steal Jodi."

"What do you mean?" said a puzzled Lucy.

"Well, Heidi and Jodi are together and Heidi thinks you fancy Jodi," Jaz explained.

"What they're together? How do you know that?"

"I've got a gaydar, it locks into the gay vibe!"

Lucy sneered at Jaz. "But Jodi's old."

"Well, you're old, but I hang around with you." Jaz chortled and received a sharp slap on her leg. "Ouch, you've left a red mark."

"You deserved it." Lucy raised her eyebrows.

Jaz parked up and kissed her. "Apologies."

"Accepted, now carry on driving."

"We're here, out you get."

"What do you mean, we've only travelled over the bridge and around the corner?"

"I know, I told you we're chilling today. I might even buy you lunch."

"Ooh, temptress. Where are we?"

"The airport," said Jaz, excited by their next exploit.

"You're not jumping out of a plane again?"

"Bloody hell no chance of that, I've given up that hobby. No, today me and you are going up in a plane, for an aerial tour of the Okavango."

Lucy got out of the pickup and looked at the wooden huts, radar tower and dinky aeroplanes. It reminded her of a scene from an old war movie.

"We're going in that blue one with Bill the pilot," Jaz told Lucy, pointing to a man who was eagerly waving at them.

Lucy stared at the plane, then at Jaz. "No, I can't."

"Can't what?"

"Fly in that plane."

"Why? What's wrong with it? It's got wings, an engine, and a decent pilot."

Lucy stared at the floor. "I don't enjoy flying."

"What do you mean? You came to Botswana on a plane."

"Yeah, but that was a big plane, and I'd had a drink or two."

"Oh boy," said Jaz. "Not to worry, I'll cancel the trip."

"No, don't do that, you go. I'll wait here for you."

"But I want to share it with you; it'll be no fun on my own." Jaz walked over toward the plane.

Lucy's stomach quivered, and a sense of sickness came over her. She opened her water bottle and took a drink. "Hang on, wait." She ran over to Jaz. "Let me look at the plane and see if my stomach stops churning."

"Okay, great." Jaz took Lucy's hand.

Lucy talked to Bill, finding out he'd been flying for twenty years, and had taken lots of tourists on flights. Then she wandered around the plane, not knowing what she was looking at. It appeared sturdy enough. "Okay," Lucy announced. "You'll stay right near me, won't you?"

Jaz nodded and held the metal door open for Lucy.

Lucy climbed inside the *small* blue plane and sat in the *small* seat next to the *small* window, gripping the camera that rested on her knee. Jaz sat next to her, fastening the seatbelt around Lucy and checking she was okay, then she strapped on her own seatbelt.

Bill did his health and safety talk and double checked the seatbelts, then he started the engine.

Lucy went pale, watching the propellers turning, and looking in panic at the locked door; trying not to freak out, she stared at Jaz.

"You're the bravest person I know." Jaz looked into Lucy's eyes, smiling calmly. "Do you want to hear a joke about a piece of paper? No, better not it's *tearable*! Do you get it, *tearable*? Never mind, we're in the air."

Lucy's eyes flicked away from the green hypnotism of Jaz. She looked through the window. Below them were miniature people, houses, and cars. Then they were over the rivers, lakes, trees, and open space of the Okavango delta. It was an incredible configuration of yellows, browns, and greens, with pools reflecting the blue of the sky. Lucy was entranced.

Bill was an excellent pilot, turning and swooping lower when he saw an interesting feature or group of animals.

"Look over there, elephants," said Jaz.

"Oh, and teeny-weeny hippos." Lucy pointed and took more photographs.

An hour later the *small* blue plane was back on the ground and a wobbly Lucy clambered out and hugged Bill the pilot. "Thank you very much that was wonderful."

"You're welcome, I'm glad you enjoyed it," said Bill charmingly, holding on to Lucy's hand. "My card in case you fancy another flight."

"Well thank you," said Lucy, fluttering her eyelashes.

Jaz shook Bill's hand and led Lucy toward a wooden shack. "Cheeky bugger, he didn't give me a card, give it here."

"Ooh you're jealous! I'll hang on to this, keep my options open." Lucy waved the card in front of Jaz's concerned face. "Oh okay, calm yourself." Lucy ripped the card in half and dropped it in the bin. "There my affair with Bill has ended."

"Lunch?" said an embarrassed Jaz opening the door to the airport's Dusty Donkey Cafe.

Jaz ate a chicken and mayonnaise wrap with a glass of beer; she felt she deserved it for getting Lucy on the plane. "Cheers, to a marvellous flight."

Lucy raised her wine glass, celebrating another fear she'd overcome. "Cheers and please don't scare me again."

"Nope, I've learned my lesson. I'll cancel the tour of the snake pit."

Lucy grimaced, not sure if Jaz was being serious.

Jaz rubbed Lucy's leg. "Sorry, I've finished my surprises now."

"Yeah right." Lucy didn't believe her.

Wandering back to the pickup, they found an outdoor supplies shop for ramblers and campers.

Jaz studied a strange gadget in the window. "That looks useful. No point in having it now though."

Lucy sensed a heaviness looming over Jaz's shoulders. "We can get one when we're back in the UK, you're bound to take me camping somewhere." Lucy opened the door and wandered into the shop until she lost sight of Jaz.

They reunited in the bag department where Jaz was trying to decide if she needed a new rucksack.

"Come on," said Lucy. "We've got a boat to catch."

"Oh yeah, HMS Heidi."

Dressed in trousers and a fleece, Lucy checked the charge on her camera battery. "It's got enough power for a few more photos. Do you want a drink?"

"I guess we've got time for one," said Jaz.

Lucy got a bottle of lager from the cool box and opened it, then she poured herself a wine. Jaz was fiddling with the focus on her binoculars, so Lucy placed the lager by the side of her chair.

"Ta very much." Jaz put her binoculars on her knee, picked up the bottle, and stared at the silver watch fastened around the glass. "Is this for me?" she said removing the watch and studying the face.

Lucy nodded. "It's waterproof to fifty metres."

Jaz set the time and the date and fixed the watch onto her wrist, then kissed Lucy. "Thank you." Jaz proudly looked at her watch. "Quarter to four."

"Time for a boat ride," said Lucy.

Holding hands, they headed to the jetty.

"Hi you two, come aboard," said Jodi, stepping onto the flat-bottomed boat, with the help of Heidi and Kabo, the driver.

Jaz was the last to board and felt the unsteady movement of the boat beneath her feet.

She surveyed the craft; there was a row of seats along each edge, a handrail around the outside, and a cotton roof fluttering above her head.

Kabo stood at the rear end of the boat, holding the steering wheel as he switched on the motor. Modise, the guide, untied the moorings and pushed the boat away from the jetty. Then he sat at the front facing everyone. Heidi and Jodi sat on the seats to his right and Jaz and Lucy to his left.

It was a lovely relaxing journey. Flights of cormorants swept above them, landing on the branches of trees, nests of bee-eaters crowded the banks and kingfishers dived in and out of the river.

"If you get a decent picture of a kingfisher, I'll give you a whole Pula," said Jaz.

"No problem." Lucy focused on a kingfisher as it dived into the river.

The boat slowed, and Modise pointed to the shore. A congregation of crocodiles basked in the shallows, lying stock still, their large dark eyes watching for prey.

Lucy took photos of their menacing faces, praying they stayed away. Then she photographed a daydreaming Jaz as she contemplated the scene. Military motorboats powered by and Lucy took another photograph.

"Watch out," said Jaz. "If they see you, they'll take away your camera."

Panicking, Lucy took her camera away from her eye, until the soldiers had passed. Then she quickly picked up the camera to photograph a white-headed eagle who dived out of the sky and landed on top of a tall wooden telegraph post.

"Oh, that's superb." Jaz watched through her binoculars.

As it set, the sun glowed orange, the golden ball sinking below the yellow horizon. Jaz's arm relaxed around Lucy's shoulders, and they gazed at the scenery as they motored back to the jetty.

From the peacefulness of the river and singing of birds, Jaz heard the roar of a motorboat. Looking over the side Jaz saw the motor boat heading straight towards the flat-bottomed tour-boat. It turned sharply at the last minute, creating waves which almost turned the tour boat over. Jaz grabbed Lucy, and they clung to the handrail. There was a massive splash and Heidi screamed.

"Jodi's in the river," yelled Jaz as the boat righted itself. "I'll get her." As she spoke the motor boat turned and powered back toward them, catching the edge of their craft, making it tip again.

"Lucy, keep holding on. I love you." Jaz slid down the deck and entered the river.

"No!" screamed Lucy in horror. "No!"

The force of hitting the water ripped Jaz's binoculars from around her neck. They glugged into the murky brown depths, tiny bubbles sealing their fate.

Jaz swam toward the thrashing Jodi. Reaching her, she told Jodi to lie still, so as not to attract the crocodiles. Jodi went into a rigid stillness while Jaz with her swift swimming strokes propelled them back to the boat.

The boat levelled out and Heidi and Kabo waited at the hull to pull Jaz and Jodi back on board.

Modise cried out as a crocodile swam towards Jaz, and he pushed the beast away with a boat hook.

Lucy grabbed a nearby paddle and whacked it into the river, hitting the crocodile's nose with the paddle's curved steel end. The crocodile stopped dramatically and stared at Lucy. With its sharp, angry teeth it grabbed the paddle, shaking it crazily sidewards. Lucy used her strength to drag the crocodile to the other side of the boat and held on for dear life.

"What have you caught?" said a soggy Jaz.

Lucy released the paddle. It shot up the river at high speed. She grabbed hold of Jaz, hugging her soaking wet body.

"Look, my watch is still working." Jaz held her arm aloft.

At the shore, Modise carried Jodi off the boat and she sat herself on a bench.

"There's no way I'm carrying you, so don't even consider it," said Lucy, glancing at Jaz.

Heidi came over and hugged Jaz, thanking her and kissing her cheek.

"Not a problem, as long as Jodi's okay," said Jaz. "The only thing the crocs got was my binoculars."

"Come on," said Lucy. "I think you need a hot shower." Lucy led Jaz to the shower block via the tent where she collected Jaz's sleeping gear, trainers, and wash-bag. "Right in you go, pass me your wet clothes and I'll wash them."

"Oh, right okay." Jaz undressed, handing over each piece of wet clothing as she peeled it from her body. Suddenly feeling chill and damp, she jumped under the showerhead.

Admiring Jaz's body, Lucy handed over soap and shampoo.

Jaz started singing an unintelligible pop tune. "Have you got a towel?" she shouted.

"Here you go." Lucy came and rubbed Jaz's back dry, kissing the warm skin between her shoulder blades, before handing Jaz the towel.

"Thanks." Jaz turned and stole a kiss on the lips, then dried her body and put on her sleeping clothes. Warm and dry, she sat on a chair, watching Lucy washing the river out of her trousers.

Lucy finished wringing out the clothes and folded each item. "Let me do your hair?" She took a brush from the wash-bag and pulled it through Jaz's hair. Each time she brushed Jaz's hair sprang back into its natural curl. "Wow, it has its own style, doesn't it?"

"Yeah, can't do much with it, and I don't want it too short."

"Oh no you can't lose your curls, they're wonderful, so very you."

At the tent, Lucy hung Jaz's clothes on the washing line. "You were wonderful, and you swim very well," said Lucy.

"Oh, it's essential when you live next to a lake."

"But you realise that your lake doesn't contain crocodiles, he was heading straight for you."

"I know but I had to do something, and an angel with a boat paddle saved me." She pulled Lucy onto her lap and kissed her passionately.

"Sorry again, only me." Heidi appeared.

"Hiya," said Lucy rapidly tearing her lips from Jaz's and standing. "Are you okay?"

Heidi started sobbing. "Yes, but that was awful, I thought I'd lost her."

Jaz grabbed a beer and pulled off the lid. "Here you go."

Heidi took a drink. "I can't swim and I'm so grateful to you."

"How's Jodi now?" asked Lucy.

"She's had a shower and gone to bed. I won't leave her too long, she's freaked out."

"Well, she's lucky she's got you," said Jaz.

"Thanks, I wanted to invite you both for breakfast at the cafe next door, to say thank you."

"That'll be nice," said Jaz.

"Good." Heidi stood. "I'll see you in the morning, is nine-thirty okay?"

"Perfect," said Lucy.

Heidi gave Jaz another hug and thanked her again.

"Don't forget your beer," Jaz reminded her.

"Thanks." Heidi smiled and walked off, bottle in hand.

"Think you've made a friend," said Lucy.

"Yeah, we're best mates now, you're not jealous, are you?" sniggered Jaz.

Lucy returned herself to Jaz's knee. "I'll have to keep my eye on you," she said kissing Jaz's tender lips. "Did you mean it?"

"Mean what?" asked Jaz.

"What you said before you leapt off the boat."

"Oh yeah, course I meant it." Jaz kissed Lucy's lips.

Chapter 23

Jaz thrashed around in her sleeping bag, before opening her pale, puffy-eyes. She stared at Lucy, then started crying.

"It's alright darling," said Lucy, holding Jaz close. "It's just a nightmare." Lucy kissed Jaz's forehead and stroked her cheek.

Jaz blinked. "I've had a dreadful night, I'm sorry."

"It's okay." Lucy kissed her lips.

"It was horrible. I dreamed you were in the water and I couldn't get to you; the croc had my leg, and you were drifting away."

"Lucky it was only a dream, because I'm still here."

Jaz touched Lucy's arm to make sure of reality and smiled.

Today was the day they were returning to Francistown, and they packed their gear into Big Red.

While Jaz was pulling up tent pegs, she vomited into the sand. "Must be the bending," she moaned, looking over at Lucy, dazed and pale.

"Sit over here," said Lucy, gesturing to a shady spot under a tree. "Did you swallow water from the river yesterday?"

"I might have swallowed a mouthful."

"Here drink this." Lucy made Jaz one of her stomach powders. "Have you got a headache?"

"Little one."

Lucy put her arm around Jaz's shoulders as she drank the medicine. "I'll finish packing the tent, you rest here." Lucy packed the tent in the rear of Big Red, then drove over to the café.

"I can cancel breakfast," said Lucy, helping Jaz stagger from the pickup.

"No, I'll be fine, we've got to say our goodbyes."

Jodi and Heidi greeted them as they entered.

"Jaz isn't feeling too good, she swallowed river water," said Lucy.

"Oh yuk, same as Jodi," said Heidi. "Here take one of these tablets, I brought them with me from Canada, they treat infections." She handed one to Jaz and gave the rest of the strip to Lucy. "Jodi's been taking them."

"Thanks." Jaz swallowed the tablet and belched.

Lucy felt guilty for ordering pancakes, and when they arrived, she looked at Jaz, who smiled and told her to enjoy them.

Heidi told them they'd been to the police station that morning and reported yesterday's incident. "You didn't see who was driving the motor boat, did you?"

"I'm afraid I was concentrating on saving Jodi," said Jaz.

Lucy shook her head, not sure of what she'd seen.

"Not to worry," said Heidi. "We're flying to Gaborone today to get Jodi checked over at the hospital, then we'll head home to Toronto."

"It's a shame to end your holiday in this way," said Lucy.

"Yes, but it's for the best," said Jodi.

"Jaz, we bought you a gift, just to say thank you." Heidi handed Jaz a box.

"Oh wow, new binoculars, thank you."

"We thought you'd need them." Heidi patted Jaz's shoulder.

"Here's our address if you're ever in Canada," said Jodi. "We live on my old family farm, lots of room for you to stay. You could come for our thirtieth anniversary next year."

"That'd be nice." Lucy glanced at Jaz's non-committal face.

"So, how long have you two been together?" asked Heidi.

"Well err, three years," said Lucy, quickly pulling a number from her head.

Jaz's head twisted, not believing how easy it was for Lucy to lie.

"Oh my gosh, still getting to know each other," said Jodi.

"How did you meet?" asked Heidi.

"Oh, you tell them, Lucy, it was so exciting," said Jaz. "I couldn't believe how fate could bring two people together."

Lucy turned to Jaz with an eyebrow raise that could have killed. "Well, I was on holiday," started Lucy.

"In the Lake District," interrupted Jaz.

"Yeah, and I headed off for a walk."

"Up Skiddaw, it's a high mountain," added Jaz.

"Yeah, I walked up Skiddaw." Lucy sneered at Jaz.

"It's a stunning mountain, the walk starts as a road built by the Victorians and further along becomes a rocky path," explained Jaz.

"Well yeah, it's the rocky path that got me, I caught my foot and fell on the floor. I was in agony and Jaz appeared asking if she could help." Lucy smiled at Jaz.

"And you couldn't say no to Jaz, could you?" Heidi winked.

"No, I couldn't say no to Jaz." Lucy gazed into Jaz's eyes.

As they finished breakfast, Jaz wrote her address in Heidi's notebook; in case they were ever in Bassenthwaite. Then after saying their goodbyes Lucy started up Big Red and drove out of town.

"What a memorable three years it's been," said Jaz.

"I had to say something, three weeks sounded odd."

"You realise that when you write or visit, you'll have to remember that you lied."

"Well, maybe I'm good at lying." The words fell easily out of Lucy's mouth.

"Yeah, guess you are." Jaz looked at Lucy then quietly stared out of the window.

"What now?" said Lucy.

"What do you mean?"

"Well, you've got a sharp edge to your voice, and what I said to Jodi and Heidi has upset you."

"What edge?"

"That hard northern ending to what you say, it gives your mood away."

"Oh, it's probably because I'm not well."

"No, you didn't have it when you sprained your ankle, but you did when you asked Hilary to sit in the front of Big Red with you."

"Blimey, are you keeping a diary or something?" Jaz snarled.

"No, I'm trying to understand your feelings," said Lucy. "Are you upset because we're heading home? To be honest, I'm terrified. I'd prefer to stay here with you and wander around Botswana forever."

"It is upsetting coming to the end of our trip, but I'm more concerned about the lies you tell. You might lie to me, the same as with Wes, Jodi and Heidi." said Jaz.

"Not informing Wes he had a baby wasn't lying. I was young and naïve and thought he'd left me. When he came back, I truly believed we'd have another baby, I just never managed to get pregnant again." Lucy pulled Big Red over to the side of the road and switched off the engine. "And telling Jodi and Heidi that me and you had been together for three years made us look more respectable."

"So, you might not tell me everything and you might exaggerate the facts." Jaz sighed. "I'd respect you more if you always told me the truth."

"Well, you'll never tell me everything that's happened in your life, sometimes people are better protected by not knowing things."

"But knowing how easy it is for you to lie makes me scared about our future, we should be truthful and honest," said Jaz.

"Okay, I promise that I will always be honest with you," said Lucy holding Jaz's hand. "Here's my truth, as soon as I get home, I will tell Wes our marriage is over and arrange a divorce. Then I'll come to visit you and work out what I want to do with the rest of my life." Lucy tried not to appear scared as she looked at Jaz. "You trust me to do that, don't you?"

Jaz peered into Lucy's eyes and shrugged. "Yeah."

Lucy sighed. "Does this disagreement mean you're going to sulk for the next four days? Because that would be a waste of your energy and our time together."

"Ugh!" Jaz jumped out of the pickup and threw up in the dry grass.

Lucy's head fell forward onto the steering wheel. "For goodness sake." She stepped out and walked round to Jaz, who was leaning on the side of Big Red crying. "Come here," said Lucy holding Jaz close.

Jaz slept as Lucy continued to drive, waking when they stopped. "Where are we?" she asked.

"Gweta, near Makadikgadi Pans and Nata. How are you feeling?"

"Bit better, the last puke might have sorted it."

Lucy turned up a road, heading toward a camping site. "I've decided we're staying here for the rest of the day and tonight."

"Oh okay." Jaz was too weak to argue.

"We'll have lunch, unpack and do something," stated Lucy.

They went into the on-site cafe and ordered two cheese sandwiches and a pot of tea.

"Wait for the food, I'm off to the reception desk," Lucy said to Jaz.

Jaz watched her leave and told her stomach to enjoy the food that was coming. It burped in response.

Lucy returned as the food arrived. "Great, that's everything sorted."

"What've you been up doing?"

"I'm doing the surprises for the next couple of days, so I don't have to put up with you moping."

"I'm not moping, I'm ill."

"Are you still off your food?" asked Lucy.

"No, I'll give it a go." Jaz tucked into her sandwich, eating it with as much enthusiasm as she could muster.

"Well done," said Lucy, seeing Jaz's empty plate. "Your pink cheeks are coming back, and look at that..."

"Look at what?"

"You smiled at last."

"Shut your face." Jaz grinned and threw her serviette at Lucy.

Lucy drove them to a mud hut. "Hey presto, we need a change from the tent, it's called a Bakalanga Hut," Lucy told Jaz as she ushered her through the straw door.

"The traditional paintings on the wall are so cool." Jaz touched the walls. "Separate beds though." Jaz lay on a narrow bed. "Still, they're comfy."

Lucy sat next to her. "Well, it won't hurt for one night." She rubbed Jaz's leg and wandered over to the bathroom. "It's en-suite, got a loo and a shower."

Jaz came up behind Lucy and put her arms around her waist. "Sorry I'm a twat."

Lucy twisted around into their hug. "Come on, we're off out, you'll need your sketchbook." Lucy let go of Jaz and got her camera and water bottle.

"Right, okay. I'd better take my stick if we're walking."

"Yeah, don't damage that ankle again, we've still got loads of driving to do, and we need to keep you fit for your duties."

By reception they met two bushmen who led them and a group of tourists through Gweta village and lands, telling traditional stories as they walked. The tour ended at a market where Gweta residents sold handmade items.

Jaz bought a small heart-shaped broach made from a cola can. "For my friend," she said in Setswana to the seller.

When they returned to the campsite, everyone sat in a circle and drank glasses of sorghum beer. Lucy found it difficult to swallow the thick brew and gagged.

Jaz felt nauseous again. "It's made from the mushed-up middle of the maize plant," she said.

Lucy laughed. "It's not Chardonnay is it?"

A bushman handed Lucy a tray of fried green delicacies.

"What are these?" asked Lucy.

Jaz belched. "They're Mopane worms, they're grubs that live on the Mopane tree. You eat one of those and I'll love you forever."

"Are you sure?"

"Definitely."

"Right." Lucy picked up a worm, smelt its garlicky odour and popped it into her mouth. She chewed repeatedly, swallowed, and stuck out her tongue. "There, gone." She raised an eyebrow in triumph.

After their wormy starter, each person received a plate of beef stew, sweet potatoes, and sorghum mash. Jaz picked at hers, trying to eat as much as possible but stopping when her stomach gurgled, pushing her plate away.

Lucy looked at Jaz's pale-face. "Are you ready to go?"

"Only if you are."

Lucy took Jaz's hand and led her back at the hut where they sat on Lucy's bed.

"I'm sorry if I upset you earlier," said Jaz.

"It's okay. It's hard dealing with our emotions, but we can only do what we've planned, and fate will sort out the rest."

"Yeah, I guess so." Jaz fished in her shirt pocket and pulled out the broach wrapped in a piece of tissue. "I bought you a present."

Lucy took it, opening the tissue and rotating the small red heart in her elegant fingers. "It's wonderful, thank you." She leaned over and kissed Jaz.

"I think I'll have a shower before bed," said Jaz. "Feeling tired now."

"Okay, I'll see you in a bit."

Jaz took her towel and pyjamas into the bathroom. The shower was a strange contraption with stone seating around the edge, a wooden shower deck, and an enormous shower head from which water poured out in a torrent. Jaz stood and let the warm water flow over her exhausted body.

A few minutes later a naked Lucy stood next to her, squeezing soap onto a flannel. "Could you clean my back?" asked Lucy.

A surprised Jaz massaged Lucy's back and neck, swishing the water over her, rinsing the soap away.

"Do you want me to do yours?"

"Yeah, thanks." Jaz turned and Lucy stroked her back with the flannel, which wandered around Jaz's front and onto her breasts. Lucy kissed Jaz's neck, turning her around and pushing her onto the stone seat. Lucy leaned into her, kissing her passionately. Kneeling, she gently parted Jaz's legs, as if she were opening a precious book. She stroked the slight curls of Jaz's pubes, her fingers tentatively exploring.

Jaz rested against the back of the seat, groaning as her energy rushed downward toward Lucy's fingertips, which were flicking through each page of Jaz's exotic novel. Making Jaz's heartbeat pound in her chest.

Lucy's tongue delicately kissed Jaz's clit, then manoeuvred itself in small circles around her soft folds. Causing Jaz's lubricating fluid to flow out of her, exciting Lucy's tongue into a luscious sexual frenzy.

The muscles of Jaz's body tensed, then relaxed as she came, a voluptuous rhythm beating around her body.

Jaz pulled Lucy up to her lips where they kissed passionately, water splashing on their heads and running down their faces.

"I don't think I can walk now!" groaned Jaz.

"Take my hand," said Lucy, leading Jaz out of the bathroom and over to her bed, where she turned down the sheet. "In you get."

Jaz climbed onto her narrow mattress.

Lucy tucked her in, giggled and sat by Jaz's side. "I'll miss you tonight," she said. "But I'd best go." Lucy kissed Jaz deeply, then walked backward to her bed, waving as she left, talking quieter and quieter as she went away.

"Stop it," said Jaz. "You're only ten feet away."

"It feels as if I'm ten miles away."

"Good night," whispered Jaz.

"Good night darling, love you," said Lucy. "Jaz?"

"Yeah."

"Will you tell me a story until I fall asleep?"

"Well yeah, I suppose." Jaz lay on her back thinking. "From my house in Bassenthwaite I can see conifer covered Dodd Wood. One day I'll walk you along the lanes through the wood and we'll come to a small rocky peak covered with tiny blueberries, that make delicious pies. From the rocky edge, we'll watch the ospreys nesting on the other side of the lake. When we've finished our walk, I'll take you into the Wood Cutter's cafe where I'll buy you a Cumberland sausage baguette." Jaz paused for a moment, listening to Lucy's shallow breathing. "We'll cross the road from Dodd Wood and visit the Mire House. Where we'll walk along the garden path to Saint Bega's church. When we pass the church, we'll have reached my lake. We can sit with the sheep, listening to the lake's waves lap over the stones. The gentle breeze will blow from the open water and ruffle our hair while I kiss you." Jaz stopped talking, Lucy breathed gently as she slept.

Chapter 24

Jaz rolled over, removing her face from the mud-lined wall, and almost falling out of the narrow bed. Her shoulders were stiff, and she groaned as she shrugged them to ease the ache. Opening her eyes, she saw the outline of Lucy in the makeshift kitchen they'd created.

Lucy tiptoed around, lighting the hissing gas and putting the kettle on the ring. She got two mugs, spooned in the coffee, and stood waiting, drifting into a daydream.

"It'll never boil if you watch it," said Jaz.

"How long have you been awake?"

"Only just opened my eyes."

Lucy threw the tea towel at Jaz on her way over to her bed, then lay on top of her. "Missed you," she said, kissing Jaz.

"Missed you too."

The kettle started whistling. It whistled for a while until Lucy prized herself from Jaz's arms and went to fill the mugs.

"Breakfast's outside," said Lucy. "Bring the bread rolls."

Jaz did as she was told and stretched in the cool morning air. She sat next to Lucy on the dusty floor and leaned on the hut wall. "Lovely day, look at them over there." Jaz pointed out a mob of meerkats who were running around a tree stump digging into the ground, another stood picking grubs off her friend's head.

"They're so cute," said Lucy.

"That diddy one is being a real nuisance," said Jaz.

Lucy stared at Jaz.

"What?" Jaz asked.

"Nothing." Lucy shook her head. "Do you need to see a doctor today?"

"I think you cured me much better than any doctor could." Jaz winked and made Lucy's face turn bright red. "I'm hungry though." Jaz spread a knife full of jam onto a bread roll. "We'll be in Francistown for lunch and you can indulge yourself in shopping." She was trying to stay positive, even though she was mourning the end of their journey.

"Ooh that sounds nice." Lucy worked out how much money she could afford to spend.

"Will you join me for dinner tonight?" asked Jaz.

"Well, I'll check my diary and let you know if I'm available."

"Cheeky."

Jaz drove and Lucy unfurled the questionnaire she'd found under the rear seats.

"Oh no," said Jaz. "Not the interrogation questions."

"Right, where were we? We've done birth sign, oh yes, your age?"

"Twenty-one," answered Jaz, her tanned face grinning.

"I wish." Lucy drifted into a daydream.

"Hello," said Jaz.

"Oh sorry, I was miles away."

"What's wrong?"

"I've realised that I'm a few years older than you."

"And that's worrying you now?" Jaz laughed. "I'm thirty-five, it's only fourteen years, nothing wrong with that."

"I suppose it'll have to be okay, after what we've done!"

"Think of the wisdom and experience you've brought to my sad insignificant life. There must be at least fifty years between Jodi and Heidi."

Lucy laughed aloud. "Don't say that in front of Heidi, she might deck you."

"Come on, old timer, next question."

A slap came Jaz's way. "You are so rude. okay, what jobs have you done?"

"Well let me see, I did farm work when I was younger, the milk run around the local villages was fun. I met Helen at college, and we moved to Leeds where she trained as a social worker and I did my art course. Then I worked in a bookshop."

"You never told me you worked in a bookshop?" said a surprised Lucy.

"Well, you've only just asked."

"That's why you know your books."

"Well, I guess so." Jaz rolled her eyes. "After Helen abandoned me, I went home to mum and dad and helped on the farm, it kept me sane. That's when I started painting, having exhibitions, and coming over here to help Uncle Bernard."

"That's such an exciting career, I've only ever worked in the library."

"Yeah, you're dull. I don't understand why I'm going out with an old librarian."

Lucy slapped Jaz again. "Do you prefer cats or dogs?"

"Both," said Jaz. "My farmhouse has got a cat; it moved in and took up residence. I wanted to get a dog, but there's no-one at home to take care of her while I'm out at work." She glanced at Lucy.

"Oh, that's a shame, well you never know."

"No, you never know."

"Well, that's my questioning finished," said Lucy.

"But you didn't even ask my favourite colour."

"Well, that's yellow ochre."

"How do you know that?" asked Jaz.

"It's the most used colour in your paint box."

"Oh well, I guess you know everything, cool," said Jaz as they arrived in Francistown. "I could eat a juicy burger."

"Sounds lovely." Lucy tried not to sound too sarcastic.

They parked at a shopping mall and wandered inside, finding a cafe where they each ate a burger with a side of fries and drank iced cola.

After eating, they walked past the shops, feeling out of place in their well-worn bush gear.

"Ooh, that's a lovely dress." Lucy stopped by a clothes shop window, where a short-sleeved ivory dress, patterned with yellow honeysuckle flowers, was on display.

Jaz stood by her. "You'd look gorgeous in that," she sighed, picturing Lucy wearing it.

"No, I was thinking of it on you."

"Me," said Jaz in shock.

"It would be stunning on your figure. Wear it for me? For our date tonight." Lucy's mouth made a pleading smile, and she fluttered her eyelashes.

Wearing a dress was a radical exercise for Jaz. "Are you trying to make me look stupid?"

"No, you'd look sensational. But I suppose you can go as you are." Lucy's eyes wandered around Jaz's body. She tutted and walked away.

Jaz stood fixed to the spot; her brain telling her that wearing a dress wouldn't wreck her life. "Okay, I'll try it on."

"You will?" Lucy dragged Jaz into the shop and after Jaz had tried it on, purchased the dress and a matching pair of sandals. Then she found a low-cut yellow robe for herself.

They continued with their shopping trip. Lucy stopped at every jewellery shop, studying the diamond rings, pointing out which ones she liked. Jaz wondered if she could afford to keep Lucy. The heart-shaped broach made from the cola can, which Lucy always wore, was cheap compared to the prices in the windows.

Lucy popped into a toy shop and bought a stuffed crocodile. "It's not for you, it's for Kgosie. You big kid."

"Best get ourselves a pitch on the campsite," said Jaz.

"I've enjoyed our shopping trip, thank you."

"It's been a pleasure." Jaz stared at the dress in the plastic bag.

At the Marang Hotel, Lucy insisted on going into reception to book their pitch. She came out beaming and directed Jaz around the site. "Over there," she said smiling.

Jaz parked up by one of the raised wooden huts. "We can't camp here; this space is for people staying in the hut."

"Yes, that's us." Lucy leapt out of Big Red and ran up the steps.

Jaz walked up after her and followed her from the balcony into the beamed, thatched room. "Oh, it's stunning," she gasped. Noticing the massive double bed, Jaz pulled Lucy onto it. "Even more stunning," she muttered.

It was a while before they both emerged from the shack and sat on the balcony drinking beer and wine. They held hands and watched the giant kingfishers sit on the trees and wail to each other.

"Jaz?" said Lucy.

"Yeah." Jaz prepared herself for another deep and meaningful conversation.

"You won't leave me once we get home, will you?"

Jaz considered the question. "No, I'll stick with you until someone else takes my fancy."

"Be serious."

"No, I will not leave you. We're seeing each other on Sunday, and I hope you're staying for few days. Then we can date by long-distance."

Lucy had a drink of wine. "I could move to the Lake District and live near you."

"Now that'd be wonderful." Jaz pondered whether Lucy might consider living with her in the farmhouse, but didn't dare to ask, in case she said no. "Well, I've got a date tonight, so I'd best have a shower."

"Do you fancy her, this date of yours?"

"Oh yeah, adore her." Jaz kissed Lucy's hand. "I mean I love her so much I'm wearing a dress!"

When Jaz returned to the hut in her shorts and t-shirt, Lucy was laying her honeysuckle dress on the bed.

"My turn to shower and get ready. I'll pick you up in half an hour." Lucy stroked Jaz's arm.

"Okay, half an hour, right?" Jaz stared at the dress. A piece of paper lay on the fabric with '*Darling Jaz, my heart is yours, Lucy X,*' written in a heart shape.

Jaz smiled, placed the note in her sketchbook, and removed her top and shorts. She pulled on the dress, finding it difficult to pull up the rear zip. "Bloody hell, these things are dis-empowering, the things you've got to do to keep a girl," she muttered under her breath. Jaz rubbed the moisturiser Lucy had left for her, onto her legs and arms, making them shine. She brushed her curly hair, strapped on her new sandals, and waited.

There was a knock on the wooden door.

"Right, here we go," sighed Jaz as she answered, and stood awkwardly in the doorway.

"Oh, you're so beautiful." Lucy kissed Jaz so deeply, Jaz thought she might die from the pleasure. Lucy took Jaz's hand and led her to the hotel restaurant.

A ground worker stood at the side of the path showing a visitor a chameleon he'd found in a tree. The chameleon blinked at Jaz, who looked uncomfortable and out of control in her unfamiliar clothes.

"Isn't she stunning?" exclaimed Lucy. "She's the same as you changing herself to suit the occasion."

When they entered the restaurant, men watched Jaz in sultry ways, and at the bar one asked Jaz if he could buy her a drink.

"Not bloody likely," said Jaz. "I'll get my own."

He shuffled off at her response.

"Bloody dresses," Jaz complained, putting Lucy's wine on the table and sitting opposite her with a pint of Guinness. "I think they're only designed to attract men; you can't even cross your legs or flirt with the waitresses."

"Well, I've got to disagree," said Lucy. "My dress might have attracted you to me at the airport."

"Um, I suppose so." Jaz couldn't argue that fact.

Lucy rested her hand on top of Jaz's. "You're wearing it for me, not them." She waved her other hand around the restaurant. "I love you in it, and out of it." She raised her eyebrows.

Jaz devoured her steak and a second pint of Guinness, while Lucy ate her fish in a buttery sauce, drinking a delicate rose wine. Chocolate cake followed with fresh cream. Lucy dabbed a touch of cream onto Jaz's nose. Jaz restrained herself from starting a cake fight in a public place.

After drinking coffee liqueurs, they wandered back to the raised wooden hut. Lucy leaned on the wooden door as she pushed it closed behind her, staring at Jaz, her eyes burning with passion. "You can undress now," she ordered as she kissed Jaz's neck, unzipping the back of her honeysuckle dress, slipping a hand beneath the fabric and around Jaz's waist.

Jaz responded at once, lowering the zip on Lucy's dress. In unison their clothing fell away and within seconds they were lying naked on the bed.

Lucy straggled Jaz's hips, overpowering her and passionately kissing her lips. Lucy's mouth moved around to Jaz's neck, which she nibbled; once again ignoring Jaz's curses. As she held and stroked Jaz's breasts, Lucy delicately sucked a nipple, massaging the tip with her tongue until it became solid. Then Lucy was below, licking and kissing around Jaz's clit, refusing to touch it just yet, driving Jaz mental.

After caressing and cajoling her way around Jaz's soft auburn hairs, Lucy's mouth and Jaz's clit fervently met. A delicate tongue stroked its way up and along Jaz's inner lips, tasting and rolling in her juices. Then the tip of Lucy's tongue slid into Jaz's entrance, teasing Jaz beyond belief. Lucy placed her thumb in Jaz's erotic zone while her mouth wandered excitedly back to Jaz's clitoral spot.

Jaz's back arched, her legs splayed, losing control she groaned and gyrated on Lucy's mouth and fingers, until her orgasm engulfed her. Gently she held Lucy's head on her pussy, not wanting to let her go.

Her mouth and chin soaked in Jaz's fluidity, Lucy slid her face up to Jaz's mouth, kissing her crazily so that Jaz could taste her own flavour. "Wow, you came easier that time," Lucy mumbled, pleased with herself. She rolled onto her back, followed by an adoring Jaz who was kissing behind Lucy's ear and massaging the wetness between her groins.

"My god it's as wet as the Okavango between your legs," said Jaz. "Lucy, can I go inside you?"

Surprised at the question, Lucy stopped kissing Jaz's neck, before nodding her head.

Skilfully Jaz's fingers aroused Lucy's opening. Then steadily, under her exquisite control, Jaz entered Lucy, delving deep into her body.

Lucy pulsated as she reached orgasm. "Fuck, oh fuck, no, no, oh fuck," she raucously cried holding onto Jaz tightly.

After maintaining her position for a short while Jaz removed her fingers and cuddled Lucy, who was sobbing on her shoulder. "Oh no, I'm sorry," exclaimed Jaz. "Did I hurt you?"

"No," whispered a sniffing Lucy. "It was wonderful."

They lay cuddled together, Jaz kissing away Lucy's tears.

Chapter 25

Ready to share another passionate experience, Lucy woke Jaz early in the morning. Her kisses were long, tender, and slow. Jaz reciprocated, working her tongue eagerly around Lucy's mouth, savouring the pleasure of their intimacy. Her hand and fingers rode their way over Lucy's body, working enchantingly. Lucy copied Jaz's actions and their orgasms happened in union, beating with a tender rhythm, creating satisfied smiles on their faces.

Jaz was completely in love with the woman lying in her arms. "Thank you for coming travelling with me," she said.

"I never thought I'd meet somebody as wonderful as you," said Lucy.

"Get out of it, you're the amazing one." Jaz beamed her sexy smile.

They showered together, breakfasted, and packed their kit away.

As Jaz scanned through Lucy's safari book, recalling the animals and birds they had seen, Lucy drove toward Palapye.

"What's this?" said Jaz.

Next to the picture of the crocodile Lucy had written: *'Jaz attacked by croc!'*

"Oh, thanks for that, every time someone looks at this book, they'll be asking what happened," said Jaz.

Lucy laughed. "Yeah, I'll be able to eat out on that story forever."

"I wonder who drove that motor boat? They didn't even stop to help."

"I don't know, probably a drunken lunatic, the police will catch up with him," said Lucy. "Jaz, you will talk to me if you get stressed by the crocodile incident? Post-traumatic stress can build up after such experiences." Lucy patted Jaz's leg.

Jaz nodded her head. "Will do, thanks."

At Palapye they bought take away coffees and food; then carried on motoring southward, with Jaz now at the wheel.

They passed the turning to the white rhino sanctuary. "We can visit there one day, see how they care for the rhinos and protect them from poachers," said Jaz. "From there we can cross the Kalahari, go over to Ghanzi and down to Lobatse."

"Oh no, here comes another grand tour, sounds wonderful, darling."

Jaz's smile turned to a look of horror as a chaotic sight filled her mirror. "Shit, fuck," Jaz shouted, swerving the pickup and stopping on the verge. "Accident, call the police," Jaz yelled as she jumped out of Big Red and ran up the road.

"What, oh okay." Lucy leaned over, turned off the ignition, removed the keys and pulled Jaz's door shut. Then she grabbed her shoulder bag, climbed out of the pickup, banged her own door shut and locked Big Red.

Lucy found her phone and walking up the road she rang the emergency services. As she saw the scene, she described it to the lady who answered her call. "A car has pulled out from the Ghanzi road and a lorry has crashed into it."

"Okay," said the lady. "Help is on the way."

Jaz helped a group of people lift a man's body from the bonnet of the car. They rested his smashed and bloodied body on the tarmac. A woman checked his neck for a pulse and shook her head.

Lucy heard a familiar voice reverberating from the ground. She looked down. A mobile phone, thrown from the man's hand as he smashed through the windscreen, lay on the floor. Lucy bent and picked it up.

"Ian, are you there? Ian is everything alright?" said a male voice.

Then a woman spoke. *"Wes, what's happening? What's he saying?"*

"He's not answering, I can hear noises. Hello, is there anyone there? I can hear breathing. Hello. No, I must have lost the signal. Look, Ian, I'll phone you later, bye."

Lucy held her breath until the phone call ended. Wes's phone number glared at her from the phone's screen, disappearing when the phone flashed back to its home screen.

A solar-powered skeleton on the dashboard of the crushed small black car waved at Lucy from behind the shattered windscreen. Lucy's eyes saw the man's remains and tears pouring from Jaz's eyes.

Lucy turned the volume on Ian's phone to silent and placed it in her handbag. Then she put her arm around Jaz's shoulders, helping her stand, and walking her toward a rock on the verge. "Sit here," said Lucy.

"That was horrible," said Jaz, trembling. "He's dead."

Lucy pulled open the shuttered rear of Big Red and filled a bowl with water. She found a flannel, dipped it into the bowl, and rubbed the splashes of blood from Jaz's face. Then scrubbed the dark red splatters from Jaz's legs, hands and arms; watery beads of redness dripped onto the ground. Lucy got a t-shirt and a pair of shorts from Jaz's bag. "Here you'd better change."

Jaz gazed at the crimson blood-covered clothes covering her body. A sudden sickness filled her throat, and she heaved to the side of the rock, choking on her phlegm. Jaz ignored the few locals who were watching, and pulled off the stained shirt and shorts, replacing them with her clean clothes. "Will you drive?" Jaz asked Lucy.

"Definitely." Lucy walked around and got into the driver's seat. She passed Jaz a can of cola. "Drink this, and there's chocolate in the glove box, sugar is good for shock." She stroked Jaz's damp thigh.

"Thanks." Jaz took the can and opened it. "I hate to say it, but the dead driver might be Ian." She took a long drink.

"Yeah, it was the same car that drove around the campsite." Lucy couldn't tell Jaz about Wes's telephone call, fearing distressing her even more.

"I'd better phone Bernard, perhaps Emma can tell Hilary." Jaz glanced at Lucy, seeking reassurance.

"Excellent idea," Lucy said, squeezing Jaz's hand tight.

Jaz got her phone from the shelf above them and dialled, repeating the entire story to Bernard through mouthfuls of chocolate and swigs of cola. "Yeah, it was horrible...Blood everywhere...Head smashed in...No, I'm okay...Yeah, Lucy's here, she's driving...Will you tell Emma and ask her to tell Hilary...Yeah, I will...Okay, we'll see you later...Yeah, we're being careful...Yeah, bye." Jaz ended the call. "I hate it when he goes gushy, he hopes you're okay."

"That's nice."

"He invited us over for tea."

"Oh, lovely, you could wear your dress!"

Jaz laughed and kissed Lucy's neck. "Not bloody likely, if I did that without warning it'd kill Bernard off, one death is enough for today." She popped a piece of chocolate into Lucy's mouth.

Jaz directed Lucy along the roads of Gaborone to the bungalow, then clambered out and opened the gate. Lucy drove through and parked Big Red by the front door.

Once inside the bungalow, they fell onto the sofa in a weary heap, holding on to each other. The hug was comforting, but Wes's phone call had traumatised Lucy; and the bastard was calling again tonight.

"Tea or coffee?" Lucy asked.

"Tea, please." Jaz followed Lucy into the kitchen. "After the horrors of today I've decided I don't want you meeting Wes on your own. I'm worried he'll hurt you. So, once we get to the UK, I'm coming to Manchester with you."

Jaz's words took Lucy by surprise, and she stared at her, upset that Jaz could make a sudden decision without discussing it with her. "Oh, you've determined that on your own, have you? You didn't consider discussing your thoughts first?"

"Well, no, I believe it's the best thing to do."

"If I'm allowed an opinion, I don't think it's your best idea. You being there will make things worse; you're too volatile. Besides, he's meeting me at the airport."

"Oh okay, well I'll come to Manchester on the coach."

"There you go again, deciding without asking me. Look, you're not the most subtle person I've met, and I know how to handle Wes." Lucy's stress was heightening each time Jaz spoke.

"I'm trying to protect you from the man who hits you when he's in the wrong mood."

"Jaz, darling, I can sort it myself, you'll complicate things. Just go home and wait for me and I'll meet you on Sunday."

"Yeah, but you're not safe," said Jaz sitting on the chair. "I'm concerned."

Lucy knelt in front of her, her hands resting on Jaz's knees. "I know, but I'll be fine, everything will be alright."

Jaz gazed at Lucy, then suddenly her eyes became more piercing. "Oh wait, I can see what's happening."

"What?" asked Lucy, puzzled by the look on Jaz's face.

"You're going back to him, this between us has been one big holiday romance.

You've fucked me, had a pleasurable time, and now you'll get on the plane and return to your normal life. I'm such a twat."

Lucy put her hand to her mouth and stared at Jaz's face. "No, you truly believe what you're saying." She walked to the sink and poured herself a glass of water. "After everything I've told you and shared with you, you think I've led you on and I'll go back to my asshole of a husband." Lucy's voice got louder and angrier. "Well, you're right, you are a twat, a fucking nasty twat."

Lucy's temper snapped, and she turned to Jaz and poured the glass of water over her head. "Why the fuck won't you listen to me." Lucy smashed the glass onto the table, slicing her hand. "How many times do I have to bloody ask you to trust me? I know I'll never ask again. I'll just go, I'll just fucking go." Lucy stormed out of the kitchen, blood dripping from her hand. She slammed the front door so hard its small window cracked.

A shocked, drenched Jaz sat in the chair, water soaking through her t-shirt and shorts.

As the house fell deadly quiet Jaz stood and made a pot of tea. She opened the front door and peered into the garden.

Lucy sat on a tree stump glaring at the house. When she saw Jaz emerge, she swung around and sat with her back to her, staring at the bright, dancing flowers.

Jaz walked over to her. "I'm sorry," she whispered, placing a cup of tea on a low wall. "Can I check your hand?"

"Just leave me alone," said a seething Lucy, her left hand gripping the bloody cut on her right palm. She turned her face out of Jaz's sight.

Jaz walked back to the veranda, poured herself a cup of tea and crumpled onto the seat.

Lucy's bloodied hand picked up the steaming cup of tea, and she drank a mouthful. It was bush tea, and it tasted delicious. But Lucy's anger took over. She stood and yelled at Jaz, "Is this supposed to calm me, a cup of fucking bush tea." The cup hurled its way toward Jaz, tea and china spreading everywhere as it crashed onto the ground, way short of its target.

Jaz ran over, trying to hug and calm Lucy.

"Go away, don't touch me." Lucy stood and walked toward the house. "I'm going for a shower."

A while later, a clean Lucy stepped out of the bungalow and sat on a veranda seat, a large plaster covering the gash on her hand.

"Are you ready to go to Bernard's?" asked Jaz.

Lucy gave Jaz a stony stare. "You are joking, aren't you?"

"What do you mean?"

"I'm not going."

"But...err...Well, I must see him, it'll be rude if I don't," said Jaz, stumped by Lucy's response.

"Good, I'd rather be on my own."

"Right, fine, I'll get changed." Jaz dressed in a pair of dusty trousers with a slight mud stain, and a crumpled shirt. "I'll see you later," Jaz smarted as she got into Big Red and drove away.

"If I'm still here," exclaimed Lucy.

With tired, reddened eyes, Jaz arrived at Bernard's flat. He answered the door with hugs and kisses, asking where Lucy was.

"Oh, she's worn out. The safari was exhausting."

"The poor love," said Bernard. "Well go in the lounge, I'll be with you in a minute."

"Surprise," shouted a group of people as Jaz entered the room. Jaz smiled feebly and shrugged as poppers popped and balloons floated through the air.

"Hi everyone." Jaz swigged most of the beer from the bottle Jeremy had just rammed into her hand. "It's good to be back. Sorry Lucy couldn't make it."

Aileen sensed trouble, giving Jaz an enormous hug before dragging her onto the balcony. "So, my dear, what's the problem?"

"Well, my life was amazing, then it went downhill," sighed Jaz.

"Your fault or hers?"

"Suppose it was mine." wailed Jaz. "I interfered and told Lucy I was going to Manchester with her to protect her from her husband."

"Why?"

"He hits her, he's violent, I need to protect her."

"Me and Naledi keep telling you to let people make their own decisions and sort things out the way they think is best," said Aileen, rubbing Jaz's shoulder.

"I was only trying to help."

"But Jaz, sweetie, sometimes you take over and sound insensitive and pushy."

Jaz started sobbing. "Then I told her she'd used me as a holiday romance."

"Oh shit," sighed Aileen.

A nervous Lucy sat on the sofa staring at Ian's mobile phone. It started to ring and Lucy allowed it to go to voicemail, then she attempted to listen to the message. But the phone was asking for a code to unlock the screen.

"Damn it," she cried, typing in 0000 and getting no response, 1234 didn't work either. Ian had told her it was his birthday on the night of the Ceilidh, Lucy entered the day and month into the phone and it unlocked. She pressed the answerphone button.

"Hi, Ian, it's Wes here. Look, I've got the photos you sent and the info about this Jasmine woman, fucking dyke. But Sue's told me what else you've planned and you're not to kill Lucy, right? It's a stupid idea; she's still my wife, you know. You've done enough. Leave Lucy alone. Okay. Phone me when you can and I'll send your money. Speak soon, bye."

Lucy sat back, shocked. A numbness filled her brain as she replayed the message and then flicked through Ian's photo gallery. She saw pictures of her and Jaz sitting close and drinking at the riverside bar, Jaz's arms around her shoulders. She dropped the phone on the floor and groaned, letting her head fall onto the cushion. Lucy couldn't tell Jaz any of this, she'd go ballistic. An icy shiver flowed through her body when she realised Ian could have killed her.

At the CD player, Lucy selected a tune, then pressed the play switch followed by the pause button. Picking up Ian's phone, she wandered into the kitchen, found half a bottle of red wine in the fridge and took it into the bedroom. She put her mp3 earplugs into her ears and sat in bed listening to Tosca, swigging wine from the bottle. Tears pouring from her eyes. She needed Jaz to come home, hold her and rid her of the nightmare.

Jaz arranged to be at Frank's house the next morning, to drop off the camping equipment. Naledi sobbed her goodbyes. Jaz told her she'd email in a few days to check up on her and the baby. There were more tears from Aileen, who made Jaz promise to sort out her problems with Lucy.

It was eerily quiet when Jaz arrived back at the bungalow; she prayed that Lucy was in bed and hadn't left her. The red light blinked on the CD player, Jaz pressed play and lay on the sofa. It was Texas, Sharlene was singing "You're all I ever wanted, loving you is the right thing to do, I'll see it through." Jaz listened and sobbed through the entire song.

In the bedroom Jaz saw Lucy asleep in the bed, her back turned to her. After changing, Jaz slipped under the covers, daring not to touch Lucy in case she exploded once more. She watched her, wishing she'd turn over so she could apologise, and this complete nightmare could end with a passionate embrace.

Chapter 26

The bed space beside Jaz was empty and the sheets cool. Jaz listened, hearing cups clanking in the kitchen and the kettle rising to a boil. Then there was a crash.

"Shit." Lucy bent to pick pieces of china off the floor. "Shit, shit, fucking shit."

"Morning." Jaz appeared in the doorway.

"I broke another cup."

"Don't worry. I'll sort it."

"No, I'll do it." Lucy picked up the cup's handle and threw it in the bin, then she sat by the table. "You came home quietly last night."

"Yeah, I hope I didn't wake you." Jaz looked at the grim lines under Lucy's eyes and the furrows across her brow. "Lucy, I didn't mean what I said yesterday, I was worried you were going to dump me. I'm sorry." Jaz sat, her hand rubbing her forehead. "I love you."

Lucy glared at her. "Jaz, you were organising my life without asking my opinion! Then you accused me of using you for sex!" Lucy placed her palms flat on the table and she stared at her fingernails. "For fuck's sake Jaz why did you do that? I slept with you because I loved you." Her hands came up to her forehead, and she rested her head into them. "Wes used to control my life, and he'd accuse me of making him rape me, because I didn't want to have sex with him. Why do the people I love want to hurt me?" Lucy put her head on the table, covering it with her arms and sobbed.

Jaz knelt next to Lucy and wrapped her arms around her. Lucy tried to wriggle away, but Jaz held her close. "I'm sorry," cried Jaz. "I didn't mean to hurt you?"

Lucy rested her head on Jaz's shoulder. "*Sorry* is a word I've heard so many times. Wes used to say he was *sorry*, but he'd still hit me and abuse me." Lucy took a tearful breath.

Nothing Jaz said could say would console Lucy.

"I want to go home; I need to get dressed," cried Lucy. "Please let me go?"

Jaz released her, and Lucy stood.

"If you're interested, I'm never going back to Wes. I so wanted to be with you." Lucy sniffed and wandered into the bedroom.

Jaz sat on the stone floor tiles and kicked the chair across the room, its wooden leg cracking as it hit the wall.

Jaz put their bags into the back of Big Red and sat in the driver's seat. Trying to work out how she could solve the immense problem she'd created; she cursed and slammed her hands onto the pickup horn, making it blare loudly.

Lucy scowled at Jaz as she came out of the bungalow.

"Sorry, it was an accident," said Jaz.

"If you say so."

They sat in painful silence and headed to Frank's house. As soon as they arrived Lucy jumped out and greeted Frank and Kgosie.

"Aunty Lucy," shouted Kgosie. "Come with me, I've drawn you another picture." He pulled her to a plastic table under a tree.

Jaz unloaded the camping gear from the back of Big Red, and with Frank's help carried it into the garage.

"Lucy looks happy," said Frank. "Kgosie loves her."

"Yeah happy, happy, happy," said Jaz choking on a sob that lodged in her throat.

"Oh dear." Frank put his arm around Jaz's shoulder. "Naledi thought you looked rough last night."

"Everything's gone wrong."

"Sorry mate, want a beer?"

"Best not, I'd better stay sober." Jaz sat on the bench and dismally watched Lucy sit on a small seat next to Kgosie and have a jovial conversation.

"Aunty Lucy, what's in your bag?" Kgosie asked.

"Well, in this bag is a dangerous animal and you must be very careful and quiet when you handle him." Lucy pulled the furry crocodile out of the bag and roared.

"The crocodiles going to eat me," shouted Kgosie as Lucy chased him around the garden, until, exhausted, she sat laughing.

Frank brought her a glass of orange juice.

"He's so lovely," said Lucy, looking up at Frank.

"Thanks, he's taken to you."

"Can I write to him, send postcards and things?" asked Lucy, watching Kgosie and the crocodile, pretend to eat plastic cakes.

"Yes, Jaz has got our address." Frank turned and wandered back to Jaz, who was depressingly sipping her juice. "She's calmer now," said Frank.

"I hope so," said Jaz downing the squash.

Frank shouted over to Kgosie. "Lucy has to go now."

"But we're playing house," said Kgosie.

"Sorry Kgosie, I've got to catch a big aeroplane and fly to England. If you look up to the sky at twelve o'clock, I'll wave to you," said Lucy, smiling.

"Oh, that will be wonderful," he said, hugging her and pecking her cheek. "Bye Aunty Lucy."

Lucy got into Big Red and watched Kgosie run over to Jaz and jump on her.

"I love Aunty Lucy," he whispered in Jaz's ear.

"She's kinda nice isn't she." Jaz smiled and gave him an enormous hug, holding on to him as she stood. "You know what? I think I'll take you home with me." She carried him to the pickup.

"Oh no you don't," said Frank laughing. "He's mine."

"Oh darn, I'll get you next time." Jaz stood Kgosie on the floor and rubbed his head. "Now you look after mummy, daddy, and your new baby." She kissed Kgosie and then hugged Frank. "Bye, give my love to Naledi."

"Take care," said Frank as Jaz got in the pickup. He looked over to Lucy. "Bye Lucy, have a pleasant journey."

"Thanks," said Lucy. "Bye."

"I love that kid," said Jaz as she drove out of the garden. "The thing with children is that they fight and the next minute they're over it and playing again."

"Hm, most of the children I know fall out and take their toys away," said Lucy.

Jaz went quiet, and the silence returned.

Bernard met Lucy at his front door. "What's going on?" he asked, sensing an air of tension.

"Me and Jaz are no longer together," said Lucy.

"But you were both so happy."

"Well, you'd better discuss it with your niece. I need to sort our packing." She entered the spare room and put her Gucci suitcase, cabin case and Jaz's bin liner on the bed.

Bernard went into the car park to help Jaz unload the pickup. "What have you done now?" he asked.

"Made a complete and utter mess." Jaz rested her head on his shoulder.

"Oh, you fool." Bernard slapped her on the back of the skull.

Jaz carried her rucksack and Lucy's canvas bag into the spare room. Lucy ignored her and continued to pack her suitcases.

"I need fresh air," said Jaz, passing Bernard in the doorway and wandering back to Big Red.

Lucy took Jaz's giraffe picture out of the camera bag and used it to mark her page in *The Price of Salt*. "You'd better have your camera back," she said, handing it to Bernard.

"No, it's yours," sighed Bernard, who came over and held her hand. "You are the most special and wonderful person Jaz has ever met, and she needs a good hiding for hurting you."

"Bernard, she's been evil to me. She tried to take over my life, then accused me of lying and of abusing her."

"She's a naïve fool," said Bernard. "Let me get you a drink."

"Thanks, can I have a wine, it takes my flight nerves away."

"Sure, I'll see you on the balcony when you're done."

Lucy wrapped the camera in a sweater and placed it in her cabin case, then she packed as many clothes as she could into her suitcase.

Repacking Jaz's rucksack, Lucy found the honeysuckle dress and recalled how gorgeous Jaz had looked the night she had worn it. She folded it, and to save it from getting crumpled in the rucksack, she packed it into in her suitcase. Then Lucy dug out a set of clean clothes for Jaz to change into.

Lucy wandered out onto the balcony, taking the glass of wine Bernard handed her. "Thank you, where's Jaz?"

"Outside putting the pickup in the garage." Bernard gestured to the car park.

Lucy sighed and drank some wine. "She needs to get changed, ready for our flight."

"Well, you'd best tell her."

"Can't you tell her?"

"No, you two need to sort out your problems," said Bernard in his very grown-up way.

"Okay, but if I kill her, it's your fault." Lucy gave a slight smile and wandered down to the garage.

Keeping a formal distance, Lucy stood outside. "I've put you a set of fresh clothes on the bed," she said.

"Thanks." Jaz walked out of the garage carrying her satchel and pressed the button to close the automatic door.

"Then we've got a plane to catch," said Lucy.

Jaz wanted to hug her and try to apologise again, but she felt helpless. "We'd better get the luggage loaded into the car then," she said.

"Yeah."

"Where's your car?" Jaz shouted up to Bernard, who was standing on the balcony.

"Over there next to the silver one," he shouted back.

"Okay chuck us the keys, I'll make room for the suitcases." The keys flew over to Jaz, who expertly caught them and went over to sort the car.

Lucy wandered back into the flat. "Best take the luggage to the car," she said. "Thank you for everything."

"It's been a pleasure," said Bernard.

Lucy walked to the car with her two suitcases and handbag, followed by Bernard who struggled under the weight of Jaz's rucksack.

Jaz saw him buckling and ran over to take the bag from him. "What you doing carrying that old timer, give it here." Jaz took the bag and swung it elegantly onto her shoulders.

"Thanks," said Bernard, huffing and puffing as Jaz placed her bag in the trunk. "Come over here." Bernard ushered Jaz to one side, away from the car. "Right, lecture time, you must apologise with as much sincerity as you've got, convince Lucy that you love her and promise to trust her."

"It's useless, she's leaving me," whined Jaz, watching Lucy put her suitcases in the boot and then lean on the car, waiting for them both.

"No, she isn't, she'll only leave if you let her and you don't want that do you?"

"No."

"You get changed and I'll send Lucy up to fetch my coat," said Bernard, waiting for Jaz to move. "Go on then."

"Right, okay."

Jaz was in the bedroom changing when Lucy appeared at the door.

"Just getting Bernard's coat," said Lucy, staring at the half-dressed Jaz.

"Oh, it's over here." At the coat rack Jaz unhooked Bernard's leather jacket.

"Thanks," said Lucy as Jaz handed it to her.

"Lucy I'm sorry for being an idiot and everything I've said and done. I love you and I want to make things right." Jaz looked at Lucy with begging eyes. "Please don't leave me."

Lucy stared at Jaz. "It's not only your behaviour that's upset me, I've also got to handle Wes and his issues. You're not helping by telling me the shit that comes into your head."

"I panicked," said Jaz pulling on her clothes and walking toward Lucy. "If you give me a chance, I'll never upset you again."

Lucy pulled her mouth into a tight straight line and her eyes perused Jaz. She looked stunning, dressed in her clean jeans, white blouse, black leather jacket and brown hiking boots. Lucy knew absolutely why she loved the crazy woman, she blinked and looked away from Jaz's apprehensive face. "Let's go," she said.

Jaz compliantly followed Lucy out of the flat and over to the car where she politely opened the rear door for Lucy.

"Thank you." Lucy got into the car. "But you've got a hell of a long way to go before you're forgiven."

"Emma just phoned," said Bernard, trying to distract them. "She hopes you have a safe journey and she'll see you in Manchester."

"That's lovely, I'll phone her when I can," said Lucy. "Bernard I've left a few clothes in the bedroom, I couldn't fit them in my bags, could you donate them to somebody."

"Oh yes, if it's alright I'll give them to my cleaner." Bernard started the car.

Jaz rooted through her satchel. "I've lost my passport and ticket."

"I've got them in my bag," sighed Lucy.

"Oh great, thanks."

They drove off with Bernard and Jaz planning what he and Emma could do when he visited the UK. Lucy sat in the rear staring aimlessly through the car window, her mind numbed by the pain that surrounded her.

When they arrived at the airport, Lucy and Jaz went through the check in process.

"I'll see you in two weeks," said Jaz, keeping her tears under control as she said goodbye to Bernard.

"Definitely, me and Emma will catch up with you both." He exaggerated the word *both*.

"Goodbye," said Lucy, hugging Bernard.

Bernard waved as they walked through security and into the departure lounge. Lucy took a small bottle of wine from her handbag, opened it and drank it in a long gulp. Jaz sat fidgeting with the buckles on her satchel, knowing exactly how the crocodile felt when Lucy walloped him with a paddle. Following a brief wait, they walked across the tarmac to the plane and climbed the steps.

"Do you want to sit next to the window?" asked Jaz.

"Is that okay, it'll be nice to see the country as we leave," said Lucy. She looked through the plane window as they took off, waving to Kgosie as they flew above the city.

Then miniature villages appeared, and they disappeared into the high faint clouds.

Jaz fiddled with the plastic tray in front of her. "Thank you for the song on the CD last night," said Jaz, tears starting to well in her eyes.

"I don't want to give up on us Jaz, but if we stay together, we have to discuss things, allow the other person to have a say and stop making horrible accusations." Lucy took Jaz's hand. "Please don't cry, we've got to change planes in a minute." She wiped the tears from Jaz's face. "Look, we're in a tricky place right now, but things can't get much worse; unless the plane crashes and we die together, arguing into eternity," sighed Lucy.

Sat on the connecting flight from Johannesburg to Qatar, Lucy leaned her head on the window and stared into the darkness.

"I wonder how many meals we'll have?" muttered Jaz, getting her sketchbook out of her satchel. "Think I'll do a sketch of the passengers."

"I'll finish reading your book, you can have it back then," said Lucy, getting *The Price of Salt* out of her handbag. Jaz's giraffe drawing fell onto the floor. They both bent to pick it up, knocking their heads together.

"Here," said Jaz. "Sorry."

"Please stop saying sorry."

"Yeah, okay," said Jaz, becoming quietly engrossed in her drawing.

Half an hour later, Lucy closed the book. "Finished, I didn't expect a happy ending, here you go," she handed the book to Jaz.

"But it's yours."

"Lend it to your next girlfriend," said Lucy.

"I don't want anybody else; I want you. I know you don't appreciate the word sorry, but it's the only one I've got. Please let me try again."

Lucy didn't have an answer, and she shook her head. Jaz loved her, she loved Jaz, but it hurt.

Chapter 27

It was midnight in Qatar, when they changed to their final flight.

Lucy settled in her seat and fell asleep. She woke at five o'clock in the morning, embarrassingly her head was resting on Jaz's shoulder.

Jaz shifted in her seat as Lucy raised her head and opened her eyes. "We're here," said Jaz. "Just about to land."

"Oh," said Lucy, fastening her seatbelt, suddenly terrified to be home and having to face Wes.

The plane steadily descended and bumped along the runway.

Jaz ungripped her hands from the armrests and took a deep breath. Gathering their bags, she followed Lucy off the plane and along the passageway, going through customs with nothing to declare. She retrieved Lucy's suitcase from the carousel and grabbed her own rucksack before it disappeared up the conveyor. They were suddenly about to go their separate ways, and the pain of splitting was showing in Jaz's face.

Before she could work out her feelings for Jaz, Lucy knew that she had to sort out her problems with Wes. She knew that she was walking into a potentially dangerous situation, but she didn't have a choice. Lucy touched Jaz's arm. "Please be brave."

"Will I still see you on Sunday?" Jaz held her tears back.

"I'm not sure."

Tears rolled down Jaz's cheeks.

Lucy dug out a tissue from her pocket and handed it to Jaz. "Okay, yes I'll see you on Sunday."

Jaz sniffed. "Where's Wes?"

"He's not here." Lucy had realised from Wes's phone call to Ian and the lack of replies to her emails, that he would not be meeting her at the airport.

"What do you mean?" asked Jaz.

"Wes didn't get back to me."

"So, what are you going to do?"

"I'll take the train."

Jaz gazed into Lucy's eyes. "I could have come with you then."

"No, you couldn't, I've told you that."

Jaz looked down to the floor and shuffled her feet. "Well, goodbye then."

"Yeah, bye." Lucy was trembling, and suddenly she didn't want Jaz to leave. Who'd know if Wes attacked her. Jaz was the only person who truly cared about her. Lucy scribbled on a piece of paper. "Here's my home address, my mobile number, and my email. If you don't hear from me each day something might have gone wrong."

"Why, what's happening?"

"Look we haven't got time to discuss it now."

"You'll phone me if you need me." Jaz stuffed the piece of paper into her jacket pocket.

"Yeah, look I'll phone you tonight, what's your number?"

"Oh yeah, here," said Jaz, writing her phone number and email on a page torn from her sketchbook.

Lucy looked at Jaz's wrist. "Where's your watch?"

"In my satchel, I'm keeping it safe."

"Well, you'd better get going otherwise you'll miss your coach," said Lucy. "I'll see you at the weekend."

"Yeah, bye. I love you. You know that, don't you?"

"Yes, I know." Lucy shook her head and sighed heavily.

"Can I kiss you goodbye?" asked Jaz.

"If you must."

Jaz gave Lucy a kiss on the cheek.

"Oh, for fuck's sake." Lucy kissed Jaz firmly and possessively on the lips. "Get your coach and don't chat anybody up on the journey."

"Right, yes, bye." Jaz waved as she hurried away.

"Bye," Lucy shouted, tears running from her eyes; she wiped them away and walked to the railway station.

Lucy dozed on the train journey, waking occasionally to find out where she was. As she slept Lucy dreamed of her and Jaz travelling around Botswana, their hot, sleepless, loving nights, and the wildness of their life together.

Just after midday Lucy stepped off the train and organised her bags; she was already missing Jaz dealing with her luggage in her methodical manner.

Lucy's flat wasn't far away, and it was quicker for her to walk than take a taxi. She dragged her case across the station car park and up a side street, passing old mills which were being converted into hotels. She saw her block of flats, and decided that when she got in, she'd have a cup of tea on the balcony, and watch the murky canal. It wasn't the same as the Thamalakane River, and would be filled with supermarket trolleys rather than hippos. But at least it was home.

Lucy typed a code into the door interface and entered the foyer. Then she took the lift to the top floor and walked toward her front door. She put her key in the lock and took a deep breath. Here we go, she said to herself, you can sort this. Lucy turned the key, but it stuck. She checked it was the correct key and tried again. No movement. She gave the door a loud knock. The sound echoed around the room.

Remembering that Sasha, her neighbour, had a spare key. Lucy rang her doorbell, but Sasha wasn't home. Frustrated, Lucy returned to the foyer and checked the post box, where she found an electric bill and a plain white envelope. "What the fuck," she muttered.

At her favourite coffee shop Lucas, the barista, brought over Lucy's usual skinny flat white. She juggled the long white envelope in her hands, before opening it and finding a letter written by Wes.

"Hi Lucy, I'm not good at letters, and I meant to email you, but I guess I'm a coward. Lucy, I've left you. I wanted to be there to hold you and say I'm sorry, but I'm a shit."

Lucy was gob-smacked, not believing Wes's words. She re-read the paragraph, and a sickening sweep of pain, bewilderment, and shock flowed through her body. Taking a deep breath, she continued to read the rest of the letter.

"I suppose you need more of an explanation. I've been seeing a girl from work and she got pregnant. The baby arrived two weeks ago, I've enclosed a photo, and I've moved in with them both. I guess you can't think this will get any worse, but I suppose it does. I needed money to get me and the family settled. So, I've sold the flat."

"Oh my god," shouted Lucy. She apologised to Lucas and the other customers. "What is wrong with you, you're a maniac?"

"I got £325K and have put half of it in your bank account. I know it's a shock, but I had to do it! Your things are in storage. The locker key and map to the storage company are in this envelope. I suppose you'll track me and we'll have a row. I'm sorry, Wes."

Lucy's head fell onto the table, and a horrendous howl came from her mouth. She started crying into a napkin. Lucas came over to check she was alright, pouring her a glass of water.

"Wes has left me," Lucy sobbed.

Lucas patted her on the back. "Oh, my goodness, I never liked him."

"But my aim was to leave him!" cried Lucy.

Lucas stood bewildered and left when a customer entered the cafe. He returned later with a fresh cup of coffee and a clean napkin.

Confused, Lucy sat and stared through the window. She took her tablet out of her handbag, switched it on and connected to the café's Wi-Fi. She emailed Wes, asking him to please contact her; she'd read his letter, and they needed to talk. Then she emailed Jaz to tell her she had arrived safely in Manchester.

Lucy paid her coffee bill and headed to the car park attached to her block of flats. Her black Mini Cooper was parked in a visitor's parking spot. She dug the car-keys out of the zipped pocket of her cabin bag, placed her suitcases in the trunk, and drove to a nearby hotel.

The only available room was a compact single. Entering the room, Lucy screwed up the letter and chucked it toward the bin, missing and watching it drop to the floor. She threw her handbag on the bed, kicked the chair, then opened the cupboard doors and slammed them shut. Finally, she crashed into an exhausted pile on the bed and fell into a nightmarish sleep.

When Jaz staggered through the front door of the bed-and-breakfast she gobbled down the dinner her mum served her, because, as usual, she was starving.

"Your packages from Botswana arrived at your house yesterday," said dad. "It's still in boxes, plenty of unpacking to do."

"We finished the decorating for you, though, and put in a few spare bits of furniture," said mum.

"Oh wow, you're fantastic, thanks." Jaz kissed each of them on the cheek, then went into her bedroom with a cup of hot chocolate.

Once there Jaz unpacked her rucksack, creating a pile of dirty clothes on the floor. Then she grabbed her sketchbook from her satchel and threw herself on the bed. Flicking through the pages, she stopped and admired each drawing of Lucy. When she reached the back of the book, she found a scribbled note from Lucy.

"Darling Jaz, I don't know when you'll read this, but I wanted to say that I've had the most wonderful time. I love you more than I've ever loved anyone, and I can't wait to see you and be with you again. Love, Lucy."

Jaz stared at the note and sipped her drink, her eyes starting to prick with tears. To distract herself, she switched on her laptop and checked her emails. It surprised her when a message came through from Lucy; she emailed back. *"Hi, missing you."*

Moments later, a brief message came back. *"I've asked to be your friend on Facebook, can you accept me and we can speak through Messenger?"*

"Okay, bit technical, but I'll have a go! Why haven't you got your phone?" Jaz logged into her Facebook account and accepted Lucy's friend request. Then Jaz's laptop rang. She studied the screen and pressed the answer button.

"Hiya." Lucy's voice filled Jaz's head.

"Blimey, this technology is amazing," said Jaz. "Hi, you okay?"

"Yeah." Lucy forced herself not to talk about her nightmare day. It had been too awful. "I'm knackered now though."

"I had a shit journey home, the Carlisle coach was running late, then I missed the bus to Keswick. Poor dad had to come and collect me." Jaz's tale made Lucy giggle. "It's nice to hear you laughing," said Jaz. "So, where's your phone?"

"Oh, it's around here somewhere, I can't find it at the moment." Lucy shuddered as she lied.

"I hate it when I lose my phone."

"Well, looking at the state of your phone, you need to lose it," laughed Lucy.

"Yeah, I'm outdated in this modern world. Have you talked to Wes?"

"No, I haven't seen him yet."

"Oh, is he at work?" asked Jaz.

"I think so."

"He's not with you?" Jaz sensed something was wrong.

"No, please could you stop asking questions, it's been a tiring day."

Jaz paused. "I looked through my sketchbook."

"Oh," whispered Lucy.

"It was a lovely message."

"I meant it," said Lucy.

Jaz's throat choked with a tear. "You sound tired, time you were asleep."

"Yeah, I suppose so," said Lucy yawning.

"I'm sorry I made such a mess of things?" said Jaz. "Are you less annoyed with me now?"

"You're asking questions again, but no, I'm not as upset." Jaz was the least of Lucy's problems.

"I'm glad," sighed Jaz. "Goodnight then."

"Goodnight."

"Ke a go rata," said Jaz. "Robala sentle."

They both pressed the call end button, their faces reflecting in the home screens.

Chapter 28

At six o'clock in the morning Lucy stood outside the rear door of the postal sorting office, waiting to catch Wes arriving for work. She watched workers coming and going, then saw Wes's friend Eric getting out of his car. "Eric," she shouted.

"Hiya Lucy, did you have a wonderful holiday?" said Eric as he approached the doorway.

"Yes thanks," answered Lucy. "I was looking for Wes, is he here?"

"I don't think so, I'll check." Eric disappeared inside, returning two minutes later. "No, he's still on paternity leave."

Lucy pushed her hand through her hair and rubbed the back of her neck. "Eric, could you phone him for me? I've phoned, texted and emailed, but he's not getting back to me? I don't know what's going on, please can you call him? Tell him I just want to talk. Please," begged Lucy.

"Okay, calm yourself, my dear," said Eric, getting his phone out of his pocket. "Wes told us you'd dumped him and he'd sold the flat because you were moving away. Is it because of Sue and the baby?"

Feeling faint, Lucy leaned on the wall. "You knew all about that?"

Eric nodded his head and dialled Wes. "Morning Wes, sorry it's so early…I'm with your Lucy and she wants to talk to you, I said I'd arrange for you two to meet…Yeah, okay, I'll tell her. Cheers, mate, bye."

"What did he say?" asked Lucy.

"He'll meet you at ten o'clock at the fish bar."

"That's brilliant, thanks Eric, you're a star."

"I hope you two can sort things out." Eric gave Lucy an enormous hug. "Best get into work."

Jaz woke early and helped her dad make breakfast for the guests. When she'd finished, she jumped in her red Fiesta and drove over to her Bassenthwaite farmhouse, relaxing in the sight of the mountains.

Turning left, she drove down the narrow lane, passing Saint Bega's chapel. A few minutes later she saw her footpath to the lake. She pulled into a lay-by and walked down to the shore.

It was a placid lake today, with a slight breeze which blew through her gloomy mind. "Right okay, I agree," she muttered to the moving air. "Be patient and wait."

Back in the car, Jaz trundled over to her renovated farmhouse. "Oh, you look amazing," she said, staring at the stone building with its new green front door which opened into the parlour. Jaz walked through the empty room into a stunning kitchen which looked as if it was posing for a country house magazine. An archway led from the kitchen into the lounge where patio doors opened onto a veranda.

Standing on the wooden decking, Jaz stared at the mountains looming over her, protecting her from the evils of life. Back inside, she sat in the only chair in the house, looking at the boxes she needed to empty.

Lucy stood at the front of the fish bar, Wes appeared and locked his bicycle to a railing. "Hiya," he mumbled.

"Hi." Lucy tried not to cry. "What's happening? I don't understand."

"Let's get food, then we can talk." Wes ordered coffee and a chip butty.

Lucy bought a cup of tea.

"Not eating?" asked Wes.

"No, as you might have noticed, I'm upset!" A hardness grew in Lucy's voice.

Sitting at a greasy table, Wes took Lucy's hand; she pulled it away. "Lucy, it's straightforward I've gone, our marriage is over," he said.

"But after twenty-seven years."

Wes started eating. "I know, we held on too long, we should have divorced years ago."

"But I thought you loved me."

"No, I don't. I think we've always just been mates."

"Wes you tried to murder me, that's not being a fucking mate!" hissed Lucy.

"What! How do you know that?" Beads of sweat formed on Wes's brow. "That was a mistake. Sue wanted your insurance money. I stopped it once I found out; I never wanted you dead."

"Oh, thanks for that, mate!" Lucy pulled Ian's phone out of her bag. "Let's hope the police understand." Lucy dialled the emergency phone number.

"No!" Wes reached out and took the phone from her, ending the call. "You can't report me to the police, you're not even dead. And don't tell me it's just me whose in the wrong because that's bollocks."

"What do you mean?" asked Lucy, grabbing the phone back and resting it on the table.

"I've seen the photos; do you want to see them? You and your lesbian tart." Wes reached in his pocket and pulled out a wad of photos, passing them to Lucy. "They helped me get my head together." He picked a piece of chip from between his teeth. "How long have you been a dyke?"

"Well, not as long as you've been fucking Sue! Who the hell is she?"

"Sue works with me at the sorting office. Look, Lucy, our marriage is over, you've got thousands of pounds out of it, check your bank, and you've got most of the furniture. You can go wherever you want, even move in with your girlfriend." Wes stood. "I'm sorry it's come to this."

As Wes walked to the doorway Lucy stared into her teacup. "Oh, I meant to tell you,

Ian's dead," she said.

Wes stopped and glanced at Lucy's face as he took in what she'd said, then he opened the door and walked out.

Through the window, Lucy watched him sit on his bicycle and take his phone out of his pocket. He dialled a number and the phone sitting in front of Lucy vibrated. She picked it up and screamed, "Fuck you, Wes."

Finishing her tea, Lucy left the fish shop and went to the cash machine to check her bank account. One hundred and sixty-two thousand pounds on top of her own savings. "Shit?" she muttered, finally realising that everything Wes had said was true.

Aimlessly, she went to the hotel car park and got into her Mini. Finding the postcode of the storage company in Wes's letter, she typed it into the car's navigation system and drove, following the stated directions.

Arriving at *Store It Here,* Lucy used the key to open a a unit crammed with furniture and boxes. At the back Lucy could see her bright pink suitcases. She worked her way over and opened them, collecting a few clean outfits and fresh underwear.

In a box she found her laptop and mobile phone. She pressed the power switch. Text message signals beeped. Most of them from her old neighbour, Sasha.

Weds. 15.30pm: "Hi Lucy, strange man looking around flat with Wes, and Wes gone off with suitcases!! Holiday?"

Thurs. 14.05pm: "Hi, me again, Wes is with a dishy man emptying flat! Get back to me!"

Sat. 12.30pm: "Lucy – what's going on – Wes is changing door lock!"

Mon. 10.30am: "OMG – Wes has taken the spare key off me – he said you'd left him! Speak to me – I'm distraught!"

Lucy put her head in her hands, and took a few deep, steady breaths. Desperate to hear a loving voice, she phoned Jaz.

"Hello," said a chirpy voice.

"Hiya," Lucy whispered, her words echoing around the storage unit. "Just found my phone, thought I'd call you."

"What's wrong?"

"What makes you think there's a problem?"

"I can hear your mind turning."

"I'm just tired."

"You've seen Wes then?"

"Yeah, I've seen Wes."

"And…?"

"And what?"

"Do you want to talk?"

"No." Lucy couldn't tell Jaz what had happened.

"Oh okay, well I'm here when you need me."

"Thank you."

"Are you sure you're alright?"

"Yeah, it was painful talking with Wes."

"I wish I was with you," said Jaz.

Lucy wanted Jaz to be with her, she needed one of her hugs so badly. "Well, I'll definitely be up to see you on Sunday."

"I'll practice my cooking."

"Yeah, that'll be good." Lucy could feel tears welling in her eyes. She needed to hang up.

"That was a joke, you'll only get a heated frozen dinner."

"Yeah, look, I'll speak to you tomorrow, bye." Lucy disconnected the call.

Jaz stared at her phone. "Fuck, just hang up, why don't you."

Jaz and her mum entered their favourite cafe.

"Bernard phoned while you were out?" said mum, putting her napkin on her knee.

"Did he get his plane ticket?"

"Yeah, he's flying over next Wednesday, and he's bringing his new lady friend to visit me and your dad." Mum sipped some tea. "He mentioned another lady, someone called Lucy."

"Oh yeah, Lucy."

"Is she nice?" asked Mum, nudging Jaz's hand.

"Yeah, you'd get on with her."

"When are you going to introduce us?"

"Well, there a problem, Lucy's married."

"To a man?"

"Unfortunately," said Jaz. "Me and Lucy fell out, you know me, I said too much. I wanted to look after her while she sorted things out with her husband. But she told me to leave her alone. Then I accused her of messing me around and planning to go back to him."

Mum tutted and shook her head.

"Yeah, but it gets worse, he's not a nice person, he hits Lucy and forces himself on her. I'm sure she's not safe. When I spoke to her last night and earlier today, she sounded odd. Something's not right."

"Blimey! That's a fine mess you've got yourself into," said mum, waggling a carrot stick in front of her mouth.

Jaz laughed. "Stop messing around, give me advice."

Mum took Jaz's hand. "Well, if you love her, I assume you do, go to her. It'll calm your mind."

"What now?"

"Well, finish your sandwich first; then you can be a hero, or a fool, suits you both ways."

Jaz ate rapidly. She kissed her mum goodbye, and ran to the bus station, jumping on the Penrith bus. As she sat rolling along on the rickety vehicle Jaz got nervous. Her mum might be wrong. What if Wes confronted her? Lucy might tell her to go away. Maybe she should go back home. No, she thought, I'll be fine, at least I'll be there.

Lucy poured a sizeable glass of wine, then transferred the texts and photographs from Ian's phone onto her laptop.

Afterward, she relaxed and wallowed in the bath, drinking a second glass of wine. Bubbles floated across her body and she dreamed Jaz was bathing with her.

"Bloody woman, get out of my head," she yelled, but the image of a naked Jaz stayed with her. "I'm supposed to be hating you." She splashed the bath-water, swirling it through her fingers. Lucy wished she could soak Jaz and have a huge soapy wet fight, then make love and be together again.

"Sod it!" Lucy jumped out of the bath, dried and dressed. She packed her cabin case, left the room and hurried to the train station.

"What do you mean no trains go to Bassenthwaite? How am I supposed to get there?" Lucy asked the ticket seller, who replied with a myriad of alternative routes.

Eventually, Lucy stood on the platform with a train ticket and a takeaway coffee, flicking through the Internet on her phone, searching for Cumbrian bus times. A train rolled in, and she walked along the platform seeking a quiet carriage.

As soon as the train arrived in Manchester, Jaz realised she didn't know how to find Lucy's flat. She stepped off the train onto the platform and dialled Lucy's number. It surprised her how she could hear Lucy's Nessun Dorma ring tone so clearly.

"Hello," said Lucy.

"Hi, the phone's here are well odd, your voice is reverberating in my ear."

"And you're mad." Lucy tried not to smile.

"How am I mad, and how do they make phones sound so peculiar?"

"It's probably something to do with me standing behind you."

"What?" Jaz turned around.

"You might as well end your call," said Lucy.

"Bye," said Jaz into her mouthpiece. "I…I…I just popped by to check you were okay."

"I'm fine." Lucy wore no make-up, her eyes were red and swollen, and her cheeks puffed out from her face.

"You don't look fine, you're a bloody mess."

"Oh, thanks for that, it's lovely to see you."

"I'm sorry, but…it doesn't matter." Jaz noticed Lucy's cabin case. "Where are you going?"

"Bassenthwaite."

"Oh, it's lovely up there at the moment. You visiting anyone?"

"Well I was, but I needn't bother now. Coffee?"

"Great."

They sat in the coffee shop staring at each other, steam rising from their cups.

"So, why are you really here?" asked Lucy.

"My mum told me to come and see you."

"Your mum sent you! You're how old?"

"Something isn't right, and I'm not leaving the woman I love on her own."

Lucy's bottom lip wobbled.

Jaz took hold of her hand. "What's happened?"

"I'm in a hotel. I couldn't get into my flat, Wes has changed the locks."

"What? Why?"

"He's left me, he's been having an affair for years."

"Bloody hell! When did you find this out?"

"When I got home yesterday."

"Oh, for fuck's sake, why didn't you tell me."

Lucy became defensive. "I needed to talk to Wes first, and I thought you'd laugh at me."

"Why would I laugh?" asked Jaz, shocked by Lucy's words.

"I'm sorry," Lucy cried.

Jaz moved next to her and wrapped her arms tight around her shoulders, allowing Lucy's tears to flow over her jacket. "Come on, let's get you back to your hotel." Jaz stood and with Lucy clenched to her side wandered out of the station. "Where am I going?" asked Jaz.

Lucy directed Jaz along the road to the hotel. "My flats over there." Lucy pointed over the road. "Well, my flat was over there."

Heartbroken and weeping, Lucy kicked off her shoes, swung her legs onto the bed and leaned on the pillows. "My life's a mess."

"Have a cup of tea," said Jaz passing Lucy a cup and lounging next to her. "Let's analyse the situation, Wes has told you he's left you."

"Yeah."

"So, now you don't have to worry about leaving Wes."

"Yeah, that's one benefit," said Lucy looking at Jaz.

"Then he sold the flat," said Jaz.

"Yeah, he sold it cheap, but it was in his name. He gave me half of the money he got for it."

"Wow, that's damned decent of him." Jaz drank some tea. "Lucy, if you want to, you can come and stay with me for a while."

Lucy looked away. "I don't know, you might only want me for my money?"

"Oh, for goodness sake, who the hell is this person I'm supposed to be. I'm here with you, I love you." Jaz kissed Lucy's forehead.

"I wanted to hate you, but I can't." Lucy gazed into Jaz's eyes. "You're the only person in the world I love and trust." She fell, sobbing, into Jaz's arms.

Chapter 29

Lucy leaned over and kissed Jaz's sleepy mouth. Her tongue then traced the rim of Jaz's ear.

Jaz's hand flapped her face. "Bloody mozzies!" she murmured, opening her eyes then closing them again.

Lucy's hand wandered along Jaz's body, feeling the pertness of her nipple as she cupped Jaz's breast. Then roaming across the curvature of her stomach, Lucy's hand reached Jaz's lower curls, where her fingers created a wetness, which Lucy playfully circled. She kissed Jaz's mouth harder now, her tongue losing control as it moulded with Jaz's.

Jaz welcomed Lucy's attentions with gusto, and she widened her legs to invite Lucy's curious fingers inside her. They slid firmly back and forth, making Jaz grab hold of the bedding as her entrance ticked and pulsed.

"Oh, for fuck's sake," cried Jaz, grinning wildly and tensing her body.

Lucy left her hand in place for a few seconds, then she glided them up Jaz's torso. "Morning." Lucy smiled contentedly and caressed Jaz's nipples.

"Morning." Jaz exhaled as she released her hands and felt her body fall into a super relaxed state. "I've just had the most fantastic dream; it was so realistic, bloody marvellous."

Lucy slapped Jaz's stomach and kissed her mouth. "Good, glad you enjoyed it." She rolled over, taking the sheet with her, wrapping it around her body while she got up to switch on the kettle.

Jaz rolled on her side and watched Lucy's movements, a fixed grin on her face.

Lucy returned to bed with two cups of tea and replaced the sheet over them both. "You can stop grinning now."

"No, I'll grin the entire day." Jaz kissed Lucy's cheek. "It's a lovely day."

Lucy stared at the window watching the rain pour down the glass, large drops chasing each other along the panes. "I don't think the weather agrees," said Lucy. "What do you want to do today?"

"Well, let's see, we could repeat stage one. Then you can show me where in Manchester we can get a tasty breakfast. I've never been here before."

Lucy put her tea on the bedside table and straddled Jaz's hips. "That's crazy, you've visited Botswana but never been to Manchester."

"I know I'm a terrible person avoiding your fair abode. I'm just too rural."

They kissed again and this time Jaz took control, her lips worked their way over

Lucy's body. It was another hour before they emerged from the sheets.

"Come on, time to stop," said Lucy. "I'm starving."

"Shower first."

"Do you need a hand?" asked Lucy, following Jaz into the bathroom.

They walked through the damp Manchester streets and sat in a window seat in Lucas's coffee shop eating a sausage bap.

"Jaz."

"Yeah."

"There's something else I haven't told you."

"Oh no, what now," sighed Jaz.

"I don't know how to say it." Lucy sat fiddling with a serviette.

"Is this a thing you should have told me and thought you shouldn't because you think I'm unhinged and you can cope better without me?"

"No, I didn't tell you because it's a horrible thing and I didn't want to upset you."

Jaz took Lucy's hand. "What do you need to tell me?"

"Well, they were trying to kill me."

"Oh, for fuck's sake no, that's not right." Jaz released Lucy's hand and slammed her palms on the table. "I was right. Wes is an evil bastard. Where is he? I'm going to fucking kill him this time." Jaz stood, ready to leave the coffee shop.

"Please sit down." Lucy pulled at Jaz's jacket, getting her back into her seat. "You see what you do, how you react."

Jaz sat, shaking her head from side to side, her foot tapping on the floor. "So, Wes was trying to kill you!" she snarled.

"Not Wes, it was a stupid idea Sue, his girlfriend, planned with Ian. He needed to cause an accident, kill me, and then Sue would claim the insurance money."

"This is crazy. When was this happening?"

"It started at the hotel, the motorbike, the boat…"

"You mean Ian tried to kill Jodi…and me?"

"Wes didn't know about it, when he found out he told Ian to stop."

"When did you discover this information?"

"Monday."

Jaz's mouth dropped open. "Monday! You've kept quiet since Monday."

Lucy told Jaz the tale of recovering Ian's phone, listening to Wes's phone calls and the shock of discovering Ian was trying to kill her.

"Jeez no wonder you got stressed, and that's the reason you didn't come with me to Bernard's flat," said Jaz.

"Yes, and you had upset me."

"Shit, what a bloody mess."

"It gets worse."

Lucy's statement didn't surprise Jaz, and her fingers tightened into fists.

"Ian took photographs of me and you together, then sent them to Wes," announced Lucy, handing the photos over to Jaz.

Jaz flicked through, admiring some pictures. The last photograph was of a man with greying blond hair and hazy blue eyes holding a dark-haired baby in his arms. "Who's this?" she asked.

Lucy looked over. "That's Wes and his new baby."

Jaz studied the picture and shook her head. "For fuck's sake," she said, passing them back to Lucy. "Can I keep this one, it's a terrific picture of us?"

Lucy nodded and took Jaz's hand. "Jaz, I'll stay in Manchester till after the divorce, I don't want you dragged through everything."

The suggestion startled Jaz. "No, you're alright, I can cope with Wes. Don't let me get near him though, the dick-head."

Lucy smiled at her superhero. "Are you calmer now?"

Jaz took a deep breath. "Yeah, as long as you're okay, I can be calm."

"Good." Lucy stroked Jaz's face. "I love how you take care of me, you maniac."

Jaz mopped up the coffee she'd spilled in her slamming incident. "Lucy, please will you come and stay with me, or with my mum and dad? We want to look after you. We've got coffee shops, you know."

"Do you want me to destroy your life as well?"

"You'd never do that; our love is too strong."

"Well, if you're happy and you'll have me, I'll come."

"I'd have you, especially if you're coming,"

"You are so rude." Lucy laughed and slapped Jaz on the arm. "I'll stay with you as long as you promise to tell me if it's not working out. I don't want to experience this trauma again."

"Fair enough." Jaz kissed Lucy's hand. "And if it's not what you want, you must tell me."

"Okay." Lucy didn't want to part from Jaz's side ever again.

Romantically they held hands, gazing into each other's eyes while they finished their coffees, then they stood and left the cafe to visit the art gallery.

The cream stone steps led them into the large Victorian building. They walked around, admiring the stunning women in the Pre-Raphaelite paintings and Brueghel's visions of eighteenth-century life. Then they both stared at the modern art.

"You've got to admit it's shit," said Lucy.

"Well, you've got to admire the shape, form, colour, and aesthetics behind the imagination that created it. Then you can stand back and say, yeah, that's shit," giggled Jaz.

Lucy guided Jaz along the hallway into the glazed tearoom, where they were excited to find they served red bush tea.

"Cheers," said Jaz, dropping a piece of lemon into her cup.

"Will you be able to come to Manchester with me and help me through this divorce shit?" asked Lucy.

"Yeah, it's easy enough on the train, and we could stay overnight. I've seen how inspired you get in hotels!"

Lucy kicked Jaz's leg.

Jaz cried out in exaggerated pain. "Oh shit," she muttered.

"What?" asked Lucy.

"Helen and her pastor."

"No way, where?"

"Hi, J...Jasmine." A woman wearing a dishevelled brown leather-jacket stood in front of them. Her short, bleached hair stood to attention, and a tattoo of a teardrop fell from her eye.

"Hi, Helen." Jaz stared at Helen, refusing to acknowledge the sturdy, tweed dressed woman standing by her side.

Lucy stood. "How do you do." She held out her hand to Helen. "I'm Lucy."

"Oh h...hello." Helen shook Lucy's hand. "This is Fiona," she said, pointing to her partner.

"Hello, Fiona." Lucy shook her hand. "Won't you join us?"

"Is th...that okay?" Helen asked Jaz.

Jaz nodded in response.

Lucy took Jaz's hand and squeezed. "So, how are you?" Lucy asked Helen. "Jaz told me about your illness, a terrible thing to happen."

"I'm a l...lot better. I had an...another str...stroke last year, but not m...much h...harm done."

"And how have you coped Fiona? It must have been difficult looking after Helen, I know Jaz found it challenging."

Fiona's pale face twitched. "We've been fine, lots of hospital visits and several tricky times. But we're okay."

Jaz said nothing, just stared from Helen to Fiona and back, allowing Lucy to carry on the conversation.

"Do you still work for the church?" Lucy inquired.

"Yes, I'm a preacher at a small LGBTQ+ church in Stockport."

"Oh, that's interesting and Helen, are you working?"

"Not yet," whispered Fiona. "She still has a few issues with her illness, her memory isn't good, and she's gets annoyed at petty things."

"Ah that's a shame." Lucy spoke steadily. "So, Helen, have you stopped wandering from one woman to another?"

Jaz choked on her tea, coughing into her hand as she admired the remarkable woman sat next to her.

"Well y...yes, I'm sorry," said Helen into Jaz's glaring eyes.

Lucy stroked Jaz's arm. "Well, I'm glad you left because it meant I found Jaz, and Jaz found me."

"We should go, got to catch the bus." Fiona stood up and Helen copied her.

"Bye." Helen held out her hand to Jaz and let it drop when Jaz ignored the invitation to shake it.

"Whatever," said Jaz.

Lucy waved to them as they left, then smiled at Jaz. "There, an awkward moment overcome."

"You are amazing. I love you?"

"Are you sure?" Lucy looked at Jaz, knowing she'd dragged her through shit.

"If I watch what my mouth says and you're able to be truthful, we should be fine."

"Okay, I promise." Lucy kissed Jaz's hand. "When do you want to travel to your house?"

"Well, I'm working on Monday, so I could do with heading back today if possible, get myself sorted."

"Right then, I'd better check out of the hotel."

They lugged Lucy's suitcases into the car park, and Lucy introduced Jaz to her car.

"It's diddy," said Jaz, comparing it to the Mercedes parked by its side.

"Yeah, but don't you think it's sexy?"

Jaz stood back and studied the curved, shiny black exterior of the Mini. It's red leather seats, making it more appealing. "Yeah, it's sexy." Jaz spelled out the number plate. "LC08BLE," she said. "That's a tidy number plate."

"Oh, yeah, a present from Wes, I can get rid of it."

"Why it's cool. I'd keep it if I were you."

Lucy smiled. "Can we drive to the storage unit and pack more things into the car?"

"We can try." Jaz tried not to laugh as she contemplated fitting anything else into the tiny vehicle.

As Lucy opened the storage unit Jaz stood aghast, staring at the furniture emporium.

"Bloody hell, you've got a houseful of stuff."

"Do you need any of it?" Lucy held Jaz's arm.

"Well, yeah, but I can't afford it."

"Stupid, you needn't buy it, you can have it."

"No, I can't take it, that's not right."

"Tell you what, you supply the house and I'll bring the furniture."

"Excellent compromise," said Jaz, examining a Tiffany style lamp. "What can you squeeze into the micro buggy?"

Lucy gathered a set of towels, a few more pairs of shoes, her jewellery box and an album of photographs.

"I can't believe he's dumped your personal stuff as if it means nothing." Jaz looked through the album, finding one of Lucy as a baby. "Oh, you were so cute." Jaz squeezed Lucy's cheek.

They pushed as much as they could into the boot of the car, forcing the door shut. Then Lucy locked up the storage unit. "I'll come back next week, see the solicitor and arrange a removal van."

"Great," said Jaz. "So, are you ready to come and visit my wonderful lake, and I'll introduce you to my parents."

"Won't they mind me showing up at their house?"

"No, they'll have the best room ready for you."

"Where will you sleep?" asked Lucy.

"Oh, they'll send me to the cellar and release me in the morning to wait on you! What do you mean? I'll be with you."

"In the same room!"

"Oh, you're worried they'll be nasty and homophobic," announced Jaz. "Not mum and dad, they're the best. I suppose they'd be happier if I married you."

"Oh…well I'll have to get my divorce sorted first."

"No, sorry…I wasn't meaning to propose," said Jaz, her face reddening.

"Good, because it's a little too soon." Lucy smiled at Jaz's worried face and kissed her cheek. "But don't forget to propose again when everything's sorted."

Lucy started the car, and they headed toward the motorway. Crossing the dirty brown river, where buildings emerged from its dreary depths, and following dull roads lined with grim-looking housing and sharp-eyed people.

They reached a large, well-tended garden surrounded by metal rails. "Queen's Park," said Lucy. "Built for Queen Victoria's anniversary of something or other. This is Bernard Manning's club; do you remember him? A crude comic, he's dead now."

"Nah never heard of him, does Peter Kay live around here? Now he's funny."

"No, he's from Bolton, over that way." Lucy pointed northward. "I learned to swim in that ancient swimming pool," said Lucy. "The cockroaches taught me!"

"Ugh, yuk," said Jaz, belching.

Lucy turned right at the lights, then veered into the supermarket petrol station. Jaz filled up the car and went inside to pay, buying Lucy a bar of chocolate and two bottles of water for the journey.

When she got back to the car, Lucy's fingers were tapping on the leather steering wheel. "Are you alright?" said Jaz.

"I'm scared, the last few days have been horrible and my life will be so different. I don't know if I'll cope." Lucy leant into Jaz's arms, juddering with tears.

"It's okay, I know it's frightening now, but I'm right here with you. If things go wrong with us you can move on. I won't hold you back, I mean, there's always Bill the pilot."

Lucy laughed a snotty laugh. "Yeah, I'll be fine?"

"Let me drive," said Jaz.

"Thanks," said Lucy, getting out of the car and walking to the passenger side.

Jaz adjusted the various seat settings and nestled herself behind the steering wheel.

Lucy pointed up the road. "I was born and bred up there, near to where Wes is living now."

"Is it alright to go that way? It'll help me get to know and understand you."

"I don't know, what if we see Wes?"

"Well, we'll drive straight past him, put our arms out of the window, stick two fingers up and shout rude words."

Lucy laughed. "Go on then crazy lady, get driving before I change my mind."

Jaz drove up the road, trying to get used to the clutch and accelerator. "Wow, she's keen."

"Yeah, I've got a car as intense as my girlfriend." Lucy sniggered as she looked at the surrounding sights. "There used to be lots of small shops and houses around here, before the council demolished them. There's the post office, and that used to be an art shop," said Lucy, pointing through the window. "See that old red building there, that's the library, can you see the begging dog on the roof?"

Jaz looked toward the sky. "Oh, that's cool."

"They call this part of town the Ben Brierley, he was a writer who used to write in old north Manchester dialect." Lucy was enjoying reminiscing. "And that park is where me and my dad went fishing and played soccer."

While Lucy continued to share her childhood memories, Jaz watched a man freewheeling his bicycle down the hill in front of them. The wind blew back his greyish blonde hair. He stared at the car as he passed, glowering at Jaz.

"Wanker," Jaz mouthed as she drove by him.

Jaz's last sight of Wes was through the rear-view mirror. She saw his rotated head glaring at the Mini, and ahead of him a green van making an emergency stop. Then she watched Wes crash into its rear end, his wretched body flying over the van's roof.

Bringing her eyes back to the road in front of her, Jaz drove on, not mentioning the incident to Lucy. "It sounds as if you had a lovely childhood with wonderful memories to cherish," she said, firmly rubbing Lucy's leg.

"Yeah, it was brilliant." Lucy gave a deep sigh. "Right back to the present, best give me the postcode of where we're going?"

A smiling Jaz looked at Lucy's contented brown eyes. "Are you still sure?"

"Absolutely, time to make fresh memories."

THE END

Thank you for purchasing and reading my first novel.

It would be hugely helpful if you could review my book,
and your actions would encourage my writer's soul.

.

Please read the continuation of Lucy and Jaz's story in my next book

"**Red Wine and Mint Cake.**"

From Jaz, Lucy had discovered true love, and slowly she was overcoming the negative actions of her abusive husband. But living away from her home town, was making Lucy feel insecure and she demanded a lot of Jaz's time and attention to help her find a way through her new life.

Being busy working, helping out her family and supporting the love of her life, Jaz didn't realise that Lucy was finding her new life challenging. Through her actions Jaz lets Lucy down, causing their relationship to fall from wonder to despair.

Will the two of them be able to reconcile and re-align their lives to take on the challenges the future may bring.

About the Author

Alysia D. Evans lives in a village in the British countryside. When the weather permits, she is inspired to be creative by the view from her window. She lives with her wonderful partner and small, brown, sleepy dog. When Alysia' s not obsessed with putting pen to paper, she enjoys watching sports and TV dramas.

Contact her at:

alysiadevans@gmail.com

Find her on Facebook and Twitter

Website   https://alysiadevans.wixsite.com/website

Printed in Great Britain
by Amazon